"I'll drop the door," J.B. offered, reaching for the outside control lever

As the Armorer touched the green lever, the sec door fell—not slowly, controlled by a mass of hydraulics and pistons, but all at once, with the infinite deadweight of solid vanadium steel. Hundreds of tons crashed to the concrete floor, nearly taking J.B. with it.

"Rad-blast it!" he cursed, jumping back with the agility of a hunting puma.

The whole place shook. Dust and flakes of stone fell from the ceiling, creating their own choking fog. Ryan dropped to his hands and knees, cradling his head, ready for a major cave-in. But the echoes of the fallen door were swallowed up in the muffling stillness. Nothing more came away from the ceiling and walls.

As the air cleared, everyone looked at the sec door. It didn't seem to be damaged, but the concrete around its base was severely cracked. J.B. tried the control lever. He pushed gently, then put more of his weight against it. The tendons in his neck tightened under the strain, and a vein throbbed at his temple. But nothing happened.

"Trapped," Jak announced.

The monosyllable said it all.

Other titles in the Deathlands saga:

JAMES AXLER

DEATHLANDS®

Time Nomads

A GOLD EAGLE BOOK FROM

WORLDWIDE®

TORONTO • NEW YORK • LONDON
AMSTERDAM • PARIS • SYDNEY • HAMBURG
STOCKHOLM • ATHENS • TOKYO • MILAN
MADRID • WARSAW • BUDAPEST • AUCKLAND

It's been thirty years since I first saw John Stewart, singing as part of the Kingston Trio. Since then I've seen him plenty of times as a solo performer and bought every one of the string of wonderful, and largely unheralded, records. This is for John, with my thanks and admiration, from one of the legion of loyal friends and front-row dancers.

Second edition April 1999

ISBN 0-373-62549-9

TIME NOMADS

Copyright © 1990 by Worldwide Library.

The past and present
are only a heartbeat apart.

—From *Tunnel Vision*
by Laurence James
Published by Blackie, 1989

Chapter One

Mildred Wyeth was at the most wonderful party of her life. The only dark spot was a nagging headache that lurked somewhere behind her eyes, giving occasional stabs of pain that left her feeling oddly weak and disoriented.

Everyone was there.

Martin and Coretta both smiled at her as she walked by and into the parlor where the buffet was laid out. Andrew and Jesse were involved in a heated discussion, both in danger of spilling their plates of gumbo on the carpet. They saw Mildred and grinned sheepishly, parting to allow her through.

Ralph was helping himself to some potato salad. "Can I serve you, Mildred?" he asked.

"No, thanks. I'll just pick a little."

"Sure?"

"Sure. Is it true that Jack and Bobby are coming along later?"

He nodded. "Surely is. Just about the biggest gathering we've seen. Your pa around?"

"Out in the garden with Mom."

"That's a pretty pistol you got there, Mildred. Not

looking for trouble, are you? Not here, among friends?"

"It's a ZKR 551, Reverend. Six-shot blaster, chambered to take a standard Smith & Wesson .38."

"That the one you used in the Olympics? It looks kind of different."

For a moment Mildred was puzzled. "Guess it does, at that."

Through the window, she could see a couple singing by the barbecue, a tall, good-looking man and an attractive girl, their voices blending perfectly.

"Who're they?" she asked.

Ralph had moved away, and a crew cut white teenager answered her. "That's John and Buffy. They're going around with Bobby, playing at all his whistlestops. They're cool."

Mildred strolled through the open doors, savoring the fresh air, catching the scent of orchids, hearing cicadas in the bushes. The garden was familiar and yet had features that she didn't quite recognize. Parts were bigger, and some of the angles at the corners seemed different.

She glimpsed her mother near a small ornamental fountain. She waved to her but got no response.

For a moment Mildred felt a strange, painful sensation, as though something had stirred deep within her brain, like a tiny metal orb revolving in the frontal lobe above the eyes.

It was sharp enough to make her wince.

She closed her eyes, then jumped as someone laid a hand on her shoulder.

"Sorry, Millie."

Uncle Josh, her father's younger brother, was the only one who ever called her Millie. Like her father, Josh was a minister.

"It's all right. Goodness, it's cold. I feel frozen. Really frozen."

For some reason, that seemed to be funny, and she smiled broadly. But her uncle didn't react. "Your father wants to speak to you, Millie. Out in the corner, under the magnolia."

That had always been his favorite place before...

"Before," she murmured.

"Over there." Uncle Josh pointed. "With some new friends."

"I didn't know he had any new friends. Who are they?"

Her uncle shook his head slowly. "Can't say I cotton to them too much, Millie. Over there. Four men and a lady."

"I'll go look."

The light seemed dimmer, but she could make out the short dark curls on top of her father's head, just visible above the back of the striped chair. And she could also see the five strangers that Josh had mentioned to her.

The girl caught her eye first. She was very tall, close to six feet, with a mane of the most wonderful hair that Mildred had ever seen. The deep, fiery crimson seemed to glow in the dim evening light. She half turned and smiled at Mildred, revealing eyes the color of melting emeralds. She was dressed in khaki overalls, tucked into dark blue leather Western boots, which had silver points chiseled into the toes, and silver spread-winged falcons embroidered on the sides.

Next to her was a well-built man with a mop of black curly hair. He stood a couple of inches over six feet, and was broad-shouldered. He also turned at Mildred's approach and she saw, with no surprise at all, that he had a patch over his left eye. The man wore a long coat of dark leather with a white fur trim, and a white silk scarf was looped around his neck.

Next to her father stood a young boy, barely five and a half feet tall, with the most amazing hair. Whereas the woman's hair was like living fire, this was like spun snow, like the frozen spray off the highest waterfall, cascading over his neck and shoulders. The boy wore nondescript pants and a peculiar patched jacket of leather and canvas.

"Hi, Mildred," he called.

It crossed her mind to wonder how the teenager knew her name, although he did seem somehow familiar to her.

She took a few steps nearer the group, then stopped, stricken.

The pain came swirling back, sucking at her mind, knocking it off center. She was suddenly dizzy, and took several slow, deep breaths, fighting off the pangs of nausea. This time the pain was like clawed fingers scraping at the inside of her skull.

"You okay, Mildred?" the one-eyed man asked.

"Yeah, thanks, Ryan. Just a…better lay off the martinis for a spell, I guess."

"Want to sit down?" asked the sallow-faced man in the fedora hat and metal-rimmed glasses.

"Thanks, J.B., but I'll be fine."

"I fear that all is not well with the doctor lady," said the last member of the group. "Perchance the physician should heal herself."

The speaker was the oldest of the group. He was as tall as the one-eyed man but much skinnier, and wore a stained and faded frock coat of Victorian cut, and cracked knee boots. He sported an ebony cane with its silver top carved into the head of a lion. He smiled and half bowed, showing excellent teeth that were at odds with his lined face and long gray hair.

Mildred bowed back. "Thanks a lot, Doc. Courteous and useless as ever."

At the back of her mind was a slight bewilderment at how she knew these five strangers. The girl was called Krysty Wroth and the boy was Jak Lauren. She knew that.

"How?" she whispered to herself.

"Your father wants to see you, Mildred," said Ryan. Ryan Cawdor.

Mildred wondered, with so many of the civil rights leaders there, why her father was sitting still and silent in his old chair. Like many black Baptist ministers in the South, Reverend Wyeth had been active on all of the marches, as had Mildred's mother.

But her father was already...

"Dead," Krysty said.

"How's that?" Mildred asked.

"Dead on my feet. Double-bushed. Could do with a rest someplace."

"Let's go get some eats, lover," Ryan suggested. "Come on, folks. Leave Mildred and her father to a little privacy."

The five friends walked away across the grass, nodding and smiling to the groups of people talking and eating in the soft moonlight. Mildred watched them go, closing her eyes against the surging waves of sickness that swam up behind her temples. Her nostrils filled with the familiar scent of charcoal and grilled chicken. The lower branches of the magnolia seemed to dip around Mildred, closing her off with her father from the noise of the gathering.

"Daddy?"

Around her the party was fading into stillness. It was as if someone had thrown a vast cloak of black velvet over Mildred and the silent figure in the garden chair.

"Daddy? It's Mildred. Mildred Winonia Wyeth, your little girl."

The smell of burning from the barbecue behind her was stronger. Whoever was in charge of the cooking had been very careless and allowed some of the meat to scorch. Mildred wrinkled her nose and swallowed to try to clear her throat of the stench of burned flesh, but it seemed to be growing thicker.

"Best move, Daddy. That smell's real horrible and it'll…"

She moved to the front of the chair and stooped down to look directly into her beloved father's dark brown eyes.

For a moment Mildred believed she'd gone insane, that the disturbing sickness inside her skull was a symptom of a virulent madness.

Because what sat slumped in the seat was not remotely like her father, only barely resembling anything that had ever been human.

It was like a thick, blackened log that had been drawn, still burning, from the center of a fire.

There were a few charred rags hanging on the outside of the log and draped off the two branches that sprouted near the top and the two that dangled from the lower half. Smoke curled upward, and parts of the log still glowed ruby bright.

The head was a like a round, black stone, with charcoal pits where the eyes had been seared from their sockets. The mouth hung open, showing the startling whiteness of her father's teeth.

"Sweet Jesus Christ!" she breathed. "Oh, Daddy…what've they done to you?"

The ultimate horror.

The head moved, and sour, ashen breath soughed from the ruined lips. A hand trembled, the fingers like twigs from an old bonfire. The leathery skin cracked open and bright crimson blood flowed down over the flame-torn flesh, dripping onto the faded stripes of the canvas chair.

"Takes more'n fire to kill a man," croaked the corpse. "Said Joe, I didn't die."

Mildred started to scream.

"It's all right," a voice insisted. "It's all right."

Chapter Two

"It's all right," the voice repeated. "It's all right. Come on, Mildred."

She kept her eyes closed. That way, she wouldn't be tricked again. If she opened them, then the charnel horror that had once been her father might rise grinning before her.

"Been a bad jump for her, lover. Gotta remember it's her first."

"Yeah." Ryan shook her shoulder. "Come on, Mildred."

Her lips moved, but no sound came out.

"Said something. Mouth opened."

"Try getting her on her feet, Ryan."

"Looks like she's in deep shock, J.B. Mebbe safer t'leave her a while."

"Could be the result of the freezing. She seemed real well when we thawed her out. But now..." Krysty's words faded away like rainwater down a storm drain.

"Slap her face. I would be the first to volunteer for the opportunity."

"Go take a flying fuck at a rolling doughnut, Doc," Mildred managed.

There was a ripple of laughter, tinged with relief. Mildred took a chance and, cautiously, eased open her left eye.

"Welcome back to Deathlands," Ryan said, kneeling at her side.

She tried to sit up, but dizziness and sickness came rolling in over her and she lay down again.

"Goddamn! Inside of my head feels like it's been put on double spin and then vacuum-packed for your personal protection."

Krysty put a hand behind Mildred's shoulders and helped her sit up. "It'll pass. Some are worse than others."

"None of 'em fucking good." Jak grinned, brushing his fine white hair back off his narrow face. "I beg leave to second that," Doc Tanner boomed. "Though I confess that I am sorry to see so little improvement in your temperament, ma'am."

"What was the problem?" Ryan asked. "You were screaming like a kid."

The thirty-six-year-old black woman shook her head. "I should've known it was a dream, Ryan. I was less than one year old when my daddy was butchered, but I've seen plenty of filmclips and pictures of him. So that's what I thought I'd see in..." She shook her head again. "Just that I saw him. Dead. Like a burned log."

"Racists killed him, did they?" asked J. B. Dix, polishing his glasses on his sleeve.

"The Klan," she said venomously. "The mid-sixties were busy times for the Knights with their white sheets and their burning crosses.''

"What's Klan?'' Jak asked, curious.

"Ku Klux Klan. Redneck bigots. Only a year or so before I was born one of them put a bomb under the Sixteenth Street Baptist Church in Birmingham, Alabama. Went off and slaughtered four little girls. Children! Dynamite Bob Chambliss, his name. The white folks protected their own, and it was fourteen damned years before he finally went down for the murder. Fourteen years!''

The silvered glass walls of the chamber let in filtered, shadowy light. The metal disks in floor and ceiling had cooled and dimmed. The five others, hardened by previous jumps, were ready to move out. But Mildred still seemed shaky. Ryan encouraged her to carry on talking awhile.

"Dynamite Bob. I was born eight days after Christmas in 1964. The Klan burned Daddy alive less than a year after. May they rot in hell.''

There was a long silence, which was broken by the teenager. "Did this just…'cos black? Not mutie or nothing?''

"No, not a mutie, Jak. Just a decent man who'd gotten angry and felt he'd eaten enough crow to last him. He got to preaching to folks to stand up. Not just sit patient. Stand up and take what belonged. And the Klan didn't like that so they firebombed our house.'' The tears came, unbidden, flowing over her cheeks, dripping to the floor of the mat-trans chamber.

"They catch them in the end, Mildred?" Doc asked quietly.

"They got caught. The law didn't do it. Sheriff was brother to one of the bombers and cousin to the other two."

"So, how did..." Krysty began.

"My father had some friends, some good, good friends who knew that the Klan had a real tight hold on things down there. So, the three men who did the bombing had an 'accident.' Real nasty. All three got burned alive. Seems a gas canister blew in the auto repair shop one of them owned. Lock sort of jammed. You know how it can be."

Ryan nodded. "Sure. I know how it can be, Mildred. I know."

NONE OF THE others had suffered too badly from the jump. Jak had a nosebleed, and Doc complained about a nagging headache behind his eyes, but apart from that they were in good shape.

Even Mildred recovered quickly, joining the others as Ryan opened the gateway door.

"Clear," he said. "I can see through to the main control. Looks all sealed and working good."

Everyone holstered their blasters.

The small anteroom that was present in virtually every redoubt was bare of furniture, as were most of them. The evacuation before sky-dark began had obviously been planned and orderly, with every shred of paper picked up. The walls showed faint discolorations where notices or posters had been, but all of that had been a hundred years ago.

All the main consoles in the larger room beyond seemed to be working perfectly.

Mildred stared around her, fascinated. "I'd heard rumors about all this—the Totality Concept, Over-project Whisper and Cerberus—but they kept it well hidden. And they're still here, still functioning."

J.B. answered her. "Sure. You have to remember these redoubts were all built in the last four or five years of the twentieth century, in isolated, hidden places. And most of 'em escaped the nuking. Most were powered by eternal generators. Atomic stuff. Nobody in Deathlands has the technology to get into a sec-locked redoubt."

"Nobody, J.B.?" asked Ryan.

The Armorer nodded. "Sure. Point taken. Mebbe a handful of powerful barons might have the tech-power. Maybe. But there's plenty of redoubts scattered all through Deathlands."

"What if the jump takes you to a redoubt where a mountain fell in? You get to reappear inside a million tons of granite."

"No. Rick Ginsburg, your predecessor as the group's freezie, was an expert on doorways. Told us there's a fail-safe locking system. Can't happen. That's what he said, anyway."

Mildred shook her head. "Hope that's right, Ryan. You can never trust a freezie's memory, you know."

THEY DIDN'T stay long in the control room. The basics, such as food, ammo and beds—if any were left in the rest of the fortress—would be elsewhere, on other levels or in other sections. Some redoubts rambled for miles underground.

Before moving out, J.B. took Ryan aside.

"I think this place is boobied. No, I *know* it's boobied."

"Who by?"

"It's original. Not local ville stuff. There's extra wires and plas-ex all over the place. I figure they were going to blow the whole place and never got around to it. Or mebbe the trigger device didn't work right."

Ryan looked up at the ceiling and saw loops of extra wire, obviously put up in a hurry. "And they never got a second chance to fire them? Yeah. Could be."

"Best step careful. Anything could be tied into the triggering sequence. Once we start it, there might be no way of stopping it. The whole redoubt could go skyway."

"Disable it?"

J.B. looked around him, whistling tunelessly between his front teeth. "No. Cut one wire and you break a circuit. Up it goes. Give me a few hours and I could probably track it through. But if they boobied the entire redoubt, we could be talking days to strip the system."

"Then we all step careful."

THE GREEM LEVER was down in the locked position. They knew from experience that beyond it they'd find a corridor that would lead, eventually, into other sections of the fortress. But there was no way of guessing what else might lie behind the heavy sec-door.

"Ready?" Ryan asked, glancing around from habit, making sure everyone had his or her weapon drawn and cocked.

Everyone nodded. Mildred had been placed third in line, between Krysty and Jak, with Doc and J.B. bringing up the rear.

Mildred had the Czech ZKR 551 in her right hand, finger on the outside of the trigger guard. She grinned at Ryan. "Bring on the bad guys."

Ryan threw the lever but kept his hand on it, ready to drop it again at the first warning of danger. In the past, all manner of unpleasantness had been revealed.

He stopped the door after a couple of inches, waving Jak forward. The boy knelt, squinting under the armored steel and taking his time checking it out.

"Anything?"

"Air's poor. Stale. Dead. Like stone."

Krysty had her eyes closed, using her part-mutie skill at "seeing."

"Jak's right. Can't feel any life anywhere. Dead as an old tomb."

Ryan raised the door another couple of feet, pausing it once more so that the albino teenager could take a second check.

"Nothing. Passage. Dust. Nothing."

Now, with the door sliding up to its full height, everyone could taste the peculiar flatness of the air in the corridor. During his life in Deathlands, Ryan Cawdor had often entered buildings that had been sealed shut since the twentieth day of January, 2001, and had tasted air like this. Even with the conditioning systems of a major redoubt, there was no way that air could remain fresh, unless there was some sort of contact with the outside.

The passage was like most of the others. In this case it was close to thirty feet wide, with a curved ceiling around eighteen feet high at the crown. Looking up at the concealed lighting strips, Ryan noticed yet more of the crudely pinned bunches of wires, part of the boobie system that J.B. had spotted in the gateway.

To the left there was a blank wall.

"Right," Ryan said.

"I'll drop the door," J.B. suggested, reaching for the outside control lever.

For a moment Ryan considered leaving the gateway open, but if anything should happen to it, and they were stranded, then he knew they could find themselves in the deepest possible trouble.

"Okay. We'll start—Fireblast!"

All of them jumped.

As the Armorer touched the green lever, the secdoor fell—not slowly, controlled by a mass of hydraulics and pistons, but all at once, with the infinite deadweight of solid vanadium steel. Hundreds of tons crashed to the concrete floor, nearly taking J.B. with it.

"Rad-blast it!" he cursed, leaping back with the agility of a hunting puma.

The whole place shook. Dust and flakes of stone fell from the ceiling, creating its own choking fog. Ryan dropped to his hands and knees, cradling his head, ready for a major cave-in. But the echoes of the fallen door were swallowed up in the muffling stillness, and nothing more came away from walls or ceilings.

As the air cleared, everyone looked at the sec-door. The fall didn't seem to have damaged it, but the concrete around its base was severely cracked. J.B. was first to try the green control lever. He pushed gently, then put more of his weight against it. The tendons in his neck tightened under the strain, and a vein throbbed at his temple. But nothing happened, not a sound disturbed the sudden silence to show the lock might be working.

"Fucked," Jak said.

The monosyllable said it all.

THE TRADER used to say, "Over, under or around. There's always a way."

Both Ryan and J.B. had joined the legendary Trader about ten years ago. They'd ridden with him, fought with him, chilled with him and learned from him.

But the massive sec-door would have been a real challenge, even for Trader.

"Over, under or around?" J.B. said, tapping the steel with his knuckles.

Ryan had folded his hands together in front of him, as though he were in prayer.

"Might find some more explosive in the redoubt. Blast it apart."

J.B. showed his disbelief. "Triple negative, Ryan. Not now it's damaged. We could have mebbe blown the lock, but it's warped some. By the time we blew it open, we'd have blown down the whole redoubt with it."

"Over?"

"No. Nor under."

"How about around?"

J.B. nodded thoughtfully. "Could be best bet. Long shot. Probably pack some plas-ex if we chip out a hole in the concrete. Way bits fell off of the roof, it's probably gone soft. Might work. Can't see any other way."

"Let's go trek out the rest of the redoubt and see what we can find," Ryan suggested. "Come back to this one later."

Almost immediately they began to see signs of serious earth movements. It was common knowledge in Deathlands that the terrible nuking of a century earlier had triggered seismic and volcanic activity across the continent.

There was virtually no recorded evidence of those

first hideous weeks when the world almost disappeared, but the evidence was still there. Half of California now lay fathoms deep beneath the Pacific Ocean. What had once been Mount Saint Helens was a whole lot less than nine thousand feet high. Wheatfields were deserts, and valleys had become lakes.

There was no way of knowing yet where this redoubt was, but there was no doubt that it was somewhere underground, in a region that had been badly hit by land shifts.

The corridor twisted and turned, with only a small number of identical sec-doors on either side. Jak, leading them, tried to open the first two or three, but it was obvious that they had been locked tight. Increasingly earth pressures had warped even the strongest of the doors, and the floor became littered with chunks of fallen debris.

"Looking bad," J.B. muttered, walking alongside Ryan.

"Yeah. Don't like this sour air. Could be there'll be a big fall somewheres ahead."

J.B., never a man of very many words, simply nodded his agreement.

If they couldn't open the jammed gateway doors, and there was no path out of the redoubt ahead of them, then it would be a slow road toward dehydration and starvation.

"WHAT DO YOU reckon, lover?" Krysty asked wearily.

They'd been moving for well over an hour. The corridor had no turnings and no exits, just a lot of impenetrable doors.

Three times they had clambered over piles of twisted concrete and frail, rusted iron that had been torn away from the ceilings and dumped across the passage. Now the lights only worked intermittently, and there would be stretches of a hundred yards or more without any illumination at all.

In his heart, Ryan was beginning to believe that they would soon come across a big fall that would totally block them off from any further progress.

Less than fifty yards farther on, they came around a sharp bend, and there it was.

Chapter Three

Floor to ceiling rubble, a tangle of stone and metal that had been there for nearly a hundred years stopped them cold.

They all stood and looked at it. For some time nobody spoke, then the silence was broken by J.B.

"I was wondering why the earth movements hadn't triggered any self-defense autodestruct boobies. Then I remembered that all the wires vanished off from this corridor early on. That was 'fore we got to any real damage. This has to be an unimportant part of the redoubt. Otherwise there'd only have been some dust around here. If the bombs had been triggered."

Mildred brushed dirt off her sleeve and laughed. "You guys are the limit, you know that? We're entombed in here like we were lost in the Johnstown floods, and you wonder why some bombs didn't go off a century back. How about doing some thinking on getting the hell out of here?"

"Because there's no hurry, Mildred," Ryan replied. "This fall's not going anywhere. Mebbe we'll have to go back and try to spring the gateway door, but that's not going away, either."

Like a hyperactive child, Jak was clawing his way

across the face of the earth fall, touching it with gentle hands, laying his head against it, listening intently.

"Do you hear any message from the ether beyond, my dear sprite?" Doc asked, leaning on his cane.

"Fucking solid, Doc. Could be mile deep."

"Doesn't much matter. If it's more than about twenty feet we'd never break through. And by the look of the ceiling, anything you move'll just bring down another hundred tons of concrete."

Ryan's words brought another long period of silence from everyone.

This time it was Krysty who interrupted the stillness.

"I can feel different air. Not a lot fresher, but different."

"Where?" Ryan asked, looking around and trying to detect whatever it was that the woman had felt. But he couldn't sense anything.

"From over...this door here."

It was a sec-door like all of the others that they'd passed. Ryan had already decided that on their return to the gateway they'd have to check out every exit with extreme care, just in case they'd missed something.

Krysty knelt against the bottom of the door, closing her eyes to concentrate. Her long red hair seemed to caress the pale gray metal of the door.

"What?" J.B. asked.

"Quake's pushed this one off the hinges. It's just

sort of hanging here. If we shift it… Like Ryan said, we could bring the roof down on top of our heads.''

Ryan gestured for her to move, and he stooped to examine the sec-door, finding it exactly as Krysty had said. The shifting of the main structure of the redoubt had tipped it away from the hinges, and it was supported only by its own weight. He pushed a hand against it and felt it move.

''Take a look, J.B.,'' Ryan said, edging out of the way.

The Armorer tested it with a gentle shove, then eased his shoulder against it. He looked up at the others. ''Reckon a good heave and it'll just fall in.''

''Then what?'' Mildred asked.

''Then one of two things happens. We can get through and find a way out of here into the rest of the place. Or we all get crushed.''

''Make it the first option, J.B., if you don't mind.''

''Yeah,'' Ryan agreed. ''Everyone else back down the passage. No point all getting flattened. Me and J.B.'ll do it.''

For a moment he thought that Krysty was going to argue with his order, but she simply laid her hand on his arm and kissed him softly on the lips. ''Don't get squashed, lover. Lose a lot of your charms that way.''

When the other four had moved out of sight, Ryan and J.B. knelt together on the floor. The slight man grinned at his one-eyed friend, and said, ''You and me again, huh?''

''Like old times with the Trader. One day we'll get

the short straw. Been bucking against the odds for too long.''

J.B. shook his head. ''Not us. We're immortal.''

''Then let's do it. First sign of trouble…you know what steps to take?''

J.B. grinned again, at the old joke. ''Sure. Damned long ones.''

''GAIA, AID THEM,'' Krysty whispered from her position around the sharp bend in the corridor.

They all heard the harsh sound of metal grinding against stone and the pattering noise of falling rocks.

''Ryan?'' Krysty shouted.

She dashed back along the corridor, seeing a cloud of white dust and two spectral figures coughing at its center.

''Ryan?''

''All right!'' he called. ''Just stay back a minute. Let the dust settle. Make sure nothing else is coming down.''

They waited, seeing the dark gap in the wall where the sec-door had been. A few more shards of concrete tumbled noisily from the cracked ceiling, but the structure seemed sound.

''Come on,'' Ryan called. ''Slow and easy, and don't knock into anything.''

It was a bitter disappointment, once they were through into a different section of the redoubt, to find that the air was only a little less stale than in the corridor they'd just left.

"Still smells like this store's been long closed," Krysty said.

"Not a touch of clean outdoors, is there? Means it's been recirculating all this time. Surprised it hasn't all vanished up its own ass."

She smiled at him. "Least the damage doesn't seem so bad in this passageway. And the lights still work."

Ryan glanced up and suddenly noticed that there were more of the festoons of red and green wire, looped along the roof. "J.B.?"

"I seen it."

RYAN HAD NEVER encountered a redoubt that had been more totally cleared. There was nothing left.

They moved from the corridor into open sections of the fortress, through echoing rooms several hundred feet long that had probably been either storage or living quarters. Not a scrap of paper remained. Not a cigarette butt or gum wrapper.

"Nothing," Ryan said, after they'd been walking for another twenty-five minutes.

"I must confess that I am feeling somewhat wearied," Doc said, wiping sweat from his forehead with his kerchief.

"Not even a plan left on a wall," J.B. complained.

"Most times you head up and eventually you find a way out," Krysty stated. "I just don't like this bad air. But after a hundred years I suppose it's no surprise, is it?"

"We don't find something or a way out real soon," Ryan told her, "then we'll just have to go back and face that locked door. We'll probably have to face it some time, anyway. It's our only way of getting away from this redoubt."

They reached what was obviously a major junction, which branched out into half a dozen different passages. J.B. pointed out that the wires that he suspected were part of an intricate defense bomb continued along only one corridor.

"And it goes upward," Ryan agreed.

"Could I remain here while you go ahead on a short reconnaissance?" Doc asked, sliding down the wall and sitting on the dusty floor.

"No. We stick together. Take five, if you like, Doc."

"I would be obliged, Ryan."

"Dead end," Jak called.

"Fireblast! Best turn around and head for the gateway."

"Shit," Mildred hissed. "My feet are killing me, and I'm hungry and I'm tired and I want out of this damned warren!"

"We all do," Krysty soothed.

"There was a side turning coming up here," J.B. said. "Worth a look?"

"Sure," Ryan agreed. "Long as it's on our way down."

"THERE'S A SIGN on the wall," Krysty called from her position on point.

"What's it say?" Ryan asked.

"Emergency Evac Supplies."

"Could be some food. Chins up and shoulders back, friends," Ryan encouraged.

It was an area of the redoubt consisting of two smallish storerooms and another larger room, which contained a dozen beds. Each bed had a hard square of folded gray blankets set on top, and a wall cupboard held twelve plates, knives, forks and spoons, and twelve mugs. Basic cooking utensils were available for use on a stove that stood in the corner of the room. And there was an emergency water supply and a locked cabinet containing medical supplies.

"Self-heats!" Jak shouted from the first storeroom, not bothering to conceal the disgust in his voice.

"Anything else?" Ryan asked. Like everyone in the group, he'd sampled more than his share of self-heat cans. Generally they only raised the temperature of the contents to a tepid sludge, and it was often difficult to tell what you were eating.

"Yeah. Packets of dried soup. Cans beans 'n stuff."

"Best eat and rest," Krysty suggested.

"Guess so. Then a recce. Gotta find if there's a way out of here."

"Nothing at all in the second storeroom," J.B. reported. "Hoped for blasters and some plas-ex. There's nothing at all. Not even any mouse shit."

The Trader used to talk about getting caught between a stone and a hard place. Ryan was beginning to think that the man had been right.

THE STALE AIR seemed to close in on everyone, and Doc voiced the general feeling.

"I feel rather like someone caught in the sarcophagus of a long-dead pharaoh. I had not thought before how wonderful is the open sky and the clean air. Even the fouled air of parts of Deathlands is better than this arid, barren filth."

When it came to examining the range of food on offer, nobody felt all that hungry. Over the years some of the cans had blown and split open, spilling their contents in sticky black rivulets. Others showed ominous signs of bulging and rusting. Many of the labels had fallen off and lay in brittle rectangular slices on the shelves and on the floor.

Everyone settled for soup. J.B. heated a dozen cans, stirring them together in a large pan.

It was a mix of tomato, vegetable, sweet corn and split pea, and it lined the stomach and raised the group's spirits a little.

"Hope none of us get salmonella or listeria or any of those poisoning bugs," Mildred said, licking her spoon clean. "Wouldn't fancy trying to cope with a serious gastric attack in a place like this."

"I've eaten worse," Ryan commented. "If I was going to get sick from bad food, it'd have happened twenty years ago."

She nodded. "Sure. But these cans, sitting around

for a hundred years.... Only the Good Lord knows what's been breeding away in 'em.''

The instant coffee was somewhat better. It tasted like burned acorns, but it was hot and there were plenty of artificial sweeteners to make it more palatable.

After a second cup, everyone rested awhile, stretched out on the inflexible beds. Ryan closed his eye, letting his thoughts wander.

He knew that this was a bad one.

Facing the very real possibility of being trapped and dying in the redoubt set him thinking.

Memories of the Trader brought back the years that he'd ridden and fought his way through the Deathlands. And not much of it was worth the pain of the mother who bore him.

So much chilling.

There'd been good times; good friends, mostly now rotting beneath the earth. But only in the months since he'd met Krysty Wroth had his life begun to have any perceptible shape or meaning. Now there was something for him personally to fight and survive for.

Ryan knew that she wanted to stop and set up a home and raise a family, and he wanted that as well. It was just a question of trying to find the right place.

And the right time.

But it looked now that it might all end in this vast concrete mausoleum.

There was enough food and drink to last them for years and years if they doled them out carefully. But what would be the point of that? If they were trapped, then sooner or later death was inevitable. Nobody was going to come bursting through and rescue them.

Ryan wouldn't wait for the last feeble choking breaths. It would be better to take a 9 mm bullet.

At least he and Krysty could go together.

Something he'd once read came to Ryan as he slipped away into a restful sleep. "I pay my price to live with myself on the terms that I will."

J.B. WOKE HIM with bleak news.

"Every possible passage is blocked by huge earth falls. Been with Jak in every direction."

"No openings?"

The Armorer hesitated. "Jak says he reckons one of the falls could be movable. Says he'd like to try and clear it out. It's the highest corridor we found. If he's right, then it could be close to the surface. Whatever that is."

"Let's go look at it."

J.B. sighed. "It's all right for you, Ryan. You been sleeping like a babe. So've Doc, Krysty and Mildred. That's okay, but me and Jak could use a rest."

Ryan swung his boots off the metal-framed cot. "Sure. Sure. Let's mebbe see if anyone feels like more food. Then—" he glanced at his wrist-chron "—then we can have a sleep. Freshen up. And then we'll go check out this earth fall. How's that sound?"

"Good."

"I DON'T LIKE the look of that, Ryan," Mildred said, shaking her head over the can that he'd just opened.

"Looks okay to me," he insisted stubbornly.

The can didn't have a label and a ring of flaking orange rust was caked around its top. One side was dented as if it had suffered a heavy blow when it was being stacked.

Everyone else had avoided the self-heats. Mildred and Krysty had both selected another mix of soups. Jak had found a pile of cans, still labeled, of all different sorts of fruit and had mixed up a compote for himself.

"That'll sour your belly, kid," Mildred warned.

"Won't. And don't—"

"Call me 'kid,'" everyone chorused.

Doc had found some tinned eggs and attempted the culinary miracle of turning them into a light, fluffy omelet.

And failed.

"I fear that my old skills have deserted me," he said sadly. "Perhaps some corned beef and chili beans might hit the spot."

J.B. had carefully gone along the shelves, picking and rejecting until he'd found something that satisfied him.

"Gumbo and minced chicken," he said. "Sounds good to me."

Ryan felt bad about sleeping for so long while Jak and the Armorer had been out on an extended recon, so he just grabbed the first couple of cans he came across.

The first one had attracted Mildred's attention. It was some unidentifiable fish, gray chunks of crumbling flesh swimming in an oily, iridescent sauce. The second can was a thick gumbo with slices of potato and what looked like turnip.

He poured the contents of both tins into a pan and stirred it over a low heat. The smell that came off the mixture wasn't terrific, but there was no way he was going to back down in front of everyone.

He was the last to start eating.

"Fuck horrible stink," Jak muttered as he washed up his dish.

"I rather think something must have passed away in one of those self-heats," Doc commented. "And some time ago, too."

"Up yours, Doc."

"Doesn't look good, lover. Doesn't smell anything but rotten."

Ryan banged a fist on the metal table. "Fireblast! Just everyone shut their flapping mouths and let me get on with my food! I've eaten plenty worse. I'll be fine."

He picked up his spoon and began to eat.

Chapter Four

It didn't taste all that good. The lumps of fish were slick and rancid to his palate, and the heavy oil seemed to have separated into its unpleasant constituent parts. The bits of vegetable were either dissolving into mush or hard as rocks.

In his hurry to stop the criticism, Ryan was aware that he hadn't really heated the gooey mess as thoroughly as he might have done. But he was determined not to show anyone any sign of weakness.

The lukewarm sludge settled in his stomach like a pool of iced lead. Mildred came and stood by the table, looking down at him when he was halfway through the pan. Ryan had been thinking about leaving the rest, but he forced himself to ladle it out and tuck into it.

"Nothing more foolish than a stubborn man doing something he knows is wrong, just 'cause he's trying to prove it's right," she observed.

There was some tangy powdered lemonade in one of the larger tins, and Ryan helped himself to a mug of it, mixed with the dusty water. It seemed to help, and he drained a second portion. The drink felt as if it were settling the unease that was simmering around the level of his belt buckle.

"How about some sleep now?" J.B. suggested. "Snatch a few hours."

"Sure. No need to set guards. If we can't get out of the redoubt, there's no worry about anyone else getting in."

RYAN AND KRYSTY had pushed two of the bunks together and laid an extra pair of mattresses over the top to give themselves something approaching a double bed.

The blankets were so dried and frail that any sudden movement risked tearing them into long, narrow strips.

There was no way of even dimming the stark overhead lights, so Ryan and Krysty pulled the bedclothes up over their heads.

"What do you figure, Ryan?"

"About what?"

"Will we get out?"

"Always did."

She laid an arm across his chest. Both of them were still fully dressed. He was feeling cold, though he could also feel sweat beading his forehead.

"But that door to the gateway... If it's really boobied like J.B. says it is?"

"If he says it's got an autodestruct linked to it, then it has. Never known J.B. wrong about something like that."

"We blow it?"

Ryan took her hand in both of his and gripped it tightly. "Could pass it. But if anything gets triggered, then we have to get out fast."

"Jak and J.B. found a possible way out of the redoubt."

"Could be. High up. But it's an even longer shot. Try and move a big earth fall and you get the world on your skull." He paused. "Saves digging a grave."

"Try the door first?"

"Yeah."

"Are you all right, lover?"

"Why?"

"You feel hot, and you're trembling."

"I'm all right. Guts are a bit... No, I'm all right."

"Sure?"

"Yeah. Like me to prove it?"

Krysty giggled, letting her free hand go crabbing down past the belt to the front of his breeches.

"You don't feel too much like proving anything yet," she whispered.

"Give me time. Can you get your pants down?"

"For you, lover, anything."

The metal frame of the bed rattled and jingled as Krysty wriggled out of her trousers, leaving them hooked around her ankles. To get them completely off would have been too much hassle.

Ryan slowly unzipped himself and pushed his dark gray pants down to his knees. He touched Krysty, fingers clumsy against the tight material of her bikini panties, sliding inside.

Her own fingers were cradling him, caressing him gently, encouraging him to his own swelling readiness.

"Never mind, lover," she whispered when he failed to respond to her. "Try it in the morning."

"Sorry," he muttered.

"Don't be a double-stupe, Ryan."

She pressed herself against him, so they lay like two spoons in a drawer, her buttocks fitting snugly into his groin.

Within a handful of minutes, they were both fast asleep.

RYAN WOKE, conscious that it was the middle of the night. The overhead lights were blindingly bright and seemed to sway from side to side as he peered up at them.

Krysty was still deep in sleep. Her bright red sentient hair was curled across the makeshift pillows, relaxed as it shared her rest. One arm lay across Ryan's shoulder, and he reached up and moved it carefully out of the way.

He was aware that all was far from well. His stomach was churning, and sweat soaked through his shirt. Ryan was shivering as though he had an ague, and his head was spinning. He sat up and looked across the room, seeing that the others all slept soundly.

A gasp of pain made him clutch himself, squeezing

his hands to his ribs. His vision seemed blurred, and his mouth was dry. The muscles of his face felt stiff, as though he'd been sprayed with some sort of numbing gas. When he tried to swallow, his throat hurt.

The one-eyed man stood shakily, steadying himself with a hand on the side of the bed. The movement brought Krysty back to the brink of waking.

"Lover? You all right?" she mumbled.

"Feel a bit sick. Going to…"

Nausea silenced him and he want to the ablutions at a stumbling run, making it just in time.

He retched a stream of bitter green bile into the toilet. The taste was so foul that it made him vomit still more. With a shock of dismay, Ryan also realized that he was on the verge of losing control of his bowels and fouling himself. With a spasmodic effort he dropped his trousers and avoided acute embarrassment.

Another bout of sickness left him weak and helpless.

"Oh, fireblast!" he moaned.

For a moment he felt a little better. With an effort he managed to clean himself up, then stood. The bathroom was going slowly around in dipping loops. Ryan grabbed at the washbasin and tried to focus his vision on himself in the polished steel mirror.

The face that stared blankly back at him was hardly recognizable. The cheeks were sallow and hollowed, the stubble showing black against the waxen skin. He leaned forward and peered at himself more carefully, noticing that the pupil of his eye was badly dilated, as if he'd been doing jolt for forty-eight hours straight.

Threads of yellow spittle clung to the corners of his lips, and his mouth tasted foul. He touched his face, aware that the muscles were stiff and resistant to the feel.

"What the fuck's wrong?" he said, but the words weren't properly controlled and sounded slurred and far-off.

Ryan's stomach revolted again, and a gusher of vomit cascaded into the basin in front of him.

"Ryan?"

He tried to speak, but he realized that he was losing his hold on consciousness.

"Ryan? You in there, lover?"

With a massive endeavor of will, he managed to call out a reply. "Yeah. Ill."

The floor came swooping up to meet him as he fell. There was a loud noise inside his head, and then everything became extremely quiet.

SOMETHING WAS tied loosely across his forehead, masking his eye, and someone had poured liquid glue into the muscles and tissue of his face and throat. He could hardly swallow properly, and movement was beyond him.

All Ryan could do was lie still and listen.

The voice belonged to Mildred Wyeth.

"It's bad. Food poisoning. But I don't figure it's

salmonella or something common. If it was, it could be treated easily with kaolin and morphine. Something like that.''

"So what is it?''

"Not sure, Krysty.''

"Not *sure*? But you got a good idea, don't you, *Doctor* Wyeth?''

"Yeah. Dilation and stiffness of cranial musculature. Eyelid eased down. It points one way.''

"Which way is that?'' Ryan thought that sounded like Doc Tanner, but he was losing touch with reality and couldn't be certain.

"Botulism. That's the bacterium called Clostridium botulinum. Rare. Normally found in home-prepared food. But I guess things in this place have been kind of unusual for medical science.''

"Is it bad?'' Ryan was proud that he knew J.B.'s voice through the slushing waves of surf that filled his ears.

There was a pause, and Ryan decided he'd finally passed into a coma. But Mildred eventually answered.

"The stiffness of the face spreads to the throat. Then to paralysis of the heart and all the breathing muscles.''

"And?''

"Some die.''

"Some?''

"If I was in a modern hospital and I was the duty intern and Ryan came in like this, I'd maybe lay good odds on saving him. Real good odds. But that's with all the latest drugs, equipment, ventilators and machinery.''

Now the blackness was becoming overwhelming. Ryan knew that the words being spoken around him were of some importance, but it was difficult and tiring to try to focus on them. It was easier to let go.

"You seem to be saying, Mildred, if I understand you correctly, that without such modern equipment you are rather less sanguine for Ryan's chances of survival? Is that it?''

"That's it, Doc. Botulism is—was—real rare. I've never even seen a single case of it myself. Just read about it.''

The words disappeared as Ryan slipped into a trough of unconsciousness.

"Don't die, lover. Please don't go and die and leave me here alone.''

The noises made no sense to Ryan.

Just noises.

"Fight it. Hold on. Fight it. Hold on.''

Noises.

Chapter Five

"Fight it!"

"Hold on!"

"You got him, Ryan. Hang on the bastard!"

Ryan had kept his eye squeezed shut, concentrating all of his energy on what he was doing. But the shouting made him open it.

Lex was sweating, the water trickling down from his receding hairline, through his busy sideburns. The man's mouth was set in a grinning rictus of effort. The palm of his hand was becoming wet and slippery, making it harder for Ryan to maintain his grip.

Everyone was gathered around them, most rooting for Ryan Cawdor. But a sizable minority of the crew were supporting the larger, heavier, older figure of Lex.

Lex was rear gunner on War Wag One.

"You got him going, Ryan," yelled Hunaker, one of the drivers. Hun was nearly as strong as Ryan or Lex. Her cropped hair was tinted a fiery crimson, and she was licking her full lips with the excitement of the spectacle.

"Hold on there, Lex!" someone else called. Ryan

wasn't sure who it was, but thought it might have been Rodge, the cook's assistant.

"Give up if you want, Ryan," Lex panted, his small, close-set bloodshot eyes swimming in their sockets.

"Man says that is close to the edge," came a quieter, reasoned voice from just behind Ryan's metal seat.

J. B. Dix was the Armorer on War Wag One. The small, laconic weapons expert had joined the team about a year after Ryan Cawdor, and the two men had become something close to friends. When you rode with the Trader you tried to avoid close friendships. Death was too constant a companion for that.

The arm wrestling tournaments were a constant feature of life on the war wags. It was a way of settling disputes and releasing tension—and also a good excuse for gambling. A load of jack rested on the result of this particular battle.

Lex had been riding the trails of the Deathlands longer than most of the crew. Ryan had been with them for a handful of years and had risen quickly to become the Trader's right-hand man and leading lieutenant. Most of the crew accepted that happily. Some talked about the one-eyed man as being the son that the Trader had never had.

But a few of the older hands on War Wag One resented his rapid rise. The same men and women also resented the way J. B. Dix had become the specialist when it came to firearms, and any other kind of weaponry. They ignored the fact that the sallow, bespectacled young man probably knew his subject better than anyone else in the Deathlands.

"Double up the odds?" Ryan suggested, struggling to grin through gritted teeth.

"Fuck you!"

"Knew it wasn't a good idea, Lex. Then let's get this over."

The hardships of Ryan's earlier life had given him a constitution like honed steel. He tightened his grip on the other man's hand, seeing the skin whiten, swell painfully. A trickle of bright blood appeared around the nails of Lex's fingers, and the man gave an involuntary moan of pain.

"Now," J.B. said, his voice barely audible above the roars of the watchers.

Both men had their free hands behind their backs, elbows on the tabletop, trying to use their hips and shoulders to give themselves extra leverage. Lex was the much heavier man, weighing in close to two-fifty pounds. Against most lighter men, that would have been enough to give him an overwhelming advantage. But against Ryan it didn't make a lot of difference in the final outcome.

Ryan had been confident all along that he could beat the gunner. There was a momentary temptation once he felt Lex beginning to yield, to use all of his own power and either break his wrist or give it a final victory twist and dislocate his elbow.

He didn't particularly like the older man, but he didn't quite dislike him enough to maim him.

Ryan simply slammed the arm down, let go and sat back smiling, while someone pushed a mug of local beer in front of him.

There was a voice in his ear, a calm, familiar voice that belonged to the man he loved and respected more than anyone else in the whole damned world.

"I'd have sapped you double-stupe if you'd crippled Lex," the Trader said.

"Never thought about it."

"Liar."

Ryan turned in his seat, grinning. "Well...I mebbe *thought* about it."

"Fireblast, Ryan. You still got a nasty mean streak in you."

"Thought that was a good thing."

"Time and place." The older man sighed. "I was born around forty years after sky-dark. I'm around the mid part of my own forties now, and you're the best I've seen, Ryan. You know it. Lex deserved a lesson. Everyone does, now and again. No reason to put his elbow out."

The grin had vanished. "I said I only sort of thought about it, Trader."

"Times you're like an old scarred fighting man, Ryan. Times you're a fuzz-punk out of the ruins. We're here in Colrada. Stickies been active. Burned half a ville up in the hills. Scabbies got a camp someplace around here. We need our best front team. Lex is our best rear gunner on War Wag One."

"Sure, Trader."

The grizzled figure rose and slapped him across the back of the head. It was a friendly gesture, but it made Ryan's skull ring like a .38 slug through an oil drum.

"Remember it, Ryan."

The black quartermaster, Otis, was waiting for a word with the Trader. "Said to remind you about gassing up."

"Fireblast! Forgot all about it watching these two crazies arm wrestling. Have to show them sometime how it was done in my day."

"Want me to go trade for gas?" Ryan offered, eager to make amends. "I could go with J.B. and a couple of others."

"No."

"Okay."

"There's supposed to be a big redoubt around here. Someone sold me an old map last time I was around Denver ville. Go scout tomorrow."

"Sure."

"I'll come and hold your hand," Hun whispered as the Trader strode off.

"Long as it's just my hand."

"You wish, Ryan. You wish."

MILDRED WYETH held the wrist of the deeply unconscious Ryan, checking his pulse.

"It's way low," she said finally. "I'm real afraid he's gone into a terminal coma."

J.B. stared down into his friend's placid, emotionless features. "I just wonder what the dark night's going on inside there," he murmured.

Chapter Six

Colrada had suffered in different ways during the heavy nuking from the Russians. Parts of the old state that had held silos and missile or military bases had been hard hit, and some regions, particularly close to where what was known as Colorado Springs used to stand, had been totally devastated.

There were still hot spots in a few places.

But the configuration of the Rockies had meant that some places, in the lee of the catastrophic explosions, had been spared. Small communities had been preserved, often completely cut off from the rest of the land for one or two generations. Villes had developed, each with their own warlord or baron.

And what had been concealed before the long winters began, often remained hidden.

War Wags One and Two had been working their way north toward Colrada for several weeks. They'd been picking and raiding down near the Grandee River, where there were still some big herds of cattle. But you had to pay the price that the Yanquis and Mexes wanted.

The Trader had left three men and two women

down there in unmarked graves as a part of that high price for beef.

Coming north, they'd managed to locate the old Phantom Canyon Highway. It wound along a narrow valley toward Cripple Creek, terminating near the little settlement of Victor.

It was high summer, and the sides of the trail were dappled with wildflowers, banks of gold and crimson splashed against the orange rocks. The two armored wags lumbered slowly along the boulder-strewn track, the men and women inside sweltering under the scorching sun. An old thermo had clicked way up into the red band beyond forty degrees centigrade, but the Trader refused to allow anything beyond minimal ventilation. The air-conditioning kept cutting in and out. Each time it broke down there was a burst of cursing from everyone in the steel boxes.

Ryan knew that the Trader had discovered the war wags hidden deep in the heart of the Apps, way north and east. The Trader had a friend called Marsh Folsom, and the two men had ridden together for many years. The wags had now been through about twenty years of hard usage, and it wasn't that surprising that some elements kept malfunctioning.

Now the Trader was leaning behind the driver's seat, his battered Armalite sitting easily in his right hand. He would occasionally lean forward and peer through the ob-slit at the dusty highway snaking ahead of them.

"Camp once we get out this ravine," he said. "Believe there's good water and wood ahead."

Ryan was at his shoulder. Both men wore similar clothes, which were similar to most of the crews of the two war wags: combat boots, mostly with steel toe caps; jeans or denim pants, and a mix of dark blue or brown shirts and jackets. The Trader had done a deal a couple of years ago, accepting a mass of ex-uniform clothes from a dealer near the Lantic coast and getting rid of a large cache of canned food he'd discovered in a small supply redoubt close to the Big River.

The port gunner was leaning against the wall, one hand resting casually on the butt of the bracket-mounted M-16A1 carbine. Her name was July, and she and Ryan had enjoyed a brief affair the previous fall. They had parted on terms that kept them good friends. Lately she'd been spending some time in the company of Hun.

"Hotter than a triple hot spot," she said, opening another button on her shirt and grinning at Ryan as she did so.

"Been here before, Ryan?" the Trader asked.

"Once or twice, passing through after I moved out of home."

Nobody on War Wag One knew where "home" was for Ryan. Nobody knew how he'd lost his left eye, or how he'd got the livid scar that seamed his face from eye to mouth, across his right cheek. It wasn't a question you could ask the one-eyed man.

"Which way?" the driver asked.

As the Trader was blocking his view forward, Ryan swiveled one of the armaglass periscopes and peered ahead. The road forked near the ruins of an old gas station. The Texaco sign had been snapped in half and rested in the dirt. The pumps had remained in place, like a row of patient sentinels, but the gas would have been long, long taken.

"Go right, here. It's about a half mile, close by a river."

The Trader was illiterate and had never learned how to use maps. But over the short years that Ryan had ridden with him, he'd been amazed at the sharp detail of his memory. There didn't seem a track or trail in the Deathlands that he hadn't traveled and remembered, and not a single ville that he hadn't visited during his life.

But like most of the crew of the war wags, nobody knew much about the Trader's background. He was in his early forties, with graying hair. When he could get them, he smoked sickeningly strong black cigars. He ate sparingly, rarely drank more than a single glass of alcohol and was utterly ruthless when the occasion demanded.

But where he originally came from… That was an enigma shrouded in mystery.

The multiwheeled vehicle lurched and pitched as it turned off the road. Through the dusty image in the scope, Ryan could make out the sheen of water, glinting silver through a stand of live oaks to the left of the trail.

Balancing himself against the rolling of the vehicle, he turned the glass around and watched War Wag Two follow them toward the campsite. It was barely visible through the roiling clouds of orange sand that War Wag One sent spiraling into the hot afternoon air.

"Slow. Left by that wrecked building. Flattens out there."

The engines coughed and cut out as the brakes were applied. For a moment nobody moved, waiting for the order from the Trader. He picked up the intercom mike off the dash.

"Clear behind?"

"Yo."

"Port?"

"Yeah."

"Starboard side?"

"Clear, Trader."

He leaned forward for a last look ahead, checking that there was no potential threat. "All right. Everyone out. Scouts establish perimeter, and cooks and helpers get water and fires going. Maintenance look at the third axle. Check the bearings. That's it, people. Let's go!"

FATBACK, okra and sweet potatoes, cooked in large iron caldrons blackened from age and long usage, comprised the meal. The food was washed down with some good coffee-sub that they'd picked up cheap from a pueblo ville on the edge of Westexas—cheap because there'd been a "misunderstanding" with the baron over how much jack he was paying for his goods, a misunderstanding that had been resolved by the Trader personally cutting off both of the man's thumbs as a lesson in honest dealing.

Ryan lay back on the stubbled, dusty grass, resting his head on his hands. He looked up through the sun-dappled branches of the trees, staring at the darkening sky. As he watched, a chunk of nuke debris came hurtling into the purple atmosphere and burned up in a blaze of ferocious silver light.

Over the years, Ryan had noticed that the amount of incidents like that seemed to have diminished. The chem-storms seemed less frequent and less violent. He'd asked the Trader about it once.

"When I was a kid? More hot spots. Storms were worse. Acid rain near some coasts that'd strip the paint off a wag in a couple of hours, the skin off a man's face in a quarter hour."

J.B. came and sat down by him, gnawing on a knucklebone of ham that he'd begged from one of the cooks.

"Good camp," he said. One of the things about the Armorer that Ryan liked was that he would never use three words if he could get away with using only two.

"Sure."

The river was clean, flowing fast and pure over

bare rocks. There was a small stretch of rapids upstream, with a cool, deep pool of stillness at its base. Some of the crew had already stripped off and dived in, snatching a rare chance for a good, safe bath.

The fringe of trees gave shelter from the falling sun, but wasn't thick enough to provide cover for any mutie attack. The low hills around, therefore, were scouted and guarded. Lots of places where the two wags stopped for a night were so dangerous that it meant all sleeping on board, battened down, with a watcher at every ob-slit.

Here in the clean air among the foothills of the Rockies, life was good.

J.B. had taken his Browning HiPower Mk 2 double-action automatic from its holster and was going through his evening ritual—fieldstripping and cleaning, and oiling and reassembling. All was done without even looking down at his scurrying nimble fingers. He'd traded for the blaster a couple of weeks ago, paying an awesome amount of jack to an old man in a log cabin near where they'd camped. The weapon was in immaculate condition. The old man said it had belonged to his grandfather, which took it safely back before sky-dark.

The magazine, with its thirteen rounds of 9 mm full-metal jacket ammo, lay in J.B.'s lap. His spectacles glinted scarlet in the last rays of the setting sun as he looked across at Ryan.

"Should get yourself a better blaster, Ryan. And you need a long gun."

"I can't afford to pay that kind of jack just for an automatic."

"Good as it gets, blaster like this," the Armorer replied. "Ambidextrous safety catch. Thirty-one ounces of efficiency. Must be way over a hundred years old. Mebbe hundred and fifty."

One of the mechanics on War Wag Two, a skinny black guy called Dexter, was a genius on a guitar and often played around the campfires in the evening. Ryan had watched the way his fingers danced over the strings as though they had a life totally their own. As he watched J.B. reassembling the blued-steel automatic, he had the same feeling, admiring a manual skill that he knew he could never achieve.

"You should clean your blaster, Ryan. Last time I looked at it I figured you'd been using it to hammer nails and stir stew."

Stung by the attack, Ryan slowly drew his pistol from the holster on his right hip. It was a battered Ruger Blackhawk revolver that he'd won in a wager in a gaudy-house in some frontier pest-hole up north, close to the snow line border.

"Look at it, Ryan," J.B. said, shaking his head. "Man like you shouldn't ever be given custody of a decent blaster. And look at it. Twelve and a half inches long. Takes a week to clear the holster. And only six rounds!"

"It's a real stopper," Ryan retorted. "Put down a charging stickie."

"Sure. Ten ounces heavier than mine. Big .357 will stop anyone. Grant you that."

"I'd back it against your little blaster, J.B. Get all six in a can top at fifty yards."

It was a sore point with the Armorer that his technical skill with weapons wasn't quite matched by his shooting ability. He knew that Ryan was the better man with a handgun, and it irked him.

"I can put a .50-caliber round through a can top at five *hundred* paces, Ryan. With my Sharps. Match that!"

"Can't. You got an ace on the line with that one. But I can't crap around with that on my back. Like carrying a shovel when you don't never need to dig a big hole."

J.B. shook his head. "You'll learn, kid."

Ryan clenched his fist. "And don't call me 'kid,' old man."

"Sorry. Nice spot Trader picked for camp."

Ryan stretched, feeling his muscles cracking. "Yeah. Times like this you forget about the chilling. Clean air and the stink of spilled blood's gone."

"How long we been together?" J.B. scratched the top of his head, where his hair was beginning to thin. Only a week ago he'd appeared from a scouting expedition around an old housing estate proudly sporting a brand-new, light brown fedora, which now lay beside him on the warm earth.

"How long?"

"Yeah. Since we met up with Trader?"

"Want the count in days, miles of firefights? Or corpses?"

J.B. sighed. "Beautiful evening, and you have been hit by the gloomy stick."

Ryan laughed. "Sorry. Just there's times that I look ahead. Wonder where we'll both be in ten more years. Still riding with the Trader? Still keeping a finger on the trigger all the time?"

"Rad-blast it! Course not. I'll be a retired gentleman of leisure running the best dealing store for quality blasters in all Deathlands. How about you, Ryan?"

"Married with kids and a spread of good land. Or dead. *¿Quien sabe?* Who knows?"

Chapter Seven

"Back in two hours and forty-five minutes, Ryan. No longer."

"Sure."

The Trader looked him up and down, like a general examining a young lieutenant before sending him off on a diplomatic mission.

"The ville died years ago, attacked by scabbies and burned out. Doubt you'll find much worth finding up there. Look out for any clues to a redoubt."

"Lovely day for a walk, Trader," Ryan said.

"Bright sun makes for a good target," the older man replied.

THERE WERE FIVE in the recon party. Ryan was leader, with Hun as second. Ben, a tall, quiet relief gunner with dark glasses, made three. Ray was a driver of War Wag Two. Lox was the shortest member of either crew, barely making it to five feet tall, but the effervescent little blond girl was a great auto mechanic.

All of them were armed with a variety of blasters. Ben toted an Uzi while Hun had a sawed-off 10-gauge slung over her shoulders. Ray carried a pair of

unmatched European .32s, and Lox had a handmade
.38 at her belt, a 6-shot revolver that she'd found on
a garbage dump and repaired herself.

Up the slope, away from the river, it was still possible to make out the overgrown traces of the side
trail, winding across the hillside, over a hogback ridge
and disappearing.

When they reached the ridge, Ryan held up his
hand for a pause, looking back to the foaming ribbon
of the river and the two dusty war wags, the cluster
of small fires.

He automatically checked his wrist-chron. Ahead
of them the trail was less distinct, obscured by low
brush and long meadow grass, but it led toward a
narrow valley.

It was a bright, clear morning, the sky flawless except for a collection of fluffy cream clouds, far away
to the northwest.

"Grizzly country," Ben commented, scanning the
higher slopes above them.

Hun grinned. "Heard there's a mutie grizzly
around here, a humpbacked sow, flecked silver and
gray. Say she ripped the side clear off a trading wag
came through here a month ago."

"Glowing night shit!" Ray exclaimed. "That the
truth, Hun?"

Ryan didn't want anyone getting jumpy on recon
with him. Tight fingers on triggers got people chilled
real quick. "You stupe! There's no grizzly like that
up here."

"You sure, Ryan?" pressed the woman, her dyed hair like fire in the sunlight. The Trader was always kidding her about her hair, and she was always promising that one day she'd dye it green. Ryan knew Hunaker well enough to guess that she might just do it.

"Sure. Let's go."

THE FIRST dozen or so houses they came across were utterly devastated. It wasn't possible to tell whether it was the result of the nuking, or whether they'd been pillaged and burned out in the past few years. Roofs had fallen in and every window gaped, glassless. A swimming pool behind one had a faded mosaic on its stained sides, and it was still possible to make out the design of interlocked human eyes. A small lizard scrabbled in the few inches of water that stagnated in the deep end. Lox aimed her blaster at the creature, but Ryan quickly checked her.

"If I want muties on our necks, then I'll give them a shout."

"Sorry, Ryan."

Hun patted her on the shoulder. "Never apologize, sweetie. It's a sign of weakness."

They continued on. A splash of yellow flowers lined a number of side trails that darted off from up the steepening flanks of the valley.

"Shall we split up and scout around?" Hun suggested.

With five of them, they could protect themselves

against any sort of mutie attack. But if they split up into smaller numbers, safety would become less certain.

"Better stay together," Ryan replied. "Don't forget there's supposed to be scabbies around here."

"I don't see no sign," Ben said.

"Then you better use your eyes better," Ryan snapped. "That looks fresh painted to me."

He pointed ahead of them and to the right, to a single-story house with a long cream-colored wall. On it, in dripping letters of dark green, someone had scrawled a message. And, as Ryan said, it looked to be fresh.

Waer Skabis, it read.

"I seen better spelling," Ray said, "but I guess the message is triple clear."

"We stay together?" Hun asked, grinning ruefully at Ryan.

"We stay together."

THERE WERE TWO corpses inside the cream-walled house. It was difficult to tell from their condition what they'd once been. One had been a woman, but the mutilations were so severe that it was hard to tell for sure. The smaller body lacked a head, hands or legs.

"Probably a child," Hun said quietly. "Like to get one of those mutie bastards in front of my blaster."

"Been dead around a week," Ryan guessed. "Drying out in this heat."

The skin was stretched taut and was such a dark

brown it edged into black. There were no eyes in the gaping sockets, and the soft tissues at the mouth, nose and groin had already been largely eaten away by a variety of predators.

"Think he'd have buried them," Ben said. "Guy left that message. Must have been his kin."

"Mebbe not." Ryan looked around. "No sign of a firefight here. Looks like scabbies crept up out of the hills and chilled them. Sign could have been done by someone passing through. Or someone lived nearby here."

The sudden voice behind made all of them jump.

"Right there, stranger. Live nearby. Old Walt lives nearby and that's a fact."

The man who stood in the doorway of the ravaged house was around five feet nine inches tall and looked like he might weigh around ninety pounds soaking wet. He was dressed in a variety of animal skins and was barefoot. His face was whiskered, revealing just a pair of faded blue eyes. The man carried what looked like a crossbreed blaster, half shotgun and half self-made bell-muzzle blunderbuss.

"You put that warning up?" Ryan asked, easing the hammer back down on the big Ruger.

"Sure did, sonny. Never got the way of letters, but I got close as I could." He peered owlishly at Ryan. "Hey, was you ever bit by a dead snake?"

"No."

"Me neither. Heard tell of it. Preacher near Leadville was with a whore. Husband came back, Preacher jumps out the back window. Lands on a dead rattler. Barefoot. Poisoned. Died. Heard tell of it, years ago it was.''

''What happened here?'' Lox asked, gesturing to the two corpses.

''The Widow Bishop and her little lad. Scabbies came a week back. I was out hunting. Seen tracks of a big mutie grizzly.'' Hun and Ben exchanged meaningful glances.

''Why didn't you bury them?'' Ryan asked, suddenly angry with this crazy, garrulous old man.

''Why'd I do that, sonny?''

''Because of fucking decency, you terminal fool!'' Hunaker spit, obviously sharing Ryan's instinctive dislike for Walt.

''Not my kin.''

Ryan shook his head. ''Sure. Just keep on walking by the other side, old man. Do the same for you, one fine day.''

''Seen the scabbies since?'' Ray asked.

It was the right question, and Ryan felt a momentary flush of anger at himself for not having asked it already.

''Nope. Hide nor hair. But I know they're still around here.''

''How?''

The dull eyes flicked around to Ryan. ''I ain't deaf, sonny. I hear 'em. Most nights. Yelping and singing. And I smell 'em cooking.''

''Where d'you live?'' Ben asked.

"Top o' the hill, sonny. Y'all come see me when you've poked around here. Going up now." He paused. "Did I ask if you was ever bit…"

"Yeah," Ryan said.

AFTER WALT had vanished, leaving behind a maniacal cackle and the lingering stink of a long-unwashed body, Ryan led the others into the next building up the canyon. They left the corpses where they were, since the recce time was limited.

The next house was larger. All the glass was gone, and the interior looked as if it had weathered a hurricane. Not a stick of furniture remained undamaged. Ryan went in first, turning to the others. "Ben, you and Lox stay here. One each side and keep your eyes open. Ray, climb up on the roof there. Don't shout if you see anything. Just get down and report."

"While you and Hun go have fun inside, huh?" Lox sneered.

"You do it, or you stay here and keep Walt company after we're gone." Ryan didn't raise his voice to her.

"You threatening me, Ryan?" she asked, her voice flat and cold.

"Don't be a stupe. You've ridden long enough with the war wags to know there's a country mile of difference between a threat and a promise. What I said was a promise, Lox."

Ryan turned his back on her and stepped inside, boots crunching over broken splinters of glass. It took a few moments for his vision to adjust to the darkness within the open-plan building.

"Nukes or muties?" Hun asked, her hair like a beacon in the gloom.

"Both," Ryan replied.

"What're we looking for? Food? Blasters? Not likely to find anything in this shit heap."

"Never know. Been places and found things."

Unexpectedly the woman, stepping in close, grabbed at his groin and squeezed gently. "I been things and found places, Ryan," she giggled.

Their coupling took less than five minutes and wasn't all that terrific for either of them. Hunaker was bent backwards over a torn Naugahyde sofa, her pants around her ankles. Ryan simply unbuttoned and thrust into her, feeling her pelvis grinding against his, her arms strong around his neck, her mouth sucking at his lips hungrily.

"That wasn't bad, sweets," she said as she clicked her belt buckle shut. "But we gotta do it properly with more time."

"It'd be good."

"That little cutie, July, might come in on a three-way fuck," Hun whispered, licking her lips in a way that made Ryan regret they'd been so hurried.

"Could be good."

A PILE OF debris stood ten feet high in the farthest room. Ryan guessed it might have been some sort of workroom. The shell of a word processor rested on top of shelves, along with files and folders. He reached out and tugged, bringing half the mountain sliding down around his feet. Something small and scaly rustled across the room and picked its way out through the broken wall.

Ryan probed the shelves and recognized a machine that was some kind of message transceiver. He'd seen them before, but never one that was in good working order. Some of the old prenuke machines had double lithium batteries that were supposed to last nearly forever.

It had a number of keys: Mess Record, Mess Rcvd, Announce Only, Rewind and Play.

Ryan pressed Play, expecting to hear nothing but silence. There was a delay, then a faint hissing sound, the gritty noise of dusty wheels meshing. Ryan turned the Volume knob around.

"Hi, this is Dave Platt. Sorry I'm out right now, and the way things are I'm not real sure what time I might get back. But leave a message for me."

Ryan let it wind on, listening intently to this voice from long ago. Another voice broke into his concentration.

"Hi, Dave. Corinne here. Denver's gone crazy. Don't know when I can get away. Catch you later. Love you." The words were followed by a noisy, sloppy kiss.

Hunaker appeared in the doorway, saying nothing, her face solemn.

"Hi, Dave. Calling at…at one-thirty on the…I

can't remember the fucking date, man. Can we come stay at your place? Here there's nothing but—''

The call ended in silence. The tape hissed on for another few seconds, then cut off with a loud, finite click.

"Not with a bang but a whimper," Ryan said.

"How's that?"

"Something I read someplace, sometime. About how the world would end."

"What I know, Ryan, is that it ended up with the biggest fucking bang the world's ever known. Or ever will know."

"Yeah. Find anything around?"

"No. Lot more shit like this, all around the place. Been cleaned up and reamed out."

"Go tell the others we're leaving. Better look in on that old crazy up on the top of the hill before we get back to the wags."

She went out, and he heard her calling to the other three. Something brushed against his boots as he moved, crackling dryly. He bent and picked up a crumpled paperback book. It was larger than usual and filled with black-and-white drawings, like a comic book.

Through a crack in the wall his eye caught a flicker of movement, but whatever it had been was gone.

The book was called *House of Raging Women* and was drawn and written by someone called Los Bros Hernandez. Inside the back were some striking pictures of some other comic called *Love and Rockets*.

Ryan had seen a lot of comics in his time. Oddly, despite their seeming frailty, they were something that survived around Deathlands better than a lot of other, tougher things.

"Here, Ryan!" The call came from outside.

Reluctantly he dropped the book back on the pile and went blinking into the bright sunlight.

The other four were grouped together, looking up the hillside.

"What is it, Hun?"

"The old crazy, Walt. He's waving his arms around to get us to go up there."

Now Ryan saw him, a tatterdemalion figure that was capering on the porch of a shack above them. Strangely Walt wasn't shouting out to them. He just waved his arms and beckoned for them to join them.

"Let's go."

But Ryan was conscious of the feeling, a faint, uncomfortable prickling at his nape. It was an itch that didn't need scratching, like someone was walking behind you, dodging every time you turned around so that you never quite got to see who it was.

"Red alert," he said quietly.

Lox looked at him as the others drew and cocked their blasters. "Red? What for?"

"Do it." The coldness in his voice wiped the sullen expression off her face almost as if he'd slapped her.

It took only a half minute for them to join Walt. Ryan stepped in close.

"What is it?"

"I seen 'em. In the draw. Scabbies. They was—"

Ryan didn't hear the crack of the blaster. All he saw was the old man's head explode, covering his own face with hot blood and sticky threads of brain.

Chapter Eight

Even as he dived sideways, Ryan's fighting brain was working overtime. His left hand wiped the warm gore from his good eye while the right drew the Ruger and thumbed back the hammer. And his mind was racing.

Walt was dead. His legs might be kicking like they were tangled in bed sheets, and his fingernails might be cracking and scrabbling at the rock, but the lines of communication were down.

Immediately after the explosion of the old man's skull, Ryan's acute hearing caught the flat bark of the blaster. It had the unmistakable sound of a smooth-bore handmade musket and probably fired a huge round; maybe even .50 caliber. And to blow Walt's head apart, the range had to be short—less than fifty yards was Ryan's guess.

As he hit the dirt, Ryan heard the sound of four or five other explosions, overlapping, the noise echoing around the steep valley.

They faced half a dozen muties, assuming that's what they were. In any part of the Deathlands, at any time, there would be gangs of roving outlanders, thieves and murderers, combining in wolf packs to harry and raid the weak and isolated. Twice in the past three years, the war wags had encountered such gangs and decimated them in savage firefights, as the discipline of the Trader brought victories.

"Cross the other side!"

That came from Ben, crouching behind a low wall to Ryan's left. Since the five members of the recce party were virtually at the top of the hill, the attackers must be below them. Poor tactics, Ryan thought as he scanned the opposite slope. He spotted a puff of powder smoke from a clump of mesquite, near a pair of identical ruined houses. He heard the thin whine as the bullet hit stone a couple of yards to his left and went singing into the clear sky.

But the bullet that downed the old man had come from somewhere closer, probably a little lower on the same side of the valley.

"Get inside the building!" Ryan yelled. "Me and Hun'll cover you. Go!"

He snapped off three spaced shots, concentrating on the area where he'd seen the smoke. Hun blasted a couple from the sawed-off pump-action 10-gauge, even though it was way beyond practical range for the close-action blaster.

Ray led Lox and Ben at a scurrying run into the relative safety of the semiderelict building behind Walt's corpse. A figure stood, long gun at its shoulder, aiming at the running trio. Ryan steadied his right wrist with his left hand and fired a single, careful shot, wishing as he did so that he'd taken J.B.'s advice and gotten himself a good rifle.

But the Ruger did its stuff. There was a muffled scream as the figure threw up its arms, dropped its blaster and crashed forward. It rolled down the slope in a cascade of stones and dust and lay still near the bottom. Ryan could make out a splash of red, spreading below the chin.

The shooting provoked yells of anger and a flurry of shots in reply. Hastily aimed, none of them came anywhere close.

"Now, Hun!" Ryan shouted, picking the pause while their attackers would be reloading their primitive weapons.

Despite the danger, he was immediately conscious of the stink of the old man's home, strong enough to make him gag. Sweat and urine were the less unpleasant ingredients of the smell.

But he was pleased to see that Lox, Ray and Ben had obeyed their training, each taking a side window to cover against a sneak attack.

Ryan nearly tripped over Walt's blunderbuss lying propped against a chair that looked to be built from rusting iron and knotted twine.

"Hun, take the front."

"Yeah."

"Keep watch. I'll support anyone under threat. All okay?"

There was a chorus of acknowledgment.

Ben hissed, "Got a bullet clean through my shirt sleeve. Never touched me."

"Think they'll have heard the shooting from the wags?" Hun asked.

Ryan considered the question and took the wind and the contours of the land into account.

"Can't tell. We're way off, and there's ground between us. Wind's against it, as well. If there's a scout in this quadrant then they might have heard something. Can't bet jack on it."

"So, we wait?"

"Yeah. We wait. We got the high ground and a good defensive fire point. If they want us, let them come after us."

TWO HOURS AND FORTY-FIVE minutes had been the Trader's orders to Ryan. That meant a search party would start after them if they weren't back within the three-hour limit. And they could walk straight into the ambush.

The one-eyed man looked at his wrist-chron. So far they'd been away from camp for about ninety minutes. No need to hurry events along. Not yet. He'd ordered the others to hold fire unless they actually got a clear chill shot. None of them had blasters that would do the business at much over thirty yards, and there was no point in wasting ammo.

"More of them coming," Ben called. His position overlooked the top of the opposite slope, where there were prenuke mining ruins.

"How many?" Ryan picked his way through the

junk to squint through the tattered cloth that covered the window. "Eight, ten."

"Fireblast!"

The game was changing. Their position was strong enough to hold easily against the half dozen muties they calculated were out there. But if the number was doubled or tripled, then the lack of any long guns might prove terminal.

He could see one of them, crawling on hands and knees, the top of his head occasionally peeking out over a weathered slat fence. It was a temptation to try to put a bullet through the skull, but Ryan possessed only twenty spare rounds in his jacket, and the odds against a hit were too great.

"What do we do, Ryan?" Hun asked.

The idea of sitting patiently and waiting for the Trader to send a rescue force didn't appeal to Ryan Cawdor, but if they left the shack and made their way down the steep and precarious hillside, they'd be totally exposed to the cross fire from the scabbies gathering around them.

"I got a plan," Ryan said.

"GOT ANY MORE ammo?"

"No. Ben? You got any bullets?"

"One round left, and I'm saving that for myself if they come at us!"

Ryan turned and pointed to Hun, who opened her mouth and screamed. "No! Oh, no! I got no bullets left for my blaster!"

The muties had opened up from all sides in a fusillade of shots, the defenders firing off about half the ammo they had left. Then they deliberately dry-fired their blasters, so that the muties' acute hearing would catch the metallic clicks of hammers falling on spent rounds or on empty chambers.

There had been spasmodic shooting from the slopes around them, but none of the muties had shown themselves, remaining safely behind cover.

Ryan found a ragged length of dirty sheet, and tied it to a broken broom handle, waving it outside the front door in the universal gesture of surrender.

"We give in! Don't shoot. We give in!"

There was silence outside. From just inside the doorway Ryan could see out across the reddish rocks down the valley. Above him he glimpsed a large bird floating effortlessly on a thermal, silhouetted against the pink sky.

"Hey out there! Can't you hear me? We're giving up! We run out of lead!"

A voice replied, thick and guttural, with an accent so thick you could've cut it with a blunt chisel.

"Throw yore blasters out!"

This was the tricky moment of the whole plan. From below, Ryan guessed that the muties wouldn't be able to see all that clearly onto the cluttered patio outside the door. Everybody had concealed their blasters, fully loaded, down the backs of their shirts, tucked into belts. They all now held a variety of chunks of the scrap metal that seemed to fill the old man's shack.

"Here we go," Ryan said quietly. "They open fire on us, then we get back under cover and wait for Trader. They fall for this, and you don't open fire until I say. Anyone starts blasting too soon, and I'll gut-shoot 'em myself."

"Throw yore blasters out, and you mebbe get t'live some!"

Not even triple-stupe muties wanted to get chilled if they could avoid it. Ryan knew well enough what the shouted promise was worth.

"Let's go do it, people," he said, leading the way into the bright sunlight, unable to restrain himself from a wincing expectation of being torn apart by a hail of .50-caliber bullets.

"Here's the blasters!" he yelled. He'd emerged with hands held low, and he chucked the remains of an electric iron on the tiled yard, where it rang with a satisfying and, he hoped, convincing sound.

The others jostled around him, all heaving out bits of old domestic tools, doing it so fast that it would be hard for the muties to be sure what they'd done.

"Get your hands up," he prompted.

The waiting was the worst.

He didn't check his wrist-chron, but Ryan's realistic guess was that only a couple of minutes crawled by while they waited, in full view of at least a dozen blasters, grabbing air.

"They're not going to buy it," Lox whispered, her voice cracking with the tension.

"If they was going to chill us from cover, they'd have done it by now," Ray said.

That was also Ryan's hope, though he didn't say anything.

"There," Hun breathed with an excited anticipation that verged on the erotic. She enjoyed killing more than most anyone Ryan Cawdor had ever met.

They could all see them.

There were sixteen in all, and if Ryan had been in command of the attackers he'd have sent only a couple of his best men to check. The whole group had wandered out from cover and was picking its way through the brush, up the slope toward the five defenders.

One of them appeared from their side of the valley, holding a long-muzzled musket, which Ryan figured was the weapon that had blown Walt's brains all over him.

Out of the corner of his eye, Ryan saw that Lox was shuffling her feet, and was just beginning to lower her arms.

"Not yet," he warned.

Slipping in the loose stones in their haste, the jubilant muties closed in on their victims. As they drew nearer, Ryan recognized the typical stigmata of the scabbie.

They maintained genetic malformations from the nuking of their ancestors, which manifested itself in appalling skin diseases. Ryan had once come across a crude book that dealt with the range of disorders that ravaged scabbies: dermoid cysts, rodent ulcers, keloids, lipomata, epitheliomata, acne, psoriasis and all manner of unnamed rashes.

Many scabbies went naked through life, unable to bear the discomfort of clothes against their weeping raw skin. Ryan had seen a scabbie, shot in a firefight, tugging off a loose cotton shirt to try to examine the wound. Half the flaking skin was pulled off his chest and back in his clumsy haste.

The leader was a tall man, carrying an Armalite rifle that was even more battered than the one that the Trader hefted. He was bearded, as most of the males of the group were. Scabbies found shaving wasn't all that easy as there was a tendency to remove part of the face along with the stubble.

There were four women in the group, all with hideously blotched and peeling skin. One was scratching at her breasts as she walked up the hill, leaving bloody furrows in the ulcerous flesh.

Ryan spoke without moving his lips. "Wait, wait, wait."

To be sure of total victory, each of them had to take out at least three of the mutie band.

Judgment was critical. The moment would come when the first of the muties would reach the crest of the hill and be able to see clear across the patio—and would be able to see the pile of scrap that had passed for blasters.

The hammer would fall at that moment.

"We gonna social some with your buddies in them ol' wags in the holler, boy," the leader of the scabbies called with a cheerful, toothless grin at Ryan.

In another ten yards they'd be in a position to see over the low wall around the yard, but they were still too scattered for an ideal slaughter. The steepness of the hill had strung them out more than Ryan had hoped.

But it wasn't going to be a situation with a second chance built in.

He watched the seamed, pocked face of the chief of the pack of muties, trying to read his eyes, watching for the second of shock when the man would realize that he'd been fooled.

"Right glad that—" The words disappeared as the scabbie caught on.

"Now," Ryan said in a calm, conversational tone, buying an extra fragment of splintered time by not shouting and warning the rest of the muties.

He reached behind himself and drew the long-barreled revolver, leveling it and squeezing the trigger in a single fluid movement. Ryan had cocked his blaster before concealing it, giving himself another moment of advantage.

That first shot signaled the beginning of three minutes of screaming chaos.

Chapter Nine

The firefight started badly. Just as Ryan fired at the leader of the scabbies, the man slipped and fell on hands and knees. The bullet sliced through the air over his head, missing him by eighteen inches.

If the mutie had called his forces back, they would quickly have been beyond effective range, and the balance of power would have remained with them.

Scabbies weren't great tacticians.

"Fuckin' kill 'em!" the leader screamed, firing a burst from the hip with his Armalite.

Hun, Lox, Ben and Ray all had their blasters drawn, pouring lead at the straggling wave of yelling attackers. Ryan aimed and fired off four careful rounds. He had the satisfaction of seeing four scabbies go down, each hit with a killing shot either through the head or upper chest.

Ryan saw Hun put down three with her first two shots, bracing the sawed-off shotgun against her hip. She quickly broke the gun and flicked out the two empty, smoking cartridges, then thumbed in two more rounds. The gun continued to boom its starred hail of death.

Ray, Ben and Lox were also issuing tickets for the

last train to the coast. Wreathed in powder smoke, the tiny girl stood between the two taller men, her handmade .38 thundering.

In the first half minute, Ryan reckoned they chilled ten or eleven of the scabbies. Then the muties were over the low wall and on top of them, screeching and firing their blasters, dropping empty guns and attacking with a variety of knives and cleavers.

One of the mutie women, bleeding from a shotgun wound, dived toward Lox, whose pistol was also empty. Ryan swung around and snapped off his last shot at the scabbie, but the bullet only nicked her ribs, making her stagger but not putting her down.

The butcher knife she wielded opened up Lox's throat, almost severing her neck. Blood jetted out like an arterial fountain, and Ryan knew at that second that the war wags would be measuring for a new shortest crew member.

Ray spun to his left and fired at the scabbie, the bullet exiting between her shoulders in a gout of shredded flesh. At the same moment a round from the scabbie leader's Armalite hit him in the thigh and he went down, cursing.

Hun's scattergun roared again, and Ryan saw two of the surviving muties vanish in a welter of smoke and crimson spray. Ben was backing into the house, followed by a tall, naked man.

The Uzi chattered, and the scabbie came staggering out, his body jerking under the impact of the bullets.

"Ryan!" Hun yelled, pointing behind him.

He turned to confront the scabbies' leader. The Armalite was no longer in his hand, and blood ran down his left arm. In his right hand he held a murderous ice pick.

Ryan threw his empty pistol at him, but the mutie's reflexes were quick, and he ducked under it. Ryan, stumbling over the junk on the patio, suddenly remembered Walt's bell-mouthed blaster and ran for the doorway.

He saw Ben and shouted at him to get out of the way. The floor was slick with spilled blood, and the one-eyed man nearly fell. In a moment he turned like a cornered wolf and snatched up the gun.

The butt was sticky to the touch, and Ryan fumbled for the unfamiliar trigger, heaved the hammer back and locked it. There was no way of knowing in advance if the heavy blaster was charged or not.

"Kill yer, outlander fuckhead!" the scabbie raged as he burst in through the doorway, the sunlight glinting off the needle tip of the ice pick.

The trigger was so stiff with caked grease and dirt that Ryan had to jerk on it twice, feeling his heart almost stop at the first failure.

The mutie was in midair when the blunderbuss finally fired.

It felt like there was a couple of cans of black powder rammed down the barrel as well as ten pounds of assorted nails and chunks of iron and steel.

The explosion was deafening, and the stock kicked back against Ryan so hard that he fell to the floor. He saw the flash and smelled the bitter smoke, but he couldn't see the effect of the blaster. All he knew was that the scabbie was suddenly on top of him, fighting, kicking and roaring in an odd, bubbling voice.

Ryan's face was flooded with blood. In the confusion of the fight and his head hitting the floor, he couldn't be sure whose blood it was. The antique blaster rolled against his leg, and he kicked it out of the way. His hands were locked tight around the suppurating, pustulant neck of the mutie, throttling him into submission. He felt the struggling body grow limp, but the one-eyed man wasn't taking any chances. He hung on until he felt a sharp kick on the hip.

"It's done, Ryan." The voice belonged to Hunaker. "It's over. You nearly blew the mutie fucker clean in half with that cannon."

Someone yanked the corpse off and helped Ryan to his feet. He wiped the stickiness from his face for the second time in the past hour.

"Over?" he asked.

"Yeah," Hun replied, managing a cold smile that never got close to her eyes. "It's over."

"Lox?"

A shake of the head. "Bought the farm. Bitch slit her throat like a pig in the slaughterhouse. Poor kid never had a chance."

"Ray's wounded," Ben said. "Bullet in the top of the leg. Went in and out, clean. He's binding himself now and reckons he can walk back to the wags."

"Survivors?"

Hun answered. "One. An older woman. Turned on her heel and legged it down the hill. Ben tried a shot, but she was gone. Rest are chilled."

Ryan looked down at the body on the tiled floor of the shack. The charge of the blunderbuss had hit the scabbie just below the belt buckle. At point-blank range it had, as Hun had said, nearly blown him in two.

"Fireblast! Look at my pants and shirt. Got half his guts all over me, and most of Walt's brains as well. I can sure use a bath."

"Best get back, Ryan." Hun glanced down at her own chron. "Trader'll be sending out a relief patrol in a half hour or so."

"Yeah. How's the ammo situation?"

"Enough," Hun said.

"Me too," Ben agreed. "Ray's low. Never carries enough, the stupe."

"Could be none of us had enough," Ryan said quietly, looking around at the scene of carnage. "Just didn't expect there to be this many of the bastards out on the hunt."

IN THE END they left Lox's pale corpse up on the hillside. Ryan and Ben carried it inside out of the sun and covered it with the cleanest dirty sheet. It was one of the Trader's cardinal rules that dead members of the war wags were to be retrieved from firefights—

as long as it didn't needlessly hazard anyone else's life.

Ryan led the way down the valley. Ray was limping along, helped by Ben and Hun. They didn't see or hear any sign of more scabbies.

"Yo, the camp!" shouted one of the scouts from the main trail. "Four coming in!"

The Trader broke away from a discussion with a couple of the mechanics near the main drive axle of War Wag One and strode across the camp to greet them.

"Lox chilled?"

"Yeah. Scabbies."

"Many?"

"Close on twenty. We chilled them all but one. Ray got a bullet clean through his leg."

The Trader looked around, catching the eye of Otis, the quartermaster. He beckoned to him. "Burial party. Six plus another six support."

"Lox?"

Ryan nodded. "Scabbie bitch cut her neck open. We took her in the highest building up the steep vee ahead over the ridge. Covered her in a sheet. There's plenty of scabbie corpses up there, and an old man with his head blown apart."

"Just Lox," the Trader ordered. "We'll bury her this evening by the river. She'd have liked that."

THE SUN was sinking beyond the snowcapped mountains to the west. The sky was a cloudless gray-purple, and the shadows from the trees lay across the racing waters of the foaming river.

With the exception of four quadrant guards, everyone from War Wags One and Two were there, standing in a loose semicircle around the rectangular hole that a working party had dug during the afternoon. Ryan, standing next to the Trader with Hun at his shoulder, could taste the tang of freshly turned earth.

The pathetically small body, shrouded in a layer of stout canvas, had already been laid in the grave. Rodge and Matt stood ready with shovels, waiting for the Trader to say a few words.

"Lox was a good mechanic. Given a few more months of riding with us, she could have become a great mechanic. Might not have been the tallest lady ever rode with us, but it didn't stop her doing her duty. And now she's gone. Don't know much about her. Don't know about her folks. But they could be proud of her. I know I'm damned proud of her, and we'll all miss her. Guess that's all. Just let's remember this moment and her grave. Any of you pass this way again years to come, put a fresh sprig of something green down for Lox. One verse of the hymn."

Ryan had seen enough funerals with the Trader to know what he meant by "the hymn." For the Trader there *was* only one hymn.

The peaceful valley rang with the mix of male and female voices, the old words rising to the evening sky.

"Amazing grace, how sweet the sound..."

The Trader turned and whispered to Ryan. "Forgot to ask you. See any sign of a redoubt up that way?"

"Nope. Nothing."

RYAN SAT with his back against a towering sycamore tree, hugging a tin mug of coffee-sub. Once the sun was down, the night became cold. The camp was subdued after the burial, with none of the usual laughter and bantering. Dexter's guitar remained in its case, and many of the crew had already gone to bed.

Hun strolled by, huddled inside a fur-lined jacket. She smiled down at Ryan and ruffled his hair. "You okay?"

"Sure. Happens. Her turn today. Mebbe my turn tomorrow."

"Least we had a good quickie, huh?"

He managed a smile. "Sure. Just got it in before the chilling started."

"Time we managed to fit in a slowie, Ryan?"

"Not tonight, Hun."

She nodded and walked away, her stocky body silhouetted against the crackling flames of one of the sentinel fires.

The Trader materialized out of the darkness like a wraith of the night, squatting next to Ryan with creaking knees.

"Dark night! Wish my joints worked a mite more quietly."

"Want me to get you some coffee-sub?"

"No, thanks, Ryan."

A few minutes later, he said, "Should have kept better watch, Ryan."

"I know it."

The Trader turned to look at him. "Figured you did. Just felt it needed saying."

"Sure."

The Trader sighed and stood again. "Changing plans. Not going farther north. Cutting east. Been hearing about a new ville with stocks of gas and ammo. Thought we'd go take us a look."

"Yeah. Why not?"

Chapter Ten

Rain glistened on the undulating blacktop ahead of War Wag One like a length of velvet ribbon. The trail east wound its way along the sides of valleys, plunging between sheer walls of quartz-speckled rocks, close by turbulent water. In the three days that they'd been traveling since the firefight, they hadn't passed a single other vehicle.

Twice they drove past fortified farms, built like medieval settlements, with a number of houses within a high stockade. Ryan had seen vids of the days of the old West, and recognized the pattern from cavalry forts. The small convoy didn't stop. Frontier people were likely to be fast on the trigger, and there was no point in risking lives.

The road was often broken, either by the effects of the old nukings, or by a hundred years of bad weather. They had to stop once, while a fallen tree was cleared off the blacktop. The Trader immediately put both crews on full red alert. It was one of the most common tricks in Deathlands for muties to fell a tree and wait to see who they caught.

It was a heavily wooded area, coming across to what had once been New Mexico. Ryan sat by one of the general crew, a man with a heavy beard and who had a passionate interest in trees and flowers. Whenever the wags hit a new ville he'd go around to the junk stores, looking for old books on his favorite subject. His name was Nick.

"Place like this, I could count off twenty different kinds trees in two miles."

"Twenty?"

"Sure."

Several of the others in the warm main cabin of War Wag One overheard the conversation, and there was an immediate surge of betting.

"How much jack says you're bullshitting us?" asked July from her position by the portside M-16A1.

Ryan was about the only one who didn't get suckered into the noisy gambling fever. Within a couple of minutes Nick had accepted enough bets to risk a month's basic pay.

Hun was at the wheel of War Wag One and she turned round in her seat, making sure that she also had a piece of the action.

"Twenty different kinds of trees in two straight miles?"

"Sure," Nick agreed confidently.

Otis pressed him. "You can say anything, my man. And we don't know trees from buffalo shit. You might lie to us."

Nick stood and faced the tall quartermaster. "Listen, Otis. I might lie about women, or blasters, or drugs, or jack, or women."

"You said women," Ryan pointed out.

"Sure. But I don't lie about important things like trees or plants. All right, Otis? All right?"

"All right. Hun, give us a count on a zero mile t'start."

"Coming up. Ready, Nick?"

"Sure."

"Then...go!"

The bearded man moved to the starboard ob-slit and began to recite names.

"Aspen. Cottonwoods. Elm. Red oak. Live oak. Silver maple."

The Trader, as silent as ever, had appeared in the main control area of the wag and was keeping score. "That's six."

"Only gone about a hundred yards," Hun called from the front.

"Hickory. Some lindens down by that patch of swamp grass. Can't tell what kind of linden they are. Higher up the hill there's lodgepole pine. And ponderosa pine, as well."

"That's ten," the Trader announced. "Halfway there already, Nick."

"Quarter mile," Hunaker said.

They went in silence for a while, and Hun ticked off the half-mile mark.

The wag went around a steep bend and Nick was able to see farther ahead, and up a fresh slice of the hillside.

"Spruce and blackjack oak."

Otis gave a guffawing laugh. "What's that last one, bro? I ain't never heard of no blackjack oak. Come on."

"Rough bark and leaves that go into wide lobes with tiny needle tips to them. Used to be common alongside highways."

"All right, I believe you, man." Otis winked at Ryan. "That's twelve. Still got another eight to go."

"Just over a mile left," Hun reported.

"Limber pine. Silver maple."

"You had that one," said the Trader. "Thirteen down. Seven to come."

"Honey locust and that's a western hemlock on the ridge above us."

"Five more."

"Only got a little over a half mile left, Nick," Hun called. "You better start reeling in some more trees."

"Sweet gum."

For the next half minute nobody on the wag said anything. Nick moved from side to side, glancing through the ob-slits. For the first time he was starting to look worried. The trail began to climb again, and a whole new section of the mountainside was revealed to him on the right.

"Ah, that's a mess of chestnuts. And up there's a stand of white pine. Other side there's a mulberry. How many's that?"

"Nineteen," Ryan said. "That what you make it, Trader?"

"One to go," he confirmed. "How close to the two miles, Hun?"

"Less'n a quarter mile."

"Spruce."

"No. Had it."

"Shit." Now Nick was pressing his face against the ob-slits, dashing from side to side.

"Hundred yards."

The wag was moving slower, gears grinding as it worked up a steep incline. A part of the blacktop had been eroded by rain, and the wag tilted sharply toward the left side. Several of the crew were already starting to crow with the scent of victory in their nostrils.

"Coming up to—"

"Poplars. Lombardy poplars!" Voice cracking with excitement, Nick pointed to the left, on the far side of a dried creek. There stood a whole long row of the tall, narrow trees. Even Ryan recognized them.

"Glowing night shit!" someone cursed. "Never figured he'd… Son of a bastard bitch!"

The hubbub died away and Dexter, the mechanic from War Wag Two, began to sing. He was riding with them because of the axle trouble, but he was a popular member of the crew.

His clear tenor voice began to rise above the noise of the engine.

"As through this life I wander
    There's funny things I see.

Some'll rob you with a blaster,
   Some'll rob you with a tree.''

THEY FOUND an abandoned farm-fort that evening. Its outer defences were virtually intact, but several of the houses had been burned down. Cattle stalls and pig-pens still remained, but there was no evidence that they'd been used for a dozen years or more.

"Make a good camp," the Trader observed.

Ryan looked around. "Bring War Wag One in and park it against the back wall. Fence looks weak there. And War Wag Two can stand where the main gates are gone. One sentry in each corner fire tower, and we're snug as can be."

J.B. jumped down and stretched, his glasses gleaming in the late-afternoon sunshine as he looked around. He'd heard Ryan's suggestions about defending the site and nodded approvingly.

"Good. No high ground to command, and a well. Best check the water. Seen plenty of wells used for dumping corpses." He nodded again. "Good place. We can sleep easy."

"JUST YOU and July?"

"Yeah."

"How come you got a shed with a roof all to your two lonesomes?"

"Charm, Ryan. Everybody fucking loves me, don't they?"

She thumped him so hard on the shoulder that he

actually staggered. Not only had Hunaker managed to sneak her way into the best accommodation in the small fortress, but she'd managed to talk July into sharing it with her. And now she was offering to let Ryan come in with them as well.

It was after ten o'clock at night. Over to the north Ryan had heard the distant rumble of thunder and seen the rich purple sky seamed with the silver lace of lightning. The idea of having a roof, even though it was only rough-cut sod, was better than having to crowd into the hot metal box of the wag. And if there was going to be any heavy rain or hail, sleep became the next thing to impossible.

"July know you're asking me, Hun?"

The tip of her tongue came out and crept along her full lips very slowly, followed by a smile that Ryan recognized from several previous encounters with her.

"It was her idea, Ryan."

"You only want me for my body," he said, returning her grin.

"Yeah, you got that right."

The storm was coming closer. Many of the crews of the two wags began to moan and bitch, rolling their sleepers and carrying them back into the wags. Several of them saw Ryan, standing in the doorway of the hut that had been commandeered by the two women.

"You shit gold, do you, Ryan?" someone shouted. It was too dark for Ryan to recognize him. "Luck like you get, wouldn't surprise me."

"Come in and prop that old door up, Ryan," Hun said quietly. "Don't want everyone watching us, do we?"

"Nope." He hefted the door that had rotted off its leather hinges years ago and stuck it into place, wedging it with a couple of tumbled bricks. Inside the small eight-by-eight hut it became suddenly, totally black.

Someone giggled.

RYAN WAS AWAKENED by the crack of bright sunlight that appeared through a small hole in the corner of the roof. He was wearing only his shirt and combat boots. His pants, like everyone's on the wags, were wide enough and slit at the bottoms so that he could pull them off and keep his boots on.

His body felt stiff, and he stretched, exploring the sore places with questing fingertips. There was a little dried blood across his shoulders, and he could feel the raised welts from one of the women's nails. One of his front teeth felt loose. It had been dealt a cracking blow from July's knee as she rolled about on top of him. There were several bruises around Ryan's ribs, and his right cheekbone was puffy and tender.

Hun played rough.

His groin felt like someone had used a rotary sander on it, and he winced as he lifted off the sleeping roll and heard the sticky sound of himself peeling free.

At his side, one of the two women groaned and

turned over. There was just enough light for Ryan to make out July, her cropped blond hair catching the dagger of golden sun.

Cautiously he sat up, licking his dry lips and experiencing a whole variety of tastes, some of them pleasant in a reminiscent sort of a way. His hand fumbled for his blaster, feeling the reassuring shape and weight of the big Ruger. He became aware of the sounds of the camp stirring awake outside. His nostrils caught the smell of frying food, and the dark tang of bubbling coffee-sub.

Though Ryan didn't usually worry much about the opinion of his companions, he was almost dreading opening the door and stepping out into the morning. Everyone on War Wag One and War Wag Two would know where he'd been, who he'd been with and what all three of them had been doing.

Ryan started getting dressed, biting his lip as he pulled up his pants and fastened the heavy brass buckle. He checked that his long-bladed Bowie knife was in its soft leather sheath on his left hip, then slotted the blaster on the opposite side.

The two women were also awake and beginning to dress.

Hun was sitting in her sleeping bag, naked from the waist up, breasts tipped with fire in the shaft of bright light. She pulled on her shirt and winked up at Ryan.

July was tugging her pants over her long, slim thighs, concealing a variety of scratches and bites as she did so. She looked at both Hun and Ryan, and then looked away without saying anything.

"Don't worry about it, kid," Hun said quietly. "We all had a good time, didn't we?"

"Yeah. Yeah, we did. I never thought I'd like to do... It was real good."

Hunaker stood up and kissed Ryan on the cheek. "Guess we gotta go face the rest of the world, huh? Get us some side laughs." She whispered in his ear. "Tell you one thing, Ryan. If all men were like you, I might even give up women."

Ryan threw open the broken door and led the way into the camp.

Chapter Eleven

As the two-wag convoy rolled toward its destination, the land opened up. The snowcaps were left behind, vanishing through the rear ob-slits, and the highway stretched straight and level ahead of them. It wasn't ambush country, and the Trader agreed to allow full ventilation for the crews. It meant that all doors and obs were left open, so that a current of fresh, coolish air came filtering through.

The weather was good, and the Trader ordered the noon meal to be served on the wheel.

Rodge, carrying a tray of plas dishes, made his way through the long vehicle, balancing from months of experience against the swaying and jolting. The biggest meal was generally in the evening, but the Trader made sure that everyone ate a good breakfast.

That morning there'd been a whole lot of muttered jokes that centered on Ryan, Hun and July. The young woman found it hard to handle and blushed deeply. In the end Hun stopped the teasing.

Lex had just offered July a fried sausage, making sure in the way he held it that she realized all the crude sexual implications.

Hunaker slapped it from his hand, as quick as a striking prairie rattler.

"Hey! What the fuck..."

She didn't speak loudly—didn't need to. Everyone in both crews knew her reputation.

"One more word and I take that sausage, Lex, and I stuff it up your ass, grit and all."

The jokes stopped cold.

Ryan sat with J.B. and the Trader at one of the metal folding tables that were fixed to the sides of the war wag. The fourth at the noon meal was the senior navigating officer. The oldest member of the team, pushing well past fifty, Beulah Webb, had joined them only a few weeks ago. Her predecessor, who'd been with the Trader for five years, had been a lean black named Jerry Craig. He'd tried to outrun a knife during a fight in a pest-hole drinker. The knife had caught up to him, and War Wag One was shy a navigator.

The same fight had widowed Beulah Webb when a broken bottle severed her husband's jugular. She'd gone to the Trader and asked to be taken on. She offered to do anything. Then she mentioned that her hobby was old maps, and she had what she claimed was the finest collection in all of Deathlands. Beulah had brought them with her and had stepped straight into Jerry Craig's boots.

She dipped her spoon into the bowl and peered at it suspiciously. "What in the land of Goshen is this supposed to be?"

Rodge was passing by and heard her. "We was going to serve cougar's balls on toast, but we done run clean out of bread."

It was an old joke, but it still brought a yelp of raucous laughter from the listening crew members.

Beulah slowly raised the middle finger of her right hand to the cook's assistant, glancing at the embryonic beard that was sprouting on the edge of his chin, which was Rodge's pride and joy.

"I don't understand, young man," she said in her precise Southern accent, "why you bother to cultivate that hair around your face when it already grows wild around your ass."

The laughter was redoubled, with Ryan, J.B. and the Trader joining in.

They carried on with the meal, which claimed to be a sort of mutton stew, thickened with flour, dotted with sliced okra and spiced up with shredded red chilies.

Through the open door Ryan watched the increasingly arid land roll by. Swept by scouring winds, the old four-lane was in surprisingly good shape, giving them an unusually smooth ride.

"They got some fresh peaches for after," said the Trader, wiping his mouth on his sleeve.

Cohn, the new radioman, had been eating his stew at his com-set, one earphone hooked in place. He took it off and glanced around to his boss.

"Nothing doing," he announced.

"Still a day and a half from the ville. Might pick up some local scramble tomorrow."

"You know these parts, Ryan?" Beulah asked, finishing her food.

"Not much. Me and Trader haven't ridden these roads together."

She looked up and tucked an errant strand of silver hair behind her ear. "You three have been together for a long time, haven't you?"

J.B. answered. "Yeah. Ryan joined a year or so before me."

"I never heard about how you actually came to ride the war wags, Ryan. Did Trader ask you to join up?"

"Sort of."

The Trader picked at a shred of meat stuck between his front teeth. "Sort of. Sort of not."

"Heavens! Why don't you just tell me? I'd be real interested."

"Okay."

THE TRADER had his own sec-locks established in a small war buggy that he used when the war wag was too slow or clumsy. Or conspicuous. Life was even more dangerous a few years ago, and a man didn't want to get in his driving seat and find someone else in there with him. So sec-locks had been fitted that would take the arm off anyone stupid enough to try to tamper with them.

He checked that they were still set before he used his own personal release code and heard them click open. The door slid back and he climbed into the small vehicle, settling himself comfortably into the driving seat.

And felt the metallic chill of a heavy-caliber automatic blaster jammed hard against the back of his skull.

The voice was as cold as Sierra meltwater, barely stirring the air inside the cramped little wag. "One move wrong and you get to see your brains all over the windshield."

"I'd figure that would give you around another thirty seconds of living. You're surrounded by my people."

The intruder laughed quietly. "They said you were good, Trader. Said it took a lot to move you. Not even a .38 in the neck bothers you any."

The Trader managed a smile. "I wouldn't say it didn't bother me. Sure it bothers me. And it bothers me how you got past the sec-locks."

"Easy."

The Trader knew a lot of men who'd have said that and made it sound boastful. The way the stranger said it made it sound like a simple, honest statement of fact.

"You want to lift the buggy?"

"Mebbe. Let's get the hell out of it so's we can talk."

The door slid open again and Trader got out. The stranger was good, not giving him a chance to swing around and knock the blaster out of his hand. He eased out of the buggy right behind the Trader.

The Trader was able to get a good look at him. He was used to summing up men and women quickly. Second chances were a rare luxury in Deathlands.

The man was in his mid-twenties, around six-two, strong, had a rangy build and weighed in close to the two-hundred-pound mark. He had a chillingly pale blue eye, the left one hidden beneath a patch of dark leather. A long scar seamed down his face, from the corner of the right eye to the upper lip. It was an old scar, which showed up pale against the tanned skin. Bushy black hair curled over his nape, and a Smith & Wesson automatic filled his right hand.

"Name's Ryan Cawdor."

The barrel of the gun was steady, aimed a little below the Trader's heart—maximum incapacitation without the final necessity of death.

"You know who I am," the Trader said. "You want to chill me, or you want to join me?"

"Join," Ryan replied.

"THAT'S REAL DRAMATIC," Beulah said at the conclusion of the story. "Kind of like the first meeting of Stanley and Livingstone."

"More like Johnny Appleseed and Irving Ragweed." J.B. grinned.

Later Beulah brought out one of her prenuke road maps, tracing their route from where Lox had died, heading eastward. Then she showed the Trader and

Ryan her own private maps, amended from her research to show only settlements that still survived.

"Here it is." Her stubby finger pointed to a neat red square. "Towse ville."

"Whose the baron there?" Ryan asked. "I got the feeling I heard some things about him. And none of them's good."

The Trader looked at the map. Though he couldn't read or write he had a rudimentary ability to follow a map.

"Worst baron I heard of was called Jordan Teague. Owns Mocsin, in the Darks. Got a sec-boss called Strasser. Kurt Strasser. No, Cort. That's it. Got a face like a skull. Figured we might go up there one day and say 'Hi.'"

"But who's baron in Towse?"

"Carson. Alias Carson. Folks called him that 'cause he had so many different names. Now he's settled in and gotten some power. Alias Carson. Married too, I heard."

Ryan nodded. "Yeah. That was the name. Didn't he burn out some Indians? Had their own kind of homestead."

"Pueblo," Beulah said. "Towse Pueblo. Lots of adobe houses and a church. Close by the Sangre de Cristo Mountains."

Trader looked solemn. "Bloody massacre. I passed through a few days earlier. Kind of flourishing community they had there. Day's end and Carson and his sec-thugs had chilled every mortal soul. Said he wanted it for his own redoubt.''

"And we're going to trade for gas and ammo?'' Ryan asked.

"Yeah. So watch your backs.''

Chapter Twelve

They were a full-day's drive from Towse ville when the lookout on War Wag One spotted the smoke. The message came back to the Trader on the control deck. The whole war wag was wired for sound, and the news brought a new edge of alertness to the entire crew.

"Condition yellow," the Trader cautioned. "Close main doors and watch the ob-slits. Lookout?"

"Yo!"

"Report smoke. Direction? What kinda smoke's it look like?"

"Gas. Black smoke, curling high. Almost dead ahead of us."

"How far?"

He hesitated. "Difficult. There's heat haze. Guess not more'n a coupla miles."

One of the relief drivers was at the controls, and the Trader passed the word for Hun to come and take over. If there was trouble, it was only simple common sense to have your best person at the wheel.

She pushed past Ryan without a word. That was one of the reasons why Hunaker had survived on the war wags as long as she had. Her personal life never imposed on work.

Ryan glanced through the front scope and saw what the lookout had reported—an oily pillar of black smoke winding into the pale pink sky.

He wondered if it was an accident, then dismissed the notion.

The engine revved and gears clattered as Hun prepared War Wag One for full battle speed. Otis had taken over the radio intercom and was talking to War Wag Two on the lip mike.

The lumbering armored juggernaut climbed to the top of the ridge, and Hun eased down on the brakes with a hissing of laboring hydraulics.

Simultaneously the lookout yelled down, "Convoy of wags under attack. One's on fire. No, there's another one burning!"

"Report properly, you triple-stupe bastard!" the Trader shouted angrily.

"Five wags, two fired. Caught by roadblock of stones. Looks like a war band of twenty or thirty around them. Hand blasters. No...just saw what looked like a bazooka or a gren-launcher. Missed target. Not seen us yet."

"Red, red, red," the Trader repeated.

This wasn't a passing frontier incident. Gren-launchers fell into the category of "serious" and meant that an organized group faced them.

At a word from Ryan, Hun applied the brakes and

brought War Wag One to a gentle halt. Otis passed
the command to the following war wag.

J.B. had taken over the lookout's turret spot. Ryan
had one of the scopes while the Trader leaned on
Hun's shoulder and stared out the armaglass front
shield.

The three men together would appraise the situation and decide what action the war wags should best
take. But the final decision always rested in the hands
of the Trader.

With higher ground behind them, the two vehicles
still hadn't been spotted by anyone in the fight below.
So all of their options remained open to them.

"Heavy blasters," J.B. suggested. "We run down
on them, and we can probably scare them off. But it
could mean losses."

Ryan agreed. "Have to try and take out the guy
with the gren-launcher first. One lucky shot from that
and we could be in some deep rad-dust."

The Trader nodded slowly. "Likely that convoy's
heading west for better lands, and they run into those
blood-eyed sons of bitches. Plenty of losses already.
Two wags burning. Longer we sit here the more
they're gonna lose."

"Got to drive through this way anyway," Ryan
added.

"Yeah, Ryan. Why not? Quartermaster?"

Otis looked around. "Yo."

"Tell Two we're going in. Independent command
and firing. Chill as many as they can."

The stocky black began to relay the message to the wag behind them.

''Ready people. Gunners! Open fire as soon as your blaster'll bear. Hun, go in fast, then slow it down. Don't want to get locked in with those burning wags there.''

War Wag One, sealed tight for action, jerked forward and began to gather speed down the straight stretch of old highway.

During the few minutes before the shooting began, Ryan hung on to a stanchion and thought about dying.

Any man or woman who said they went into a firefight feeling calm and under control was lying. The mouth began to feel dry and the palms of the hands started to feel moist.

Nobody wanted to get chilled, but there were times when it looked as if the only option was to go out as best you could. Pretty up and walking good, like someone once said.

Ryan still woke up shaking in the long hours of early morning, when the heart beats slowest and the sick are nearest to death, thinking about a snow-veiled gulch up north. The ground was frozen so hard that your boot heels rang out on the packed earth.

It hadn't been that long since he'd run from home, and he was still a callow kid.

Now, in the confines of War Wag One, he remembered the cross-trees gallows and the feel of the rough hemp against the skin of his throat, the knot lumped under his right ear.

His breath had come fast, hanging in the air in front of his face like wind spray. He'd been surrounded by a ring of blazing torches and the smell of the burning pitch, faces muffled in scarves and hoods, with only the eyes showing.

The trouble had been about the ownership of a horse. A pinto pony, Ryan recalled. An argument had ended with the other man on his back in the dirt, flakes of snow settling on his staring eyes.

The lynch mob hadn't taken long to reach its decision about who was guilty. The stranger kid with one eye was as good a victim as a person could look for.

It had been a woman who'd saved Ryan, bustling to the hanging tree, calling out that the boy was innocent. She'd seen it all. They couldn't top a young lad who'd been provoked into the deadly fight.

She'd persuaded them, and she'd taken Ryan back to her widow's shack and kept him there for a couple of weeks until the anger faded away from the ville. And she'd gotten him to pay a price for his life, in her bed, every night.

Now, only about ten years later, Ryan couldn't remember a single thing about her.

The sharp pinging of a slug against the armored steel of the war wag jerked him back to the present.

"Hold fire," came J.B.'s voice over the intercom. "Not until my word." The Armorer judged range with a calm expert's eye.

The shell of War Wag One was now beginning to

ring as lead beat a savage tattoo outside. But inside, everything was still calm and controlled.

Ryan watched the approach of the raiding band through the scope, counting heads and trying to make out the level of their weaponry. It was a surprise to see how many of the attacking band had high-powered rifles. He spotted a distinctive Colt Sporter II, and a couple of conventional Whitworth sporting rifles.

Now they could hear the sounds of the blasters. There was a burst of venomous chatter that splattered along the starboard side of the war wag.

"Beretta SC 70, short assault rifle," J.B. said. "These guys have got them some serious power out there."

"Close enough?" the Trader called.

The wag continued to crawl forward in a lower gear. Ryan could see that the group of men—he couldn't make any women—were moving back into a rough perimeter, keeping up a steady fire at the new enemy. The two ordinary wags were still blazing fiercely. There was only sporadic defensive shooting from the other high sides.

"Go," J.B. said.

FROM RYAN'S point of view, the firefight wasn't particularly satisfying. His function during this kind of action was simply to be available, and to be ready to lead any countercharge. In this case, it was quickly obvious that the raiders weren't going to hang around and become drawn into an exchange with the overwhelming power of the two war wags. They were already beginning to withdraw in an orderly manner toward the line of bluffs and buttes a half mile or so to the east. Ryan could see, by switching the scope to high-mag, that the land was seamed with a maze of narrow draws and arroyos. It wasn't the terrain to pursue on foot an enemy who knew the land.

War Wag One was filled with the racket of chattering blasters. The machine guns mounted on the roof and on the starboard side all opened up. Their targets had concentrated on that flank, and the gunners on the port pods were left with nothing to shoot at.

J.B. kept up a terse, running commentary to make sure everyone was informed. Only the Trader, Ryan and some of the gunners were in positions to see for themselves how the firefight was going.

"Couple trying a charge from one of the wags. Stupid. Yeah, both down. Some good eyes out there. Still pulling back. Nice. Good shooting whoever that was. Bowled him like a rabbit."

The Trader ordered Hun to bring the wag to a total stop, about three hundred yards from the small convoy. Gradually the firing died away on both sides, only an occasional bullet ringing off the steel flanks of War Wag One.

"Stop firing," J.B. called. "They're all way gone. Taken their gren-launcher with them. Don't think any're staying behind."

He was right. When the Trader finally gave the command to move down the slope, there was no sign of any of the attackers—except for seven corpses, lying where they'd fallen.

Ryan wiped sweat from his forehead and buttoned the flap over the Ruger. It wasn't going to get fired that day.

RYAN'S responsibilities as war captain for the Trader didn't include having to hang around and socialize with a group of double-stupe settlers who were lucky not to have all been slaughtered. His responsibilities *did* include taking out a working party to search the corpses for any clues of where they'd come from, who their leader might be, how many of them there were and what kind of blasters they toted. He was also responsible for collecting any weapons they might have been carrying for J.B.'s expert assessment.

He also had to post a circle of sentries, particularly over toward the line of dusty orange cliffs where the raiding party had vanished.

Ryan was briefly conscious of a tall woman glancing in his direction with eyes of the most piercing green he'd ever seen. And there was a slender girl beside her who he assumed was her daughter. What had the bearded old man told the Trader her name was? Chrissy? Krysty?

"Yeah, Krysty," he said, and promptly forgot the name.

Chapter Thirteen

The two women stood on either side of the bed, looking down at the unconscious figure of Ryan Cawdor.

Mildred Wyeth glanced across at the flame-haired woman, wishing she could offer her some sort of solace in her desperate misery.

"How long have you known him, Krysty?" she asked. "When did you first meet him?"

Krysty shook her head. The bright curls seemed dulled, pressing in tight around her face. "I'm not sure."

"Not sure?"

"No. Part of me thinks I met Ryan first up in Mocsin, when he sprang me from that iron-hearted bastard, Strasser."

"But..."

Krysty sighed. "You know I've got the power...of seeing. Learned it from Mother Sonja, back in Harmony. I mean that things aren't always that clear to me. Past and present. The lines sometimes get kind of blurred."

"So how's that affect when you met Ryan? You saying you might have met him before? In some kind of previous existence?"

Krysty managed a wan smile. "Not really that, Mildred. More that I have this heart-feel that I may have known Ryan before. I don't know. Maybe our paths crossed once."

They stood together and looked down. Ryan was in a deep coma, his heart beating slowly, his breathing so shallow that it was difficult to make out any movement of his chest.

"Will he make it, Mildred?" Krysty asked.

The black woman didn't answer. She watched Ryan's face, seeing how the right eyeball was flicking to and fro against the trembling lid as though he were dreaming.

Chapter Fourteen

By the time Ryan returned to the war wags, the situation had been resolved.

The travelers had collected and buried their dead and rescued what they could from their burned transport. The women had vanished inside, while the men went about their business.

There was no more information about the band that had attacked them. The men had come out of the desert and disappeared in the same way. They'd been particularly well armed and disciplined, and Ryan had found, once he led out the party from War Wag One, that they'd also taken their dead and wounded with them.

The old man with the white hair wasn't able to offer any real help.

"One thing, I noticed," he said.

"What?" the Trader asked.

"Man leading the chillers."

"What about him?" J.B. pressed. The Armorer had already spoken to Ryan about the way the raiders had been so cleverly organized. They'd not wasted time on trying to fight off the more powerful war wags, just held them up a little so they could make their orderly withdrawal into the hills.

"Well…" He glanced sideways at Ryan, licking his lips.

"Come on, man," the Trader prompted.

"He lacked an eye."

"Which one?" Ryan asked. "The same one as me? Which?"

"Same one. I could see him very clearly. Apart from that there was nothing to note about any of the gang."

"You'd better get moving, mister, in case they got wags and try and circle around and hit you again. Plenty of daylight left."

The white hair blew across the old man's face as the northerly wind gusted. He brushed it back from his eyes. "Very well. Our thanks again, Trader, to you and all your people. Had you not come along… then things might have gone badly."

Ryan shook his head. "Get farther and live longer if you don't talk soft shit. They wouldn't have *maybe* gone badly. You'd have been chilled. All of you. Everything stolen worth stealing. Women raped. Children too. All chilled. Not 'things might have gone badly.' Understand?"

He spit in the dirt and walked away to where Hun had War Wag One ticking over.

Behind him there was a cold silence. The old man mumbled something about getting back on the highway for Harmony. A cursory shake of the hand with

Trader and J. B. Dix, and then the two groups parted company.

They went on a few miles under a condition red, before the Trader relaxed it to yellow. It was close to evening before they dropped eventually to green.

THE TRADER, Ryan and J.B. sat together around one of the small cooking fires, each with his bowl of stew and a hunk of bread.

"You spoke harsh against the man," Trader said.

"Yeah," Ryan replied through a mouthful of the thick stew.

"Why?"

"Had it coming."

"No." The Trader shook his head. "Not true. Old man had lost friends and kin. You spoke harsh against him."

Ryan put his spoon down. "I get tired of folks like him. They move around the Deathlands, full of wind and piss about a new land, new home and new hopes. Don't even bother to get themselves any serious weaponry. Drive blind into an ambush. We bail them out of the hot spot."

J.B. interrupted him. "Come on, Ryan. Those raiders had a real ace on the line. Gren-launchers and some sophisticated blasters. Most convoys would have dropped the flag for them."

"Yeah, sure. But there's a lot of stiff ones out there now. Could've been we might have taken a lucky shot from a gren. Then there'd have been some serious chilling. It's just that I don't like that kind of stupe out here.''

The Trader patted him on the arm in an unusual gesture of affection. "Gotta give the other man his space, Ryan. Right to space. You see the villes out east, don't you?''

"Drop it, Trader. Just drop that kind of talk. You made a point. Now let it lie.''

There was a sudden moment of bitter tension between the two men. J.B., sensing it, slowly put his spoon down.

"You want to go find a quiet place to punch each other's lights out? Or do you wanna talk about where that raiding gang came from?''

Ryan smiled. "I'm not much at saying 'sorry.' You're right, J.B. Just something got to me. Maybe seeing the women and children and knowing what they were risking. Sure, let's drop that side of it. Way they was organized I could almost put them as secmen.''

One of the crew came around and pushed some more wood into the fire, making it flare with a bright yellow flame. A starburst of sparks rose in a whirling circle into the black velvet of the sky.

The Trader rubbed at his chin. "Could do with a shave. Hate looking in the mirror and seeing gray hairs sprouting on my chin. Like seeing my father's face looking out at me.''

"More stew, Trader?'' Ryan asked, glad that the

tension had eased and that his own dark mood had lifted along with it.

"Nope. Don't relish food way I used to. Times my guts starts feeling like I swallowed a sewer rat. Claws at me."

"Should see a doc about it," J.B. said.

"If there's one in Towse I might. I guess it'll be interesting to check out their sec-men."

"See if they got a one-eyed man," Ryan said. "Yeah."

"What if they have, Trader?"

"Then, J.B.," the older man said, grinning, "we'll just have to step even more careful." He stood. "And now I'm for sleep."

DESPITE ALL OF Beulah's best navigation, the two wags were forced to take a circuitous route to get close to Towse ville, eventually making a great circle and coming in from the north.

"Big gorge, hereabouts," she warned, peering at her road atlas by the light of one of the opened ob-slits.

The morning had started with a ferocious shower of cold, driving rain, beating in on the teeth of a blue norther. It had turned the campsite into an instant quagmire, but the big driving wheels of the war wags had got them moving without any serious difficulties.

They'd driven on through drier weather, with the sun eventually emerging from banks of dull, brown-ish-orange clouds. The highway steamed in front of them, and it was a relief when the Trader ordered all doors and ob-slits thrown wide open.

"Bridge ahead," called Peachy, one of the relief drivers. He was only in his midteens and had joined the group less than a month ago, near the Grandee River. His nickname came from his attempts to grow a macho beard. The pale result resembled nothing more than the fuzz on a fresh young peach.

"Slow it down," ordered Ryan, who was in the command position. The Trader was relaxing in his bunk.

Gears ground noisily, and the young man fought his way to take the edge off the speed. The front of the wag dipped as he used the brakes.

At one time there had obviously been a massive bridge with painted iron railings over what looked from a distance like a deep gorge, the one that Beulah had mentioned earlier.

Through the mag-scope, Ryan could see that there was now a bridge of wood and ropes. Whether it would bear the enormous weight of the armored war wags was uncertain. Through the scope Ryan could also see a small group of men carrying blasters.

He pressed the button on the intercom that linked him to the Trader's tiny cabin.

"Sec-patrol in sight," he reported. "This side of a big bridge."

"How many?"

"Four."

"Stop a quarter mile off. Be right there."

War Wag One halted. Ryan had put the crews on condition yellow. There wasn't any serious threat from the four men, so he held off from red. In hot weather, conditions inside the metal boxes could quickly become intolerable for the crews.

The Trader was at his elbow, looking out through the armaglass shield. "Toll collectors," he said. "Must be on the edge of Towse ville."

"We'll pay," J.B. said. It wasn't really a question. Trails and bridges into villes were commonly subject to toll payments.

"Sure. Long as it isn't too much."

How much was too much tended to vary from ville to ville, and also depended on how many blasters the toll keepers could muster.

Ryan gave Peachy the order to drive forward slowly, watching the tiny figures of the four sec-men grow larger until one of them held up a hand as a warning sign.

"Stop," Ryan whispered, and the war wag came to a smooth halt.

"Talk to them, Ryan," the Trader told him.

The door was already half-open and Ryan jumped down, feeling the heat of the sun striking at the left side of his face. He saw, for the first time, that the gorge was spectacularly deep. As he walked toward the guards, boots crunching on the sand, he was also making a mental appraisal of the probable strength of the bridge. He decided, once he was close enough, that it was sturdily built and would easily carry the two war wags, as long as they took it one at a time.

"Hi," said the tallest of the waiting quartet.

"Hi. Heading for Towse."

"Baron Carson controls the ground you're walking on, outlander."

There was a confidence and arrogance that Ryan didn't take to. Nowadays he managed to control his razored temper better than when he was younger, but he could feel the scar on his face beginning to burn with the pale beginnings of rage. With an effort he swallowed and steadied his breathing.

"That so? How much does he want to let us come and trade with him?"

"Cross the Gorge Bridge? Two big wags like them two? Whole lot of jack."

Ryan knew that the Trader wanted to avoid any argument and offered a lowish figure, which the sec-man promptly tripled—and Ryan halved.

"Baron Carson don't like to hear about outlanders fucking with his regs."

"We got enough weaponry on those wags to take out any ville in the Deathlands," Ryan replied. "But we come in peace. Want to trade for gas and ammo. So I'll pay the last figure I named and add another ten percent on top."

The man glanced at his colleagues, who were all carefully studying the distant white peaks of the Sangre de Cristo mountains. Eventually he nodded to Ryan.

"You settle when you get into the ville. I give you this ticket—" he wrote slowly and laboriously on it with a worn stub of green crayon "—and you show it and pay."

Ryan took it, checking that the amount of jack was what they'd agreed. "We go across the bridge now," he said.

"Sure. Try it both at once." The guard grinned, showing that most of his teeth were missing. "Long way down and no way up. I'd like it real good if that happened."

"I see you on the way out of here, and I'll break both your knees," Ryan said with a friendly grin. "Remember that."

Fifteen minutes later, War Wags One and Two drove along the well-maintained blacktop and found themselves within sight of the adobe buildings that made up the ville of Towse.

Within the hour they made the acquaintance of the baron and his lady.

Chapter Fifteen

Baron alias Carson of Towse was an inch or so over six feet in height. He was somewhere around the middle forties, lean, and wore a lightweight gray suit and a homburg hat. His horn-rimmed glasses had thick lenses that showed up the weakness of his pale blue eyes. His face was skinny and weathered by the New Mexico sun into deep furrows around the mouth, nose and eyes. Baron Carson's voice placed him somewhere to the east of Towse, a slow, nasal, Texas kind of a drawl.

Under the instructions of two more of the laconic sec-men the wags were parked in the square of what had once been the Indians' pueblo. The burned-out shell of a church stood stark at one end, the adobe smeared with long streaks of soot. A narrow river ran through the middle of the ville, spanned by a slender wooden bridge.

Baron Carson, with his wife and a dozen heavily armed sec-guards, came striding out of the largest building on the east side of the open plaza.

"You're Trader. Heard you was coming to pay a call on us. Welcome."

Ryan took an instinctive dislike to the skeletal figure, despite the apparent friendliness of the greeting.

"Come to deal for some gas and some ammo. Word south was that you had some stocks."

Carson nodded. "Word's right. Living here I'd be a terminal fool if I didn't keep supplies. There's some relatives of the Indians who used to live here that'd be real glad to come and visit one dark night."

"You drove them all out?" Ryan asked.

The baron turned his incurious, dull eyes in his direction. "Didn't catch your name, young man," he drawled.

"Didn't throw it, Baron. But I'm Ryan Cawdor. War captain to the Trader."

"Really. How very interesting," Carson replied, the tone of his voice making it clear as a slap in the mouth that he meant the opposite.

The tall, gray man folded his hands in front of him like a priest at prayer, and Ryan noticed that the tip of the little finger on the left hand was missing. It looked as though it had been neatly severed, many years ago.

"You chill the folks that lived in the ville, Baron?" J.B. asked.

"They don't live here anymore. That answer the question?"

The Trader tried to take the abrasive edge from the conversation. "This your lady, Baron?"

Alias Carson stared impassively at him, his face

totally without emotion. "Well, she sure as shit isn't a camel, mister."

The baron ran a finger round the inside of his collar. Despite the ferocious heat in the square, he wore a vest under his jacket, and a tightly knotted tie that was so dark a blue that it was almost indistinguishable from black.

After an uncomfortable pause, the woman spoke up for herself.

"I'm Sharona Carson. Like to welcome you all to Towse ville."

"Thanks, ma'am." The Trader bowed stiffly from the waist, in a strangely old-fashioned gesture that Ryan had never seen him use before.

But Sharona Carson, woman to Baron Alias, wasn't like any female that Ryan had seen before.

She looked as though she'd stepped straight out of the pages of a prenuke clothing magazine. Ryan's guess put her within an inch or so of six feet, but it was difficult to tell because of the spike heels on her open-toe shoes, highly polished and the color of crushed lapis lazuli.

Her dress was some kind of lightweight cream wool that clung to the gentle contours of her body like it was made for them. A slim gold chain was buckled around her waist, and a thinner version was clipped about her left ankle. She wore a gold wrist-chron and every finger carried a fine gold ring. Ryan wasn't particularly an expert on gems, but he recognized the ruby and the emerald, the sapphire and the huge fire opal, and a tulip-cut diamond that caught the sun and threw it back in myriad knives of rainbow brilliance.

Around Sharona Carson's elegant throat was a single strand of perfectly matched pearls. Her hair was cornfield blond, tumbling in sinuous curls to her shoulders.

She was stunningly beautiful.

Her eyes, an unusually pale lilac, were breathtaking. It was rare in Deathlands to see a lady wearing makeup, let alone the state-of-the-art perfection of Sharona Carson. Sluts in gaudies might daub some black around their eyes and smear some crimson grease on their lips, but here was a delicate and subtle use of shades and textures and tints.

When Baron Alias Carson had come to meet them with his bodyguards, his woman had been standing among the sec-men. Now she stepped forward so that they could all see her.

Ryan had never seen such a walking example of enormous wealth. The jewelry alone would have kept an entire frontier ville in supplies for ten years.

"Is something wrong with your one-eyed friend, Trader?" she asked.

Ryan started and looked away, embarrassed that she'd caught him staring at her, openmouthed.

"Young men nowadays, lady," the Trader replied with a grim smile. "All gall and no backbone."

"Thought he was trying to catch swallows in his

open mouth,'' Baron Carson said without the faintest
trace of a smile.

Ryan was relieved when the conversation shifted
to a dinner invitation for himself, J.B. and the Trader.

THE ARMED sec-men were everywhere. The Trader
had insisted that the wags should be guarded only by
his own people, keeping the baron's heavies away
from them.

There was a table of scrubbed pine that was large
enough to seat thirty people, but it held only six place
settings. The baron was at the head, with the Trader
on his right and Ryan on his left. Sharona Carson sat
next to Ryan and opposite J.B. Between the Armorer
and the Trader there was an empty chair.

''For my sec-boss,'' the Baron said. ''Ferryman's
out on business for me. He radioed in that he'd be a
little late. The business didn't quite go according to
plan.''

''You'll like Ferryman, Ryan,'' Sharona said.
''You and he have something in common.''

''What?''

''Wait and see,'' was all she would say.

The earlier inordinate affluence and ostentation of
the woman's clothes and jewelry were repeated at the
meal.

Baron Alias wore the same clothes as before, sitting
ramrod straight, narrowed eyes darting behind the
thick lenses to whoever was speaking. He occasionally interjected a comment in his slow, nasal drawl.

Sharona had changed.

Her hair had been piled on top her head and secured with a pin of beaten silver, holding in its clawed end a large bead of rough amber. Her necklace was also of unmatched lumps of soft amber. A bolero jacket of light cream suede was draped over her shoulders, pinned at the front across her breasts with small silver clips. Every time she leaned forward to help herself to one of the dishes of food, Ryan was aware that he could very nearly glimpse the nipple on her left breast.

Sharona's skirt was dark green leather, buffed to a dull sheen, its hem reaching to her knees. Her shoes were of matching green leather.

The plates and dishes were of fine china, with a delicate floral pattern etched around the edges. The glass was crystal that rang like a bell if tapped with a fingernail. The cutlery was plain steel, unadorned, but with handles of carved bone.

The food was ornate and was served in tiny portions, surrounded by artistic little pools of bright sauces, and vegetables carved to resemble flowers.

Ryan craved a decent hunk of meat that he could get to grips with, and a realistic helping of potatoes. He helped himself to some honest gravy instead of the endless array of sweet and sour sauces that spoiled every dish.

He and J.B. made some effort to follow the example of their hosts, who picked at their food, constructing color-keyed mouthfuls for themselves. The

Trader didn't bother. He simply picked up his spoon or fork and attacked every course with them, scraping up the meat or fish or game and jamming it into his mouth along with the frail florid vegetables. He used a hunk of bread to mop up the sauces.

"You seem very hungry, Trader," Sharona observed, not bothering to hide the patronizing note in her voice.

"I'd need to be to keep eating these double-small portions of overdressed duck, wouldn't I?" he replied, picking at his teeth and hardly bothering to smother a belch.

Eventually, after what seemed like hours, the servants cleared away the last dishes and brought in a silver samovar resting over a blue spirit flame. They settled it in place, ready to make coffee. And at a signal from Sharona, they withdrew.

"Your sec-boss, Ferryman, looks like he's not going to join us," J.B. said.

"He'll be here. Probably attending to the burying first," the baron replied.

"The business cost some?"

"All business costs, Ryan," Sharona replied. "It's a question of whether the price is worth the paying."

"Or the prize worth the having," the Trader added, leaning back in the antique oak chair.

"Oh, yes. How true, Trader. But if you truly want a thing, then no price is too high. What do you think, Ryan?"

The candles in their silver sconces were beginning

to gutter and flare, making the rectangular room shrink in the gloom. Ryan wasn't sure how well Baron Alias could make out the faces of his wife and guests.

He hoped that his own face was impassive and his voice pitched normally as he replied to the woman's question.

"There's times that the price could be out of reach," he said.

Her fingers tightened on his thigh. As the meal had worn on, the woman had gradually eased her chair a little closer to Ryan's, until she could rub her right foot up and down the calf of his left leg. It had been during the array of biscuits and fruit ices that her right hand had dropped beneath the level of the linen cloth. She started at his knee and feathered higher.

And higher.

Her fingers caressed the top of his thigh, feeling his raging erection. Then they cupped his balls and squeezed firmly.

At that moment Ryan had dropped his spoon onto his plate with a resounding clatter, receiving curious glances from both the Trader and J.B.

It was the Trader who changed the subject. During the meal he'd made several attempts to steer the conversation around to business, but the baron had always insisted on keeping the talk to other matters— the recent warm weather, the fortifications of the old Indians' pueblo to make it a secure ville, the difficulty of training the local peasants to serve at table.

Now, with the thick, sweet coffee poured into tiny cups of thin porcelain, the baron was ready to discuss business matters with his visitors.

To Ryan's relief, his wife needed her right hand to hold her coffee, and he was able to relax.

"We need ammo and gas."

"And we have ammo and gas," the baron replied, placing the tips of his fingers together like a cathedral steeple.

"Any caliber?"

"Within reason—.22 up to .45. We also have a supply of grens. Mainly frags and a few implodes, I believe."

J.B. shook his head. "We got plenty of grens. Low on 9 mill and .38."

The baron nodded. "Lots of men know what they don't want, Mr. Dix. Refreshing to meet a man who knows what he does want."

"Good octane gas?"

"Process it ourselves," Sharona said. She'd finished her coffee and, to Ryan's alarm, her right hand was crabbing its bejeweled way to the edge of the table.

"Price?" the Trader asked.

Baron Carson sighed. "Always the talk comes around to jack. That isn't the way we choose to deal with such matters here in Towse."

"How come you got so much silver and stuff?" Ryan asked. They had been served a rich red wine that tasted of summer fruit, glowing in tall crystal goblets. And it had loosened his tongue.

The woman turned to face him, shrugging her shoulders and giving him another glimpse of the dark tip of her breast.

"Alias stumbled on a redoubt years ago that was filled with old paintings and stuff. Like a place where treasure had been sent for safety. Then the long winters came and nobody remembered it. The jewels and clothes and all…sealed airtight. And some of the blasters the sec-men use. Once you have plenty of jack, Ryan, then it's childishly simple to use it to obtain more jack. And then more. Now you have come to force still more upon us for gas and ammo."

The way the Trader had talked about Towse, it had sounded a darker story, a story whose pages were dappled with spilled blood.

Ryan was aware of the scent of Sharona Carson's body, a feral, musky odor, with her perfume overlaying the flavor of her skin. He wanted her more than he'd ever wanted any woman.

The door at the far end of the room swung open, interrupting his dangerous train of thought.

"That you, Ferryman?" Baron Carson asked, peering into the shadows.

"Yes, Baron."

Boot heels rang on the old flags of the dining room, and a burly figure approached the table, gradually assuming features.

"Had trouble. Everything was going to plan, then

we got interrupted. Another five minutes and we'd
have had—''

The baron stopped him with a raised hand. ''Before
you go on, Ferryman, we have visitors. Two war wags
and the Trader himself.''

''War wags!''

The draft from the door made the candles flicker
more brightly, illuminating the face of the sec-boss.

And revealing the black patch that covered the
socket of his left eye.

Chapter Sixteen

Ferryman didn't speak as he took his place at the table, but he nodded to the baron and to Sharona. He poured himself a glass of the red wine and drained it in a single draft.

"Ah! That cuts the dust better than a gallon of mule's piss."

Ryan and J.B. waited, ready to hit leather and draw their blasters, waiting for the word from the Trader.

But the older man didn't speak for some time, sipping at his own glass of wine. Eventually it was the baron himself who broke the tension.

"How many chilled, Ferryman?"

"One from the outlanders. Lucky shot. Bullet hit Kendo clean through his left eye. Then the war wags came along and we lost us another five. Six if you count Shel. Got three rounds in the middle of his belly, and he won't make it through the night. Call it seven chilled in all."

"It's not a piece of arithmetic that I much care for, Ferryman," Carson said, dragging the words out.

"Me neither, Baron."

Alias Carson tapped his index finger on the table,

six sharp raps. Then he waited and looked around the room.

"Six, Ferryman. And what's the profit? These war wags drove you off and inflicted casualties among my sec-men."

"That's right, Baron."

Ferryman was smiling. Ryan put his age around thirty, with a dark skin that whispered something about Indian blood someplace in his background.

Ryan was starting to get a bad feeling. It was like a game where everyone knew the objective, but only one person knew the rules.

"And why were you out there beyond the gorge trying to stop a convoy of wags?"

Ferryman hesitated, as though he were waiting for some sort of guidance. And the baron gave it to him.

"They hadn't paid the tolls, had they, Ferryman? Was that it?"

"Yes, Baron."

The Trader cleared his throat. "Folks paid a mighty high price for walking from some tolls, Baron. Plenty of them fell into the dark. Burned wags. High price, Baron."

"Come within a hundred miles of Towse ville, and cross me or cross any of the boys that work for me, and you can find yourself paying a high kind of price, too."

The Trader stood, the palms of his hands flat on the tabletop. "Conversation like this could lead to some real serious misunderstandings, Baron," he said quietly. "Best keep to the business. When can you let us have the gas we want?"

Carson remained seated. "Take a few days. When's the next delivery of gas-wags coming in, Ferryman? Four, five days?"

Once again, Ryan felt that the sec-boss was simply acting as a mouthpiece for the baron, nodding his agreement to the suggestions, which tended to point toward some kind of trickery on the part of Alias Carson.

Then again, it was a common enough saying throughout the Deathlands that if you wanted to talk about something that was rotten or untrustworthy or potentially dangerous, you'd say that it was "Good as a baron's promise."

Now everyone was standing except for Sharona Carson, who was wiping her mouth with one of the embroidered damask table napkins.

"Four or five days, then," the Trader said. "I'll get our quartermaster to do some buying of food and supplies while we're here. How about water?"

"You can drink from the river that flows through the middle of the ville," Ferryman suggested. "If you want to get a bloody flux."

The Trader nodded. "So we'll buy water off you, as well."

Baron Carson shook his head. "No, Trader. While you're here, the water comes free. Man should be ready to step aside a little for a friend."

"Thanks." The Trader looked at J.B. and Ryan.

"Time t'move back. We thank you for the meal. Not like nothing I ever seen before. Start doing the trading in the morning."

The gray monotonous voice drawled, "Good to have company. Heard a lot of words about the Trader."

Ferryman nodded to them all. "You want anything or you got a problem...you come to me. Anyone knows where to find me."

Finally Sharona got to her feet, smiling at the three men. "It's been an evening of greater pleasure than I had thought. It more than came up to my expectations."

The word "up" had the faintest, most subtle emphasis, and she looked directly at Ryan as she spoke.

As they walked away from the heavily guarded main building of Towse ville, the Trader turned to Ryan and slapped him on the shoulder. He grinned broadly, his teeth white in the sliver of moonlight.

"That lady can be banged," he said.

THE TWO WAR WAGS always needed some kind of attention. Since they were closing in on a hundred years old, it wasn't that surprising that they were constantly malfunctioning. The bearing would go in an axle, or the gears would begin to disintegrate. Whenever the Trader ordered a stop in a ville that had some sort of workshops, the engineers would pester him for requisitions for parts and labor.

Dexter wanted time on a big steam-powered lathe

to repair the main doors to War Wag Two. War Wag One had been having difficulties with its radio, so Cohn wandered around Towse until he found a store offering all manner of com-parts.

As war captain, Ryan never had too much to do when they were located in a ville, even one that was as potentially hostile as Towse.

Once a rotation of guards had been established, the shifts ran themselves like clockwork. All members of the crews took their parts, two hours on and then ten hours off. That was the way that the Trader ordered it.

Ryan decided that he might as well explore the ville.

The sky was overcast, with the sun veiled behind endless banks of dark clouds. There were no shadows, just a gloom that settled over the adobe buildings of the ville.

On an impulse, Ryan wandered into the ruins of the old church. The splintered remnants of what had once been rows of wooden pews were scattered about. All the windows were shattered, and where the altar had once stood was the bent shell of an old television set. The roof had been partly destroyed by fire, and the charred beams sank into the clay walls. Someone had scrawled something on the one wall, using a burned length of wood, but it was completely illegible.

He walked to the far end, picking his way carefully among the rubbish. As he kicked a length of a smashed bench to one side his eye was caught by something that had been hidden beneath it—a glint of vivid green.

Ryan stooped and picked it up. The light was poor in the ruined building, and he had to hold the object up to make out what it was.

It was a severed finger. Desiccated and mummified in the heat, it felt dry and leathery to the touch. The green was a small ring of molded turquoise chips, held in a crude silver setting. From the size of the finger, it had belonged to a woman, almost certainly one of the original dwellers in the old pueblo.

With an expression of disgust, Ryan dropped the finger back among the rubbish, but first he slipped the ring off and put it in his pocket. The original owner wasn't likely to ever ask for it back, and he could easily trade it with one of the crew of War Wag One.

As he moved toward the rectangle of brighter light in the doorway, Ryan spotted two of the baron's secmen, waiting outside the devastated church. Each man had a hand casually resting on the butt of his blaster.

"Spying around, outlander?" one of them asked in a sneering voice.

"Go fuck a dead pig," Ryan replied.

"Oh, that's real friendly. That's the way the Trader's ass-lickers talk!"

"Better'n being ass-licker to the baron of some border pest-hole."

The two men had badges, plas-covered, pinned to the lapels of their shirts.

The one on the right, who toled a Charter Explorer 3, chambered to take a .357 round, was called Long Dog Hodgson. His colleague, Remmy Stedman, had a Renato Gamba Trident Fast Action .38. Both blasters looked to be in good, clean, working order.

Ryan kept his right hand well clear of his own Smith & Wesson. If these two sec-men were simply trying to talk tough, then he wouldn't need the blaster. But if it went that one short step further, then any sudden movement could prove terminal.

Across the far side of the main square Ryan thought he caught a glimpse of the distinctive figure of Ferryman, behind a half-shuttered window. But the person moved back and he couldn't be certain.

"Think we should take this fat-lip in for a coupla hours' interrogation?" said Long Dog Hodgson. "Sorta teach some manners."

His companion giggled. "Best kind o' teaching's spread over the table with his cheeks greased. Learn him good."

Rape was a common, everyday occurrence for anyone who was unfortunate enough to fall afoul of sec-men.

It didn't much matter either way if you were male or female. Sec-men weren't picky when it came to abusing any of the bodily orifices.

"Yeah," Hodgson agreed. "Hand over the blaster, outlander, and come talk to us about looting one of Baron Carson's buildings."

"And a fucking church, too," added his giggling companion.

"No."

"No? Did I hear that boy right, Long Dog? Did he say what I think he said?"

"Yeah, Remmy. I believe he did. Turning down a bit of interrogation with us. That's not the right kind of attitude."

"Calls for a spanking, does that," Long Dog said.

"Easy or hard, outlander?"

"That answer's still the same."

Ryan's original anger had cooled as he fought successfully for self-control over himself. The Trader often said that a man who stayed calm was a man who stayed alive.

"All right. Talk's over. You want it hard.... Blast-blindness! You'll fucking get it!"

The two sec-men both went for their blasters together.

Ryan didn't hesitate. All his reflexes had been straining for this moment, his fighting experience telling him it was inevitable. He didn't try to draw, knowing that he was framed in the doorway as a perfect target. Movement came a hot first.

He dived to his left, breaking his fall with his arm, gasping at a sudden shock of pain as his elbow hit one of the jagged chunks of torn wood that littered the floor of the church. His right hand was already beginning to draw the long revolver from its holster while he was still in midair.

As Ryan rolled over into a crouch, steadying his right wrist with his left hand, he heard a calm, familiar voice from outside on the plaza.

"Some sort of trouble?"

"In here, Trader!" Ryan yelled.

"I know that. Come on out."

Rubbing his bruised elbow, Ryan emerged cautiously into the dismal morning.

Long Dog Hodgson and Remmy Stedman were standing sheepishly on either side of the doorway. Each still held his handgun, but the barrels were pointing toward the dry earth.

The Trader was behind them, cradling his beloved Armalite. Half a dozen members of the crews were with him, including Ray, a walking stick in his left hand, one of his .32s in his right. Ben was casually holding his Uzi, grinning at Ryan.

"Trouble, Ryan?" the Trader asked.

"These guys wanted to start playing double rough," he replied.

"Looting a church! Ferryman told us special to watch for thieving bastards from the war wags' crews. Warned us."

The Trader looked at Long Dog, staring pointedly at the revolver in his hand. "Well, he ain't looting now. And you'd best put that toy cannon back in your pocket, before someone gets hurt."

"Good advice." Ferryman had appeared silently from nowhere. Ryan noticed that he was wearing a different patch over the blinded eye. It was soft maroon leather with some silver embroidery—an ornate letter *F*. The affectation diminished the man in Ryan's view.

"But you said they—" Stedman began, shutting up when the sec-boss lifted a hand.

"What we have here, Trader, is simply a failure of communication," Ferryman said, turning to the sheepish couple at his side. "Come see me in a half hour. I'll make it plain."

They holstered their blasters and shuffled off toward one of the main adobe buildings on the far side of the wooden bridge.

"Thanks," the Trader said.

"Boys get a little eager. Mebbe better if you tell all your boys—" he looked directly at Ryan "—to keep close to the wags. Avoids misunderstandings. You take my meaning?"

"Sure." With a narrow smile, the sec-boss turned on his heel and followed his two men across the fast-flowing river.

The Trader turned to Ryan, who slowly holstered his weapon.

"Look for more care from you, Ryan," he said.

"I told them that—"

"Talk comes cheap. Action costs. Be more careful while we're here."

"Yeah."

Chapter Seventeen

Three days drifted by.

On the second day there was the threat of a chemstorm, with towering thundertops clustered around the white-tipped peaks of the Sangre de Cristos. Lightning ripped into the forests that smothered the lower slopes, starting a couple of small fires. But the torrential rainfall that followed quickly extinguished the orange flames.

"Could've been worse," Ferryman said, standing next to Ryan near the fortified outer wall of the ville.

"You get some big winds down here?"

"Sure."

"Acid rain?"

"No. That's farther south, near the sea. And down the acid lakes to the east, around Norleans. But we get the hurricanes."

"Strip paint?"

Ferryman spit tobacco juice in the gray dust by his feet. "You bet. Most animals out wild know when the wind's on the way and get into the canyons. Man gets caught out in it and you don't recognize him. Clothes go. Skin. Eyes. Lips. Hair. Most of the hair. Cock and balls, too."

"Thanks, Ferryman. More than I ever wanted to know about it."

Beyond the gate they could hear the sound of a high-pitched engine, running rough and hot, whining toward the ville.

"Sounds like one of our recce boys coming in off patrol in one fucking son of a hurry," said the sec-boss.

Ryan recognized the noise as being an old two-wheeler wag. It was surprising how many of the ancient Harleys still survived around Deathlands.

The main sec-gate was thrown open on the yell of recognition from the main lookout tower, and a dusty motorbike came into Towse, skidding sideways in a shower of grit and sand. The rider was goggled and helmeted and wore what looked to be a flak jacket over a dark blue T-shirt. He turned off the engine, dismounted and walked toward Ferryman and Ryan.

"Hi, there, McMurtry," the sec-boss greeted. "What put you in such a tire-wrecking way?"

"White lion," the man replied, pulling off the helmet and easing up the goggles, showing twin rings of clean skin amid the caked grime.

"White line?" Ferryman looked puzzled. "What white line?"

"No." The man shook his head so vigorously that it almost disappeared in a cloud of pale dust. "Lion. A white lion. Cougar. Puma. Don't matter what the fuck you call it. A white lion."

Albino animals weren't that unusual throughout the

Deathlands, but Ryan knew that some of them were valued for their rare pelts.

"Baron'll be interested in that, McMurtry. Go get cleaned up and the report direct to him. Where'd you see this white lion?"

"Didn't see it myself. But I caught this ole Indian woman and took some of her water. Was going to give her a kicking for being near a highway. And she started talking on about this animal."

Ferryman sucked at his front teeth. "And you believed her, McMurtry?"

"Sure."

Somewhere on the far side of the quiet plaza there was the sound of breaking glass, and all three men turned in that direction. But a child came running out of a doorway, pursued by its angry, cursing mother.

McMurtry tried again. "Listen. I didn't just take the old slag's word, did I? I'm not a triple-stupe, boss. Took her to her hogan and asked the others. Old man and some women and kids. All told the same story. One of them women had seen it only yesterday. Scared the shit out of her, way she looked."

"Where?"

"Beyond the big sand dunes. I figured out from her words and gestures that she meant the head of Trick Canyon. By Dry Falls Creek there."

The sec-boss rubbed at the side of his nose, looking at Ryan. "You heard anything about a white lion? On the road?"

"No, but we move on through. Don't stop much. The Trader doesn't like the stopping."

"Yeah. He's already been bitching to the baron about the delay in the gas."

"Should I go tell him about this, boss?" McMurtry asked.

"Yeah. He'll want to get a hunting party up soon as possible."

The scout pushed his two-wheel wag away, leaving double tracks in the sand. Ryan and Ferryman watched him go.

"You a hunting man, outlander?"

Ryan didn't answer immediately. When he'd been a boy, in Front Royale ville, hunting had been an everyday activity—partly for food, but mostly for what passed as sport.

"I'm hungry, then I'll kill. I'm cold, then I'll kill."

"No other reason?" Ferryman leaned so close to Ryan that he was enveloped by his sour breath. Their faces were almost touching.

"Yeah. I kill when I have to."

IT WAS MORE LIKE a military expedition than a hunt for a single animal. Wearing his inevitable three-piece suit and gray hat, Baron Alias Carson rode in an armored jeep at the head of a procession of a dozen vehicles.

The Trader had asked him whether the mythical white lion was worth all this amount of logistical trouble for his ville.

"If a thing is worth seeing, sir, then it is worth killing" was his drawled reply.

There had been a brief discussion between Ryan, the Trader and J.B. about how many from the crews of the two war wags should be allowed to go along on the hunt. In the minds of all three men was the ever-present possibility of treachery from the baron.

"The men and women are getting hot-pissed about hanging around for the gas," J.B. said.

"Baron says he'll lend us two of his smaller wags," the Trader said. "That way they can watch out for backstabbing."

"How about the wags here?" Ryan asked.

They were leaning against the starboard side of War Wag One. The Armorer had managed to get hold of a supply of his favorite thin black cheroots, and he puffed a cloud of aromatic smoke into the cool, damp air.

"Can't all go rushing around the desert after some bleached puma," he said. "Need enough crew to guard them safe."

In the end they agreed that a total of a dozen, split between the two wags and drawn by lot, would go out hunting.

The two borrowed vehicles would be commanded by the Trader and J. B. Ryan hadn't been very keen on going out into the wilderness as part of a mass hunt, and had volunteered to stay in charge of War Wags One and Two.

"Watch out for stray bullets," he warned the

Trader. "Ferryman's got a score against us. Go up a blind arroyo and you get a full-metal jacket through the middle of your spine."

The Trader gave his thinnest smile, one that barely touched his lips and never approached his eyes. "Not with you and the war wags right smack in the middle of his ville. Blood price'd be too high for him to risk."

"Guess that's right."

Ryan got a pat on the shoulder from the older man. "Part of learning, Ryan. Young man gets to see a little part of the picture. Grow up some and you can, mebbe, take in the whole picture."

THE EARLY RAIN was absorbed so quickly into the earth that the mud became dust within a few minutes.

The wind had risen again, obscuring the tracks of the Harley across the main open area of the ville. Most of the men and women going on the hunt had goggles slung around their necks in anticipation of the weather to come, and everyone had a scarf of some kind tucked about their throats.

Ryan stood by the war wags and watched the final preparations being made. Ferryman strode across to join him.

"Sure you can't be tempted, outlander?" he asked. "Don't see a white lion every day. Might be something to tell your grandchildren."

"Need children before you get grandkids. And I aim to avoid that for as long as possible."

"Man should leave something behind him. Read something once about footprints in the sands of time. Know what I mean, Ryan?"

"Yeah. I buy the farm now and what've I left?" An engine roared into life, revved up, then fell away to a gentle rumble. "Not a lot, Ferryman. No brats. But a shit-load of corpses. That's what I leave behind me."

Sharona Carson had come out to join her husband. She was wearing comparatively dull clothes: skintight jodhpurs tucked into highly polished riding boots, a blouse of milk-white silk and a kerchief of maroon satin around her neck. Her blond hair was pulled back into a short ponytail and held in place with a silver clip shaped like an eagle's claw.

Ryan was exchanging a last few words with the Trader, nuts-and-bolts details about the running of the war wags—food and drink, and oil changes and sentry patrols; who should cover for whom; what changes they might make to the normal timetables and duty rosters.

They'd been told that the hunters should return to Towse before sunset. Ferryman had grinned at the news.

"Folks left outside after dark likely won't ever be coming in," he said. "Like the baron mentioned— the ville's not much loved." He spit again in the dirt. "Not that it matters. Long as they fear you. That's what matters."

Baron Carson pressed the button on his musical jeep horn.

The discipline was impressive. All of the sec-men going out with him on the hunt fell silent, allowing his words to ring clear.

"Let's to it, men. Ride on the nova express to hunt the legendary white lion. I want his skin, and I want it intact. Man that scars the pelt gets to chew on broken teeth."

Sharona was about to climb into her husband's wag when her eyes were caught by Ryan, standing away by the other vehicles.

"Not coming on the hunt, outlander?" she called. "You'll miss all the excitement."

"It's a dirty job, lady, but someone has to do it."

She laughed. "Then we shall meet up at supper tonight when... Oh!" As she was stepping up into the jeep she seemed to slip and twist her ankle, nearly falling. She grabbed on to the seat of the small wag to save herself. "Oh, my leg!" she cried, her face contorted with sudden pain.

Her husband looked down at her without the least change of expression or concern, but his words carried in the stillness. "You had better rest that, my sweet honeycomb. I suggest that you find some way of taking weight off it."

"I will."

"Best be well by the time we get back with this white lion."

"Of course."

Ryan sensed that all things weren't as they appeared, but he couldn't work out what was going on. It was almost as if the baron and Sharona were acting in some little drama, a play that they'd perfomed before and were giving a repeat performance.

Ferryman, in the second of the baron's command vehicles, turned very slowly and looked directly at Ryan. He held his glance for a moment, then looked away.

At a signal from the baron, the hunting party drove out of Towse ville, dust boiling around them. The main sec-gates slammed shut, and the settlement went about its business.

And Ryan Cawdor and Sharona Carson were left alone in the main plaza.

"Well, outlander," she said. "I've been told to take the weight off my ankle. I'd best do that. Will you give me a hand to my room?"

"Sure."

Chapter Eighteen

Ryan didn't know much about furniture, but he guessed that the four-poster in Sharona Carson's room had to date back well over two hundred years, to the early 1800s.

It was oak, so dark and weathered that it was almost black, and carved in an ivy-and-acanthus pattern. A large chest and a side table matched the bed. The walls were pale cream adobe, a couple of feet thick in order to keep out the scorching heat of New Mexico summer.

The room contained a single square window, the glass of which was crazed by the scouring desert wind. Iron bars were set firmly into the walls as a security measure. Additional safety was provided by metal-bound shutters that locked tightly across the window and turned the bedroom into a darkened cavern.

The floor was a pattern of rectangular tiles, iron-blue, slightly uneven, and a single Navaho rug of black, white and crimson was set in the middle of the room. A similar rug was hung on the wall opposite the window.

The door was iron-studded and had three large

black bolts at top, middle and bottom. All of them were slid across. There was an inner door that opened onto a small, well-appointed bathroom.

A pair of highly polished black riding boots stood like sentries against the oak chest. On it, folded neatly, was a blouse of milk-white silk and a crumpled pair of jodhpurs. A maroon satin kerchief had been tossed on top of the blouse.

Sharona's badly sprained ankle lasted just long enough for Ryan and herself to hobble together across the plaza of Towse ville, through the entrance of the baron's living quarters, along the corridor that arrowed down the middle of the cool house and into the bedroom of the mistress of the ville.

She pushed Ryan's supporting arm away and turned quickly to slam the door, ramming each bolt across with what seemed a particular venom.

"There! Keep the prying eyes of them Mex slut-bitches off of us!"

She smiled at Ryan, making a half move toward him, glanced around and realized that the shutters were open and anyone walking by could look straight into the room.

"White light!" Her heels clicked across the stone floor. The shutters clamped tight shut, making the room seductively dark. "There. That better, Outlander Ryan?"

"Better." He hesitated. "You sure?"

"Am I sure what?"

"Baron's often kind of... Your husband didn't

strike me as a man who'd be that generous with lending out his possessions.''

''Meaning me?'' He could just see her face as a pale blur in the dimness, but he could hear the sharp edge to her voice and knew that he was walking on treacherously thin ice.

''Sort of. That's the way some barons think about their women.''

The sharpness blunted a little. ''Long as *you* don't look at it that way, Ryan.''

''I don't want to wake up in that bed and find there's a .44 Magnum pressed behind my right ear.'' He paused. ''Or my left ear, if it comes to that.''

''Alias won't be back for at least four hours. If they've got to go scour Trick Canyon all the way to Dry Falls Creek, it could be close on dark. Nobody in the ville would speak to him about what I do. Sure, he might kill me and might reward an informer. But they know I'd get to them first and chill them.''

Ryan risked firing off a round at random, after a guess. ''And even if he knew, mebbe he wouldn't care *that* much, huh?''

Her white teeth flashed. ''I was right about you, Ryan Cawdor. You are something a little special, aren't you?''

''Everyone thinks that. That they're special.''

''Sure. But you... Why don't we get on and find out just how special you might be?''

RYAN HAD ENJOYED his fair share of sexual encounters in his twenty-five or so years, but a lot of them had been with scrawny little whores in frontier gaudies, places where you kept as many of your clothes on as you could and only handed over the jack after it was all over.

Of course, he'd had plenty of women who hadn't wanted paying, but never anyone remotely like Sharona Carson of Towse.

For a start, Ryan wasn't used to finding a woman who insisted on making all the moves—not that she actually put it that way. But that was the way it turned out.

"You take your clothes off first, Ryan. I like to see a man while I'm still dressed. Makes it more of a turn-on for me."

Ryan looked at her for a moment, considering the request. He'd checked out the room. Nobody could get in without making a whole lot of noise and taking a lot of time. Unless the woman was going to kill him herself—and that didn't seem logical or likely—there wasn't any immediate danger. But the habits of a lifetime still made him hesitate.

"Let me help you," Sharona offered, standing close to him and kissing him long and slow on the lips. The tip of her tongue probed between his teeth with a sensual urgency that removed the last pathetic shreds of his hesitation.

He sat on the bed while she knelt before him and unlaced the steel-toed combat boots. She pulled them off, along with his wool socks, brushing his bare feet with her lips.

He took off his shirt and laid it on the chest, drawing the Smith & Wesson from its holster and tucking it carefully beneath the fluffy white pillows at the top of the bed.

The belt was unbuckled by Sharona's long, strong fingers, and the front of his pants yielded to her. Ryan stood still while she knelt again, pulling them down over his ankles, followed by his shorts, which got a little snagged up.

"Sorry about that," she whispered. "Hope it didn't do any serious harm."

"Doesn't look like it," Ryan replied, a little more hoarsely than he'd intended.

"I'll just give it a little kissing to make sure."

The room was surprisingly cool, and Ryan suddenly shuddered.

Sharona looked up at him, smiling. "Cold, lover? Or someone wander by your tomb?"

"Cold feet."

"Soon get warmed under the sheets." She stood up. "Now it's your turn to get me naked and ready."

While he knelt down, she sat on the bed, legs slightly apart, allowing him to slide the mirrored boots off. On an impulse Ryan lowered his head and kissed her bare feet, as she'd done for him. Sharona sighed with pleasure.

The blouse came next. It was no surprise at all to find she wore nothing beneath it. The pressure of her nipples against the smooth material had already told Ryan that.

He stood away from her a little then reached out with both hands, stroking the tips of her breasts with his callused fingers. Sharona closed her eyes and sighed again. "That's real nice, Ryan. Real nice."

He unknotted the maroon kerchief and dropped it on top of the blouse.

The riding breeches were more difficult. They fitted her so tightly that it was a struggle to remove them. In the end she had to lie on her back on the bed and brace herself while he pulled them down, unrolling the material over thighs and knees until they eventually came free over her bare feet.

"Careful with those, lover. They're Armani, and there's only one more pair left in my closet."

She stood again and made sure her blond hair was still snug in the silver-clawed brooch. Ryan gazed at her naked body, shimmering in the half-light of the shadowed room. All she wore was a tiny pair of turquoise silk panties.

Sharona hooked her thumbs in the waistband, pouting at him.

"Want to take these off for me, Ryan?"

"Yeah. Sure."

"I'd like it a lot if you took them off with your teeth, lover. But real slow and real careful. Come on."

He felt the cold of the tiles against the skin of his bare knees as she swayed toward him. Once again his breath was filled with the scent of her body.

AFTERWARD as they dressed, Sharona peeked out through the shutters. "No sign of any dust trail. Still a couple of hours to dusk."

Ryan holstered his blaster. "I'll go check out the guards."

"Breathe a word, Ryan, ever, and I'll see you down and dead. Remember that."

He nodded and quietly slid back the bolts, walking from her bedroom without another word or a backward glance.

Chapter Nineteen

It wasn't a white lion—it was a tired, old, dusty, yellowish puma, half its teeth broken or missing, with a barely healed spear wound along its flank.

As they walked near the wags, the Trader asked Ryan what had happened in the ville while they were away.

"Nothing. No trouble."

"Nick said they didn't see much of you during the afternoon. You went off, helping the woman, after she...hurt her ankle."

The pause in the middle of the sentence was measured and deliberate, but Ryan chose not to surface to the lure.

"That's right. Saw her to her quarters and let her people look after her."

"Was it bad, Ryan?"

"The ankle?"

"Yeah. Her ankle. Was it bad?"

Ryan shook his head. "No. Kind of swelled over the side bone. She got one of the women to bathe it in cold water."

"And then?"

"Then I went walking."

"See anyone?"

"No." He was unable to conceal the edge that was creeping into his voice.

The Trader smiled and wiped dust off his face. "Slow it down, friend, slow it down. Just want to know how my war captain passed a few hours in the middle of a strange ville."

"I passed them, Trader, if that's okay with you. Fireblast! What's the questions for?"

The Trader's smile disappeared like the shroud of dew on a summer meadow. "Just want to be sure I left a man in charge of the war wags, Ryan. Not some green kid that'll go sniffing around the skirts of the baron's slut!"

Ryan blinked, trying to clear the crimson mist that had suddenly drifted across his vision and clenched his fists at his side.

"Not fucking fair," he said, keeping his voice pitched low so that the whole crew wouldn't hear their quarrel.

"No?"

"No! Sure I went with her. Dark night, Trader! She has to be the most beautiful woman I ever seen in my life."

"Won't argue with you there, son. But that doesn't change the fact. You were gone for three…close on four hours."

The fog of anger began to fade. Ryan swallowed hard, recognizing the inevitable truth that Trader was right. He shouldn't have left the wags like that. Nothing had gone wrong, but that could be put down to luck, not judgment.

Finally, slowly, he nodded. "Guess that's right," he admitted.

The Trader's smile flooded back, like sunlight filling a dark valley.

"Sure it is." He moved closer. "Ryan, you're a good man. Why d'you think you're my right hand when there's older, more experienced men and women in the crews? Because you're the best I ever saw. But that don't mean you're real perfect."

"You made the point," Ryan said eager now to get away.

"You want to fuck anything that moves, then you go do it. Your cock'll rot off, but that falls into the area of being your business. You risk my wags or my people, and then it falls into being *my* business. I know you know that, Ryan. But I gotta say it when I see it. That's all."

Within a day or so there was a far more serious problem to be confronted.

Despite Baron Alias Carson's repeated promises, there was still no sign of the gas supplies. The Trader, accompanied by J.B. and Ryan, demanded a meeting with the baron, who saw them in his council room, with Ferryman at his side and a half dozen well-armed sec-men positioned casually around the room.

Carson, as ever, was wearing a conservative suit of 1980s cut, and in his buttonhole was a tiny pink flower.

He noticed their eyes go to the small adornment and touched it with a lazy hand. "Guess I'm sentimental after all. Five years t'the day that my first wife, Consuela, went off on the last train west. Sorry business, that was."

Ryan had immediately been aware that the room smelled heavy from drinking, and Carson's speech was a little more slurred than usual.

"Little bit of Mex in Consuela. Pretty as a doll. But she was kind of crazed. Too much tequila and not enough control. Got me riled once about my shooting, she did."

Ferryman coughed. "You want to talk about that, Baron?"

"Why not?"

"Times past. Not worth remembering, Baron. What happened five years back...it happened. Weren't nobody's fault."

"Sure, sure, sure." He sighed. "But I've started this so... I'd been drinking some. Don't hardly touch a bottle now. She pushed me. Kept damned pushing at me. Put a glass jug of red wine on her head and stood out that door. Dared me to shoot it off her head. Dared me."

One of the first things that Ryan had noticed about the baron was that he didn't seem to sport a blaster. It wasn't unique in his experience, but it was unusual for the baron of a frontier ville like Towse.

"Had an Astra .44 Magnum in those days. Good with it, wasn't I, Ferryman? Yeah, I was good with it. I sat here and I drew down on her. On my wife. And what happened, Ferryman? Tell the outlanders. Tell Trader.''

''You shot her, Baron.'' The sec-boss's face was as blank as a granite wall.

''I shot her.'' Each word was drawled out to an almost unbearable length. ''I squeezed the trigger of my good old Magnum. Still feel the jolt that ran clear up my arm. Saw her fall. Saw Consuela go down in the dirt. Had on a long white dress of cotton. She hadn't raided for clothes like Sharona with... I stood up and walked to that door there and looked down at my wife.''

The light wasn't good in the long, cool adobe room, but Ryan was sure he saw the gleam of a tear among the leathery furrows of Carson's lizard skin.

''I thought it was the wine. The red all over her. The glass was broke. You thought it was the wine, didn't you, Ferryman?''

''Wine like blood, Baron.''

Carson lifted his face from his hands to stare at his sec-boss. ''What? What's that you said, about blood?''

''The wine looked like blood.''

''That's right. That's right, it did. She was kind of moving around, like a gutted fish. Jerking. Bare feet in the sand. She'd pissed herself. Saw that. Then I seen the little black hole in the middle of her forehead. Little.'' He held finger and thumb apart, almost touching. ''That big. Didn't look like that could've harmed a strong woman like Consuela. I knelt down. Put the gun in the dirt and never picked it up again. You destroyed it for me, didn't you, Ferryman?"

"Yeah. I did that, Baron."

There was a fly darting erratically around the council room, seemingly bemused by the darkness and the number of men. But everyone ignored it.

"I lifted her and held her head in my hand. This right hand. And...and the back of her skull was like cornmeal mush. Her brains just spilled out into the palm of my hand."

The only sound in the room was the wings of the insect, humming backward and forward. As it flew past the sec-boss, he moved with a deceptive, casual speed, plucking the fly out of the air and crushing it.

The movement broke the spell of the stillness. Baron Carson looked up. "Why, Trader. How may I help you?"

"By getting us the gas."

"You got food and water?"

"Sure."

"Ferryman."

"Yeah, Baron."

"Have the outlanders been supplied with all of the ammo they wanted?"

The Trader spoke. "I don't much care for playing games, Carson. We got food. Got water. Got the ammo, and you got the jack for all of that. We don't have the gas, and time's wasting. You keep telling us it's coming. It don't come."

There was rising irritation in the Trader's words. Ryan knew from their morning conference, before this meeting, that he was becoming seriously concerned, that Carson was getting some sort of plan into operation that might win him the invaluable war wags. Guards had been doubled, and every man and woman had been warned about keeping alert.

"Why not go away and then get back here in...in a week, Trader," Baron Carson suggested. "Man sits on his ass too long he suffers from piles. Go out hunting someplace. There's that redoubt the Indians talk about, isn't there, Ferryman?"

"Many Wolves Canyon?"

"That's the one."

Ryan knew the suggestion of a redoubt was the one thing that would switch the Trader aside from his purpose.

"Redoubt? If it's there, then how come you haven't opened it up?"

Carson stood up, smiling past him. "A fine good morning, Sharona. Come join us."

Ryan hadn't set an eye on her since their lovemaking.

Today she wore an elegant dress in a soft green velvet that reached just below the knee. The black leather belt was fastened with an ornate golden letter G. Her hair was loose and flowed down either side of her perfect, heart-shaped face. She smiled at everyone in the room.

"Did I hear someone talking about that old ghost fortress in the mountains?"

The Trader nodded formally to her. "That's right. Just asked the baron how come you hadn't cleared it out if you know it's really there."

She sat on a chair held for her by one of the armed guards. "Oh, I believe it's there, but it's in the Blood of Christ mountains, stronghold of the Indians. Ferryman here has a good map, don't you? You could let the Trader have it."

Ryan looked sideways at the Trader, seeing the gleam in his eyes, the set of his head, the squaring of his shoulders. The gas was almost forgotten. What mattered now was the chance to find and explore a new, lost redoubt.

"How far?"

The baron looked at the Trader. "Still worried about the gas? Guess we can advance you a few gallons, can't we, Ferryman? And I'm sure and certain that the shipment'll be here anytime soon. Take five days break. Do your people good to be on the road again. When you get back here, I'm positive the gasoline'll be flowing like milk and honey in Canaan."

DESPITE HIS eagerness, the Trader hadn't earned his reputation by sticking his head into a noose. As soon as they got back to War Wag One he sent Beulah Webb over to talk to Ferryman and check out the map showing the route to the supposed hidden redoubt in the Sangre de Cristo range. And he joined with J.B.

and Ryan to discuss this unexpected new development in the game.

"He shitting us?" he asked.

Ryan shook his head. "Don't see what he wins. The gas is coming or it isn't. Either way, why send us off on a fool's chase?"

J.B. had taken off his glasses and was polishing them on a strip of cotton, holding them to the light and peering through them. He took his time before replying.

"Only two things. Baron's straight, so we go check out the redoubt. Come back and get the gas. Or he's a misfire. No redoubt. Way of setting up some kind of ambush on us."

The Trader lighted one of the cigars he relished, offering one to the Armorer, who shook his head.

"It's about trust," the Trader said. "We got men and an overkill blaster capacity with the wags. No way he'll front us out of them, though he's got some good weaponry and a strong ville." He was almost thinking out loud, rather than talking directly to J.B. and to Ryan.

Beulah appeared, carrying a hand-drawn map. She saw that the three men were in conference, and turned on her heel.

"So far, there's been nothing to show he's a misfire. I figure the white lion hunt was for real. Never seen so much disappointment in a man. So if we go off and find the redoubt, for better or worse, when we come back we'll mebbe trust him all the way. Mebbe we will...mebbe.''

Ryan saw the way the older man's tactical brain was moving. ''And that'll be the time to be triple-guarded, Trader.''

''That's an ace on the line, Ryan.''

A little after dawn on the following morning, War Wags One and Two rumbled out through the gates of Towse ville and rolled steadily northeast toward the Sangre de Cristo. The rising sun had colored the jagged peaks, turning the patches of fresh snow into pools of crimson blood.

Chapter Twenty

They crossed the wooden bridge again, but this time the four-man patrol stood back and simply waved them by.

The map showed a main highway to the north, with a cutoff east on a narrower road near an old settlement called Questa. Beulah had found all that on her ancient *Rand McNally Road Atlas and Vacation Guide.*

"Red River Ski Area, up this little red line," she said, pointing it out to Ryan.

There was no point in showing the Trader, who found reading and writing about as easy as juggling a handful of eggs.

Ryan looked at the scuffed, faded print, angling it to catch the morning sunlight that came in through the open-roof ob-slit.

"Hey! What's that say?" he asked, pointing to some pale green lettering—Carson Nat'l Forest.

"One of the national recreational areas," Beulah said. Then the significance of the name struck her as well. "Oh, Land O'Goshen! Named after the Baron of Towse himself."

"But that map's a century old," Ryan said wonderingly. "How can it be named after Alias Carson? He wasn't even born."

It was Matt, the relief driver of War Wag One, traveling with them for the morning to gain more experience, who supplied the answer. His collection of comics covered all kinds of superheroes, but he also had a small number of fragile Western mags.

"Kit Carson," he suggested, overhearing the conversation. "Real famous cowboy and Indian fighter. Mainly around these parts. More'n likely that forest was named after him."

Ryan felt vaguely disappointed at such a mundane explanation.

FOR THE FIRST few miles it was obvious that the two-lane blacktop had been well traveled. But gradually the going got tougher.

The saturation use of missiles by all the countries involved in the brief but terminal Third World War had caused devastation far beyond anything that the military tacticians and logistical experts had ever predicted. Even in the "worst worst" scenario, there'd been forecasts of some kind of eventual rebuilding of society through minimum levels of survival.

But nobody had taken into account the way that the land itself would react to the total assault.

Hundreds of thousands of square miles of what had been the United States of America had vanished into the oceans. Low-lying areas had become measureless lagoons or lakes. Mountains had crumbled and new peaks had thrust skyward. The land had rippled as though it were soft and liquid. What had changed across the face of the continent had changed forever.

The earth tremors had affected the northern parts of what had been New Mexico, diverting rivers and turning highways into ribbons of broken, corrugated stone.

Hun was at the driving controls of War Wag One, her ob-shield open. A current of fresh air washed through the stuffy interior of the huge vehicle. Their speed had been slowing down ever since they crossed the deep gorge. Nobody really knew how fast a war wag could go under ideal circumstances, mainly because they never encountered anything remotely resembling ideal circumstances.

Ryan had known Hun to push them up over fifty miles an hour, when they'd been fleeing a forest inferno started by some suicidal muties near old Wyoming. A more normal kind of average speed was a whole lot closer to twenty-five.

Immediately north of Towse they'd gotten up to thirty-eight miles per hour. Beyond the wooden bridge that had dropped to the mid-twenties and a few miles farther Hun had eased back into third gear and slowed to around fifteen.

"Getting worse, Trader," she reported, her voice crackling over the intercom.

"Bring it to a walk," he replied. "I'm going up top for a look. Ryan?"

"Yo?"

"Come up."

It was a warm, sticky kind of a day, with the clouds obscuring the sun. Above the mountains on their right they could see the dense shape of a dark storm.

The war wag rattled and heaved as Hun pushed down to a lower gear. Behind them, linked by rad-com, War Wag Two also slowed, keeping station around two hundred yards behind. It was far enough to avoid an ambush, but near enough to provide emergency assistance for War Wag One if needed.

Ahead of them the two men could see what had worried Hunaker.

"Switchback time," Ryan said.

The relatively level pavement disappeared a quarter mile ahead of them and was replaced by an undulating series of dips and bumps, some of them twenty feet high. At the bottom of the nearest hollow they could both make out the glint of water, which probably meant swampy ground.

"Won't get over some of them," the Trader mused. "Don't relish getting us stuck in this kind of place. Towse is the nearest ville, and I guess there's plenty of locals that'd welcome some killing."

In their conversations with Ferryman and some of the sec-men, the recurrent theme was the danger from hostile Indians who were the scattered survivors of Carson's massacre at the old pueblo.

Ryan stood up, waist-high out of the top of the wag, and braced himself against the pitching and jolting. He tried to make out what the ground was like on either side of the ruined highway, deciding that it could be passable.

The Trader called down to Beulah, trying to find out how much farther before they were due to turn off toward the mountains.

"Close. Any sign of Questa?"

Both the Trader and Ryan peered ahead. The Trader had a battered pair of Zeiss glasses, and he called down for Hun to stop while he checked the vicinity.

The engine ticked over quietly. Ryan spotted a lone coyote, head and tail down, scurrying along a shallow ridge a half mile to the west. Apart from that, there was no sign of life anywhere. Not even a buzzard circling optimistically overhead.

"See anything?"

The Trader shook his head and lowered the binoculars. "Nothing. If there was a town there once, it sure ain't there now. Can't see no sign of any road going east, neither."

"Want me to go on?" Hun asked. "Left or right?"

"Right's clearer," Ryan said.

"MUST'VE BEEN LIKE this in the old frontier days of the Conestoga wagons," J.B. said a couple of hours later.

"Ox-drawn, weren't they?" Ryan asked, coughing as he swallowed dust.

The trail was so rough that most of the two crews had gotten out of the wags after the Trader had given

them permission. They preferred to walk rather than
ride in the sickly, sweltering metal boxes that the war
wags had become. Speed had dropped to a little less
than a steady walking pace.

"Mostly oxen. Some mules. Not many horses.
Funny. Most old vids show horses pulling their can-
vas-topped wags."

J.B. had tugged his fedora down low over his eyes
and knotted a scarf around his mouth and nose to
make breathing easier.

"You told me once that a lot of the cowmen were
black, didn't you? Never see that on the old vids,
neither."

The wags were now going due east, with the lowering sun at their backs. The Trader was sitting out
on top of War Wag One, his head bare, smoke curling
from his cigar. He looked completely relaxed.

"Look at the old bastard," Lex said, panting and
sweating along with J.B. and Ryan. "Like the baron
of the whole fucking world."

"If he wanted to be, I guess he could," July said
quietly, joining them. "I never met anyone like the
Trader."

"You never will," Ryan said.

It took them two whole days to cover the miles
into the foothills of the mountains. Beulah was de-
lighted to find that the rough map that Ferryman had
given her was accurate. It had showed the breakup of
the highway as well as the point where the forest began to encroach toward the road. If there'd been trees

in close a few miles farther back, the journey would have come to a sudden halt. As it was, the war wags were able to move back onto the ribbon of highway. The seismic devastation lower down on the plain wasn't repeated in the hills, and they picked up toward ten miles an hour.

IT WAS EARLY in the morning of their third day that the first Indian was spotted. He was a lone man, ragged-trousered, bare-chested and clutching what J.B. swore was a nineteenth-century Springfield carbine. He stood for a few moments in the clear sight of the waking camp, on a steep slope above a rushing stream of clean water. By the time that the nearest guard had shouted a warning and begun to draw a bead on the intruder, the Indian had vanished again.

"Best go to yellow" was Trader's comment.

The finest scout on either war wag was a rear gunner in One, named Garcia. He had once kept a campfire crew entertained for an hour while he tried to explain the mix of grandparents that had resulted in his dark skin, blond hair and eyes so dark that they almost disappeared in their sockets. Ryan couldn't remember that complex web of relationships, but he did recall that there was a bit of Crow Indian in there someplace. Garcia had joined them on a previous expedition south of the Grandee.

Now he was out front, kneeling in the middle of the track, the noon sun pouring his black shadow tight around him. J. B. Dix and Ryan stood a few paces behind him. The Trader had sent them out to try to check if anyone had been using the old lost highway through the woods.

Garcia finally stood up and looked around. He grinned at Ryan, flashing his solitary gold tooth. "Look empty to you, amigo?"

Ryan had some skill at tracking, but the dusty, leaf-covered stretch of road didn't share its secrets with him.

"Sure does."

"Las apariencias engañan."

"How's that, Garcia? You know I don't speak that Mex stuff."

"You must not decide how good a book is by just looking at her cover, amigo. This road, she tells many stories to me."

"Wags?" J.B. asked. That was the big question. Carson had said the redoubt hadn't been visited by anyone from the ville, that it was just local tales. If there were wheel marks, then he'd likely been lying to them.

"No. No wags. Not since the long winters, far as I can see."

"Horses?" Ryan asked.

"Ponies, off trail. Shoeless, so you wouldn't ride 'em on this hard pavement less'n you had to. Ponies. Mebbe Apache."

"Apaches? This far north?" Ryan couldn't conceal his surprise.

"Sure. Nothing like a holocaust to change the hunting grounds. Lots of the plains people got chilled. An Apache, he live in the canyons. Now they moved ways north. The warrior we seen looked Apache to me. Mebbe wrong. But I know one thing, Ryan.''

''What?''

''Less my guess wrong, we see them again, before long.''

FINALLY the trail simply ran out, as all trails eventually do, the track stopping at the bottom of a sixty-foot cliff. There was a clearing in the trees with an open flank to the north and dense forest to the south. Double patrols were set on the southern side, some a quarter mile into the woods, and another line about a hundred and fifty yards from the wags. If they were attacked, then it would surely come from the trees.

The Trader called J.B. and Ryan, this time asking Beulah to join the discussion.

''Map's still about right,'' she said. ''Shows this place as where the main track vanishes. From here you have to walk on for around four miles. Kind of steep, I figure. But the scale's not always consistent. Could be more. Doubt it'll be less.''

''Best split up and take a foot party. No more than a dozen, well armed.''

The Trader looked at both J.B. and Ryan, and they grinned back at him. The two young men had ridden long enough with the Trader to have a shrewd guess at what he was going to say next.

When there was the most remote scent of an undiscovered redoubt, the Trader tended to get his priorities a little scrambled. Though he was now well into middle age, he became like an enthusiastic young cub.

Today was no different.

They were in an unknown and potentially very hostile environment, which called for him to remain with the wags and delegate the patrol to either J.B. or Ryan.

Or to both of them.

"I'll lead with Ryan. J.B., you stay in command here."

"What a surprise, Trader." Beulah smiled. She'd already been long enough with the pair of war wags to predict how the Trader might react when he was within walking distance of a redoubt.

THEY SCRAMBLED UP the steep path, with Garcia on point. The Trader and Ryan were at the front of the supporting group of nine men and women, with Otis bringing up the rear.

They found the entrance to the lost redoubt about thirty seconds before the Apaches found them.

Chapter Twenty-One

There were signs of a massive earth slip. It looked as if there'd once been a well-maintained blacktop leading directly across country from the main road toward Raton and the Colrada line, but the land had reared up and swallowed it whole. Now they stood near the last few yards of that road, which ended in a sharp drop down a sheer cliff. At the other end, twisted and buckled, were the remnants of a pair of dark green vanadium steel sec-doors.

"Doesn't look very promising," Peachy said, rubbing a tentative hand over his sprouting beard.

The arrow hit him through the wrist, pinning it to his neck, and Peachy went down with a bubbling yelp of shock and pain. Ryan had a moment to see that the feathers on the arrow flights were notched from a gray goose. Then the boy was kicking in the dirt, and the air around them was humming with more missiles.

A spear buried its point in the sandy earth just in front of Ryan as he drew his pistol, missing him by less than a foot.

"Inside!" the Trader yelled. "Bring the wounded!"

Apart from Peachy, whose lifeblood was seeping

out of him, other members of the patrol had taken hits. Garcia was cursing in Spanish as he tried to pull a shaft out of his shoulder. Janine, a radio operator from War Wag Two, had taken an arrow in her left arm, just above the elbow. Instead of panicking and trying to pull it out, ripping the muscle away on the barbed tip, she calmly knelt and snapped the narrow shaft, pulling the jagged point clear without harming herself.

"Good one!" Ryan shouted as he paused near her, in case she needed help.

"Bastards," she hissed. As she stood, a bullet hit her in the left side of her chest, knocking her to her knees again. Before Ryan could move, a second bullet smashed into her head, just above the left ear, killing her instantly.

"Fireblast!" Ryan cursed.

The worst of it was that there was no target available for his own blaster. The rain of arrows and the occasional bullet came from the shelter of the surrounding trees and boulders.

The entrance to the redoubt gave them temporary relief from the attack. Apart from Janine, whose corpse was left where it had dropped, they all made it safely. None of them, except Peachy, had injuries that were likely to prove terminal.

As soon as they were out of sight, there was a harsh shouted word of command. And silence fell.

The Trader beckoned Ryan to his side. "I never seen a one of 'em. You make who they are?"

"Sure as shit aren't sec-men. They only got single-shot blasters. And only four or five of them. Rest got bows. Must be Indians."

"Main thing is, make sure they can't get around behind us. Now that we're snug in here we can leave a couple with automatic rifles, and they can hold off the entire damned Sioux nation."

"Apaches, Trader," Garcia interrupted. "Saw one moving around. Apache. Sure of it."

For the first time there was a moment to survey their surroundings.

Ryan had been with the Trader on a few previous occasions when they'd scouted a newly discovered redoubt. Most of them had been like this.

The destroyed sec-doors were the giveaway. It meant that the fortress had been opened up, maybe within the past year. If the entrance was peeled open, then the chances of finding anything worthwhile inside stood between one and zilch. Probably nearer to zilch.

With the Trader, deciding and acting were only a heartbeat away from each other. Once he'd made a plan he'd act upon it.

Two members of the group, along with the worst wounded, stayed just inside the entrance. The remnants of the doors, combined with a lot of fallen concrete, provided excellent cover. With Uzis and a British Enfield Support Weapon, they had all the firepower they could need to hold off even a direct frontal attack. Nightfall was still a long way off, so they were secure.

The Trader and Ryan, with the rest of the party, moved inside, the hand lights they'd brought with them at the ready.

The ceiling had fallen in several places, revealing the mesh of rusting iron above it. Water had seeped through from somewhere higher up the mountain and dribbled down the moss-covered walls. The floor was ankle-deep in stagnant pools of water, covering a tangle of tumbled rubbish.

"Air's bad," Garcia said, stopping and sniffing. "Don't seem like another entrance."

Ryan could tell that himself. All over Deathlands there were ruined buildings, and some of them had never been entered since the day of sky-dark. You got used to telling the difference in the air. This redoubt smelled of decay, of urine and animals. Often there'd be a link with other parts of the huge fortresses, and there'd be some kind of air flow. In a few redoubts the nuke power units still functioned, and you had lights and heat.

Those were the ones where you looked for some kind of trading treasure.

"Want to go on?" Ryan asked the Trader.

"No point. I can smell the rotten stillness. No point."

They'd only gone about two hundred yards into the cavern, but the weight of the earth above them was already becoming oppressive. It was like being inside your own tomb, with the worry that someone outside was about to slam the door and turn the key on you. It wasn't a good feeling.

Behind them they all heard a sudden thin cry that rose and fell, fading away into a soft bubbling sound.

"Guess that's Peachy," Ryan said. "Off to buy the farm."

The Trader punched one hand into the other. "Radblast it! I truly hate to lose a young one."

THEY QUICKLY made their way back to the main entrance. There'd been a single, brief burst of fire from Giardino, who had the Enfield.

"Coupla them showed up between them trees. Think I hit one. Mebbe both. Mebbe not."

Janine's body lay where it had fallen, and the corpse of Peachy had been dragged to the side of the redoubt entrance. Ryan only glanced at it as he went by. The pile of meat and clothes wasn't the bright, laughing kid anymore. He'd gone forever.

"Standoff," the Trader said, squinting around the corner of one of the tumbled sec-doors. "They can't get in at us, and we'll find it hard to get out safe. What's the moon?"

Ryan's job as war captain included keeping up with that kind of knowledge. Being certain if you had a full moon or only a thumbnail of a sliver could easily mean the difference between breathing and choking. Being trapped in the old redoubt was exactly that kind of situation.

"Quarter," he replied. "Most likely the clouds'll clear after dusk. Be enough for them to make us if we try to move."

A few pebbles rattled down in front of the entrance, pattering on the concrete. The Trader looked around at Ryan.

"Above us," he said.

"Yeah," Ryan agreed.

Some more stones and a couple of larger boulders came crashing down. It seemed like a good move from the Apaches. If they could start a slide that would fill the doorway to the redoubt, they wouldn't have to risk anything. A few hundred tons of bedrock would seal in the invaders and leave them nowhere to run.

Ryan went inside to look again at the broken remnant of the plan of the redoubt, hoping that he might somehow find a clue that would open up an avenue of escape. But the air remained still and stagnant.

He walked slowly back to rejoin the others, waiting in the dripping gloom. Outside, there was bright sunlight and no sign of the men behind the ambush.

The voice was sudden and grating. "We will break stones and make the mountain fall. But you go alive if you send us out the man with one eye."

Everyone, including the Trader, looked at Ryan.

Chapter Twenty-Two

Doc Tanner was praying. It wasn't an activity that came naturally to the old man, not lately. He'd prayed a lot, wildly, after he was trawled forward from 1896 to the alien year of 1998, plucked from the side of his beloved wife and two little children. Doc had tried all sorts of desperate entreaties to any kind of deity that might be listening, knowing all the time that it was futile, that there was no possible way of jumping him back through time to rejoin his family.

Now he prayed for Ryan Cawdor.

"Please, Lord, hear me. I know that this man, Ryan, might not have been what some folks would call a good man. I know he's butchered many of the ungodly, but the overwhelming majority of them truly had retribution coming. He's totally loyal to his friends, and he upholds the right. Isn't that what it's all about, Lord? About upholding the right? Ryan Cawdor is a man who walks through the valley of the shadow of Deathlands and fears no evil. He doesn't pass by on the other side, Lord. So, now he needs you...now he's slipping into the darkness...aid him with thy rod and thy staff, Lord."

On his knees in the dimly lighted room, Doc wasn't

aware that the others had come in to stand behind him, listening to the sonorous, measured voice.

Jak raised a silent hand to brush an errant tendril of snow-white hair off his high forehead.

J.B. leaned against the edge of the door, face lined and tired. He'd been searching desperately for some other way out of the redoubt, for something that might save the life of his oldest companion.

Krysty stood by him. She and Mildred had been experimenting for a day and a half with the limited supply of drugs, trying to hit upon some combination that might drag the deeply unconscious man out of his coma.

Mildred had explained to her that the damage to Ryan wasn't caused by the bacteria from the food. So a normal course of antibiotics would be fruitless. It was the toxins that the bacteria had left in the stew that were killing him. Antitoxins would save him, but the medicine cupboard didn't contain what Mildred needed.

Experimentation was the only hope—to stumble upon something that would ease the progress of the fatal disease.

Now he lay there, as still as a carved statue. His chest was barely moving, and his breathing was stilted and labored. Twice already Mildred had been forced to help him breathe through a crisis, and feeding was out of the question.

Doc, face buried in his hands, was ending his prayer.

"I think that this might be fruitless as whistling in the dark. But if there is someone beyond the veil, someone listening to the rambling words of a damned old cretin, then help me. Help us. Help Ryan Cawdor, Lord. I beg you. In the name of the Father, the Son and the Holy Ghost."

The chorus of "Amen" from behind him made the old man start and look around, nearly losing his balance and falling in the process. Krysty stepped forward and helped him to his feet, his knee joints cracking like distant pistol shots.

"Thank you, my dear. I do hope that you don't think the old chap's losing his marbles?"

She smiled and squeezed his hand. "Course not, Doc. If it helps...if anything'll help, then it's worth a try."

"Why not Earth Mother's power, Krysty?" Jak asked.

She shook her head. The curls of dazzling scarlet were bunched and dull. "Can't, Jak. Not the way Gaia's forces work. I could lift him up and break metal and...and do anything that needs 'power.' But it's more strength, Jak."

"Ryan needs strength."

"Sure. But from inside him." She managed a wan smile. "Sure I can help him a little. Hold him and talk to him. It helps some. But when you get to the ace on the line, Ryan'll make the score...or he won't. That's all."

Doc looked at Mildred. "Any joy with the medicines?"

She rubbed her eyes and sighed. "If I never look at another mix of powders, pills and liquids it'll be too damned soon. I don't know, Doc. I've worked out something that might do the trick. Got it in this syringe here. It could combat the poisons. If it does, then Ryan could pull through. Like Krysty said, he's got the inner strength."

"If needle doesn't work...chilled?" Jak said.

"That's about it. The paralysis of his muscles is almost total. Face is like granite. The heart's slowing all the time, and I don't think his breathing can carry him through another three, four hours."

"Then I suggest, madam, that you use that needle. And let us hope that your medical skills and my poor prayers combine to aid him."

Mildred took the stopper off the end of the needle and squirted a tiny silver spray in the air to remove any risk of causing an embolism. She knelt by the bed. Ryan was completely still, the gray blanket over his body seeming motionless. His eye was closed, his lips slightly parted, and his skin had a deathly waxen pallor.

"Not easy to hit a vein," Mildred muttered, flicking at his forearm with her index finger. "Ah, we got us a live one here." The needle slid into the skin, and she steadily depressed the plunger. Withdrawing it, she gave a quick wipe to the puncture with a strip of cotton that had been soaked in surgical disinfectant.

"Now?" J.B. asked.

"We wait."

"How long."

"How the—" She controlled herself. "I don't know, J.B., and I don't want to guess. But if it hasn't worked in, let's say four hours, then I think Ryan will be dead."

They stood in a silent circle. Ryan had an oddly withdrawn, faraway look, as if he were listening to some distant voice calling to him, calling out to the one-eyed man.

Chapter Twenty-Three

"The man with one eye. What the hell you done to upset them, Ryan, got all their women pregnant? Deflowered every virgin on the ranch?"

Otis was laughing, oblivious to the mortal danger that they were in. If the attacking Indians kept their word and managed to lever down half the cliff and block the redoubt entrance, then everyone's life expectancy was going to suddenly get really short.

"I never been down this way before," replied Ryan. "Why'd they want me?"

"Ten minutes, killer of the helpless! We will give you the quick death you gave our women and our babies. The others will walk free."

The Trader slapped his hand against the side of one of the doors, making the steel ring. "Fireblast! Of course."

Ryan was only a moment behind him. "Sure. That's why."

Some of the others were much slower on the uptake, still looking at one another in bewilderment.

J.B. explained. "Those guys out there want the one-eyed man. They've seen Ryan, but he's not the one-eyed man they really want."

"Ferryman," July said. "Course."

There was some laughter and relieved chattering, but the Trader shut them up.

"They could take some persuading, my friends. We can tell Ryan from the sec-boss. I wonder if these men can. Or even want to. They got them a one-eyed man snug in the nest. Why worry about whether he's the right one?"

"Two minutes then all die!"

"I'll talk to them," the Trader said.

Very cautiously he edged toward the entrance, waving a hand and shouting that he wanted a truce, wanted to speak to their chief.

Nobody shot at him, but nobody answered him either. He glanced around at Ryan, who shook his head. "Don't risk it, Trader. Wait there."

"One minute. All die!"

"Listen, you dumb-ass piece of double-stupe shit! I wanna talk!"

"Tactful, Trader," Ryan said. "Real tactful."

"Why talk?" The voice was doubtful. "Give One-Eye to us. All live. He die. Keep him and he die. All die. What is to talk?"

"We come out and mebbe we all die, but some of you get chilled. You know it's true. Talk and it could be that nobody gets to die at all. What's wrong with that? Sounds a good idea to me."

The Trader took another half step, so that the light threw his shadow back into the dank cavern. Ryan and the others had fingers on triggers. If the Trader had gone down, Ryan would have led the charge outside. That would be the last and only option.

"I talk. Me. You. No others. No bows. No blasters. You come two hands of steps."

"Ten yards forward," Garcia interpreted unnecessarily.

"You come same distance," the Trader insisted, turning and calling into the redoubt. "Rest of you stay ready."

Ryan moved to a position where he could cover the Trader. Part of his mind was conscious once again that J.B. was right, and that he really ought to get himself a long gun. If the Indians appeared and started blasting, his own Smith & Wesson revolver wouldn't be the best weapon to have in his hand.

The Trader moved out into the open, counting his steps out loud, toward the sheer drop where the blacktop had been severed.

After a brief delay, a stocky figure appeared near a single tilting lodgepole pine, holding an old carbine at the trail. The Apache wore cotton trousers and a loose shirt and had his long hair tied back in a green bandanna.

The two men stopped a few paces apart, but the day was still and it was easy for everyone to hear their conversation.

"I'm Trader. Who're you?"

"Slow Eagle. Of the Mimbrenos. Why do you come to Many Wolves Canyon?"

"Why not?"

"I have lost a brother to your blasters. You have two who will not ride tomorrow. Why?"

The Trader coughed. "My business. Better question is why you attack us like sneaking back-stabbers? Tell me that."

"This is our land."

"Doesn't give you any right to chill folks minding their own business."

The Apache's voice rose in anger. "*Your* business! The business of Butcher Carson is death!"

"Business of Baron Carson's no concern at all of ours."

"Liar!" The word was shouted so loud that it echoed from the surrounding cliffs.

For a moment Ryan really believed that the Trader was going to draw down on the Indian. There were things you could kid his boss about, but the one thing you never did was question his honesty.

With an obvious effort he controlled himself and kept his voice surprisingly calm and gentle. "It is not a thing of honor to say another man lacks honor."

Slow Eagle had taken a half step back and lifted his blaster to his hip. Then he lowered it again. "You are the men of the baron."

"We are not. Told you. I'm Trader. These are my people. We're at Towse to buy and barter for gas and ammo."

The Apache shook his head. "I still say your words are the glitter of light upon a fast river, carried away and not worthy of notice."

"Now, why the dark night d'you keep saying that, mister? You got no call."

The Indian's finger pointed out like a striking rattler, aimed at where Ryan was waiting in the shadows of the redoubt.

"There is Blind Night," he crowed, "the butcher of babes. Carson's sec-boss! Do you think us fools that we do not see him?"

"Oh shit," someone said behind Ryan. "That empties the tank on us."

"You think that's Ferryman?" the Trader asked. "His name's Ryan Cawdor, and he's my war captain on the two wags."

"Blind Night," the Mimbrenos chief insisted. "He is well remembered."

The Trader turned and beckoned Ryan toward him, asking the Indian first if he would let him come without shooting him from cover. Slow Eagle nodded his permission and called a guttural warning to his hiding warriors.

"Look closely," the Trader urged. "Ryan has lost an eye. Ferryman has also an eye missing, but Ryan is taller. His skin is not so dark. Can't you see that for yourself?"

The Apache stared intently at Ryan through narrowed eyes, shaking his head doubtfully and then coming a few steps closer. From the cliffs above the sec-doors someone shouted something in the Indian tongue. Slow Eagle didn't reply.

"What did he say?" the Trader asked.

"That no person of the Apache has ever seen Blind Night close to the face and lived."

"Must be some way of settling this," Ryan said. "Isn't there anybody who seen Ferryman who'd know him again? Anybody?"

The Apache shook his head again. "The man is walking death to all. He led the raid on our pueblo and torched the church. Buried babies living. Drove our women into the fires so they ran and burned and screamed. They screamed, Blind Night!"

He spit at Ryan, who slowly lifted a hand and wiped the spittle away.

"One time more, you stupe bastard...I'm not fucking Ferryman! Not Blind Night! What do I have to do to prove it?"

The moment stood astride a razor, and Ryan's fingers twitched for the butt of his blaster. It was clear as crystal to him that talk wasn't going to sort this out. It was going to be sorted by fighting and by chilling.

No other way.

The voice from the top of the cliff rang out again, obviously asking a question. The chief replied, then a general, bellowed conversation developed, questions and suggestions raining in from all around them.

The Trader took the moment to whisper to Ryan out of the corner of his mouth. "Gut-shoot him when I say, and fly like goose shit off a shovel. I'll bring the others."

Ryan knew it was the best plan there could be. He

was obviously the main target for the anger of the Apaches. Put their leader down in the dirt, and you could make them stop and think.

Slow Eagle held up a hand for silence, looking once more directly at Ryan.

"The oldest of our warriors makes me think you can test your word."

"Test?"

"Is it not real word?"

"Yeah. But I don't know what you mean. How can I test if I'm telling the truth about who I am? How?"

"By blood."

The Trader looked at the Apache. "Stop talking behind your hand, mister. Just tell us what you mean."

"Blind Night—man who says he is not Blind Night—can fight to death against our best warrior."

"Blasters?" Ryan asked.

For the first time there was a hint of relaxation from the Mimbrenos chief. "Your long and small guns are too strong. If you fight it will be knife against knife."

"Fine by me, Trader," Ryan said. "Back myself against any scrawny, half-assed little Indian son of a bitch with steel in my hand. Yeah. Tell him let's get to it."

"Go into the redoubt. Make ready. I'll set out some rules with the chief here. Like what happens when you win."

Ryan appreciated the confidence in the Trader's voice.

IT DIDN'T take long. The Trader strode back, his grizzled face looking slightly puzzled. He stepped into the darkness, blinking. "Where's Ryan? Ah, there."

"Something wrong?"

"No. Well, yeah. If they're so rad-blasted scared of Ferryman, I don't get how they're so eager to have one of their fighters come against you with just steel. There's something...."

"Trap?" Otis suggested.

Garcia interrupted. "No. They give their word, then they keep it." The torn material tied around his wounded shoulder was already starting to leak fresh blood.

"If you lose, they say we go free," the Trader continued.

"If I win?"

"Chief says we all go free. You as well. I kind of pressed him on that. He said the gods would decide if you spoke the truth. Some kinda heathen bullshit about the spirits of truth sitting on the shoulder of the guy who wins."

"Me." Ryan grinned.

"Sure. No rules. One knife each. Kicking, gouging and all that...anything goes, Ryan. Start on a word from Slow Eagle. I said we'd be ready in a coupla minutes."

"Ready now. Where's the little bastard I have to chill?"

The Trader sighed, rubbing the small of his back. "Think I jarred something when I dived in here. Who d'you fight? Some Apache with a real weird name. Man Who Tore His Mother's Belly Apart. Chief says they also call him Dark Cloud.''

''Man that slashed open his own mother's stomach!'' July shuddered. ''What a psycho sicko! Better watch him, Ryan.''

''I'll watch him.'' Ryan drew his long-bladed Bowie knife from the sheath at his left hip, checking to make sure it was honed to a whispering edge. He resheathed it, drew his blaster and handed it to July for safekeeping. He then peeled off his shirt and chucked it to Otis. The damp air struck cold against his skin, and he felt the goose bumps rising.

''Bring on the mother-chiller.''

RYAN MADE SURE he was out in the sunlight for long enough to get his eyes well accustomed to the brightness. All members of the recce party were lined up with their backs to the devastated redoubt, far enough away to make sure nobody started dropping boulders down on top of them. The Trader had asked the Apache leader to bring his warriors from the cliff face, and he had obliged.

The Indians had slowly filed out from their various hiding places. It was an odd situation, with the threat to the Trader's group almost vanished. In an open firefight now, they'd massacre the poorly armed Apaches. Two or three of the crew had suggested it to Ryan and the Trader, and Ryan had given them the answer.

"Could chill them easy, sure. They only got five old blasters 'tween them. But we don't know how many more there might be. Could do us some damage on the way back down the mountain. No. Better I beat their man and we walk easier."

The morality of betrayal didn't bother anyone in the Trader's party, not with two corpses beginning to stiffen.

The sun warmed Ryan's muscles, and he felt loose and ready. He'd considered taking off the heavy combat boots, but the ground where they would fight was good and hard. It was a natural arena, about one hundred feet across, with the Apaches on the wooded side and the Anglos by the redoubt. One flank was a blank wall of steep rock, and the fourth side was a sheer drop to some broken crags.

"Where's your man, Chief?" Ryan called. "Time's passing."

"Dark Cloud is praying for strength," Slow Eagle replied.

"He'll sure need it," Ryan said to the Trader, who was at his shoulder.

"Looks like he's coming," Otis said.

The row of Indians parted to allow their champion through.

"Fireblast," Ryan breathed, shocked.

Dark Cloud was just about the biggest man he'd seen in his entire life.

Chapter Twenty-Four

Ryan stared at the hulk, only vaguely aware of the buzz of chatter from his companions.

"Seven foot six if he's an inch."

"Got to weight three-fifty."

"Four hundred."

"Yeah. Four hundred, easy."

"Lookit the knife."

"Fell a pine with that."

"One blow. Whoosh! Timber!"

Slow Eagle waved a hand toward the warrior. "This is Dark Cloud. He will fight against your man with one eye who you say is not Carson's man with only one eye."

The Trader looked sideways at Ryan, who shrugged his shoulders and nodded. What else was there to do? They hadn't told him he was going to have to fight this menacing giant. Why should they?

"It's fine," he said.

The Trader looked straight at him. "Don't mix up big with slow, Ryan. Could be a real serious sort of mistake if you did."

It was a fair point, well made.

Dark Cloud stood completely still, holding his

knife in his right hand, except it wasn't properly what you might call a knife. Ryan's Bowie knife was a substantial weapon, its blade sixteen inches long. The Apache was gripping what looked like a honed-down cavalry saber. It had a brass grip and a slightly curved blade, fully forty-five inches long.

He wore the same kind of cotton shirt and pants that the other Indians were wearing, the legs tucked into soft fringed boots of brown leather. The other mistake that could be made was to mix up being big and being soft. Ryan's fighting eye weighed up the Apache warrior and couldn't see an ounce of fat anywhere on the huge body.

"It is to the death," Slow Eagle pronounced.

"I know," Ryan replied.

"Your man is ready?" the chief asked, turning to the Trader.

"Sure is. Let's get to it. Good luck, Ryan. Do it to him, 'fore the double-big son of a bitch does it to you."

The only sound was the wind as it sighed through the slender tops of the surrounding pine trees and the shuffling of the feet of the two fighters.

While he'd been waiting, Ryan had been slowing his breathing, trying to relax, knowing the fight wasn't likely to last more than three or four minutes.

"Go," Slow Eagle said.

The Apache didn't come rushing in, trying to overwhelm the Anglo with his superior weight. He stood off, narrowed eyes watching Ryan. His broad face showed no trace of emotion—no anger or hatred, no lust for blood. Just a serene, calm confidence.

The spectators were silent, watching the two ill-matched men as they moved cautiously around each other. It wasn't like a fistfight for jack, with odds on one or other of the men. Everyone who rode with the Trader knew that concentration was vital, and if one of them called out to Ryan it might just distract him for that one vital, life-robbing second.

Neither Dark Cloud nor Ryan wanted to make the first move. With blades, it was often better to use a counterstroke, rather than risk the first vulnerable lunge. Ryan held his own knife point up, hoping for a chance to thrust at the Indian's stomach, the classic winning blow that was amplified by a savage twist of the wrist.

But the Apache's reach was so much greater than Ryan's that it was a difficult problem to get close enough without being cut to ribbons.

It crossed Ryan's mind to risk it all on a single throw of the heavy knife, but the Bowie wasn't particularly well balanced for an underarm pitch. And with a man as enormous as Dark Cloud, you had to hit him in a vital spot or he'd just walk on through and hack you to pieces.

Ryan tried to maneuver his opponent so he had him with his back to the sheer drop, but the Mimbrenos was ready for him, sliding sideways, balancing easily on the balls of his feet. Slowly he started to close in toward the smaller white man, the saber probing at the air in front of him.

The longer Ryan waited, the slimmer his chances became.

"Let's go," he gritted to himself.

He slid in, crabwise, ducking under the first whistling cut of the saber and feinting at the Apache's groin. Dark Cloud was even faster than Ryan had guessed, and his backswing with the long blade was lethally quick—quicker than such a big man had any right to be.

As Ryan dodged backward, his heavy boots slipped on the loose gravel and he stumbled for a moment. The Mimbrenos warrior didn't follow him in, but Ryan caught the flash of excitement in the deep-set eyes. It had nearly been a chance for the Indian, and he'd let it go by. And Ryan knew that he *knew* he'd let it slip.

"Next time," the white man breathed.

Again he danced in, ducking and weaving, allowing his own knife to paint a whirling pattern of polished death, coming closer to Dark Cloud, readying himself for the attack.

This time he feinted to cut at the hand that held the saber, but again the Apache was lightning fast. Ryan was forced to duck away, and again his combat boots slipped. But this time the slip was infinitely more serious.

This time he actually fell, crashing down in a clumsy tangle of arms and legs. As he struggled to get to his feet, something went wrong and he dropped the Bowie knife. It skittered eight or ten feet away from him, mockingly close, but an eternity beyond his reach.

The drama dragged the crowd of watchers from their silence.

The Apaches gave a great yell of encouragement to their man, seeing that victory was a scant handful of heartbeats away.

"Roll, Ryan, fucking roll!" shouted a voice that Ryan recognized as Otis's. It was good advice, but he ignored it. He lay on his back and watched the giant Indian looming toward him, the saber raised for the death thrust that would pin him to the bedrock.

Dark Cloud's impassive face cracked into the beginnings of a smile of triumph.

Ryan moved, so fast that the Apaches were still cheering his death.

Instead of trying to wriggle despairingly away from his opponent, Ryan made his move *toward* him, pushing off the palms of his hands like an acrobat, kicking out at Dark Cloud with the heel of his combat boots.

The giant had come a half step too far, lured in by Ryan's apparent helplessness. He reared back, trying to avoid the kick, but this time he was too committed, too slow.

In that frozen moment of time, Ryan felt the exultant flush of victory, transmitted by the solid crack as his heel made a violent contact with the right knee of the Mimbrenos. His ear caught the sound he'd been hoping for, the sickly crunch of the delicate joint imploding. Protective bone splintered, tore cartilage, ligaments and tendons. The damage was so radical that the Apache would be a cripple for as long as he lived.

Dark Cloud screamed then, the only sound that Ryan had heard him make. He toppled sideways, arms out, the saber flying from his crooked fingers.

"Timber," someone said behind Ryan, voice awed and quiet.

Ryan was dimly aware that his opponent was falling, but he was too busy following through on the next step of the combat plan. He tumbled away in a sort of slanted backward roll, coming up poised on hands and knees, his hand automatically finding his own Bowie knife where he'd dropped it.

The Indian was still trying. Despite the blinding fire of agony that blazed in his knee, he was struggling to get up on his left leg, hopping like a stork. But the pain had fogged his fighting brain, and he couldn't find his fallen blade.

"Take him, Ryan," the Trader urged.

Ryan didn't need telling. He moved in with lethal grace, easily dodging the clumsy flailing arms of the huge man. His razored steel pecked at the hamstring that corded the back of the Indian's left thigh, and blood seeped through the thin cotton pants. Dark Cloud fell again, clutching at the knife wound and rolling in the dust.

The watchers were silent.

Slow Eagle and his warriors were stunned by the

sudden and horrific defeat of their utterly invincible tribal champion.

Ryan cautiously circled the stricken giant, located the long saber and picked it up. He shook his head with amazement at its weight. To wield it the way Dark Cloud had done spoke of an almost unbelievable strength of wrist and arm. He turned back again to the Apache.

Dark Cloud's face was beaded with rivulets of sweat, and a trickle of blood oozed from his mouth—he'd bitten his tongue in shock and pain. His eyes were screwed up, nearly closed.

Ryan moved closer in, not taking any chances on coming within reach of those crushing arms. Dark Cloud's eyes opened wide, staring intently up at him. His lips parted, and he spoke to him, a short, harsh sentence.

Watchful of a trap, Ryan glanced away, looking for the face of Slow Eagle. "What'd he say, Chief?"

"He said he wished for swift passing to the mountains beyond the darkness."

"Yeah."

"Give it, white man. You have won. I believe you are not the creature of Carson."

"You reckon?"

He paused a long moment, then said reluctantly, "Yes. The gods have shown it so."

"No need to chill your man, then."

"It was to the death, Ryan," the Trader reminded him.

"Wouldn't want it said all through Deathlands that Ryan Cawdor butchered a helpless man, Trader. Not for no reason."

The helpless warrior repeated the same pleading sentence, but Ryan shook his head and began to walk away, toward his waiting friends. A shout from Slow Eagle stopped him.

"No!"

"No what, Chief?"

"It must be done."

"Chill him? Like slitting the throat of a penned steer? No thanks, Chief. Not my style."

"You must. Word was given that the fight would be to the death."

Ryan was insistent. "Won't do it, Chief. I'd have chilled him while the fight was going on, not now. Not after."

He'd sheathed his own knife, having wiped it clear of blood in the dirt. Holding the saber in his left fist he went to the wounded man and offered a hand, knowing that nobody would still expect him to chill Dark Cloud after that.

The monolithic warrior watched him, eyes puzzled. Finally he recognized that the one-eyed man was reaching down with a gesture of friendship.

Wincing in pain, he stretched up and gripped Ryan's right hand. Then, snarling with a savage ferocity, he tried to draw Ryan down, the fingers of his other hand clawing for his face.

"Fucker!"

The final struggle lasted less than five seconds. The moment Ryan realized the murderous intention of the crippled warrior, he reacted with a lethal speed. He pulled away from the clutching hands and thrust the needle point of the saber at the center of the Apache's muscular neck. He then leaned on it with all his weight.

The steel slid into flesh like a cormorant diving into water.

Ryan could feel the tip as it grated past the vertebrae. Dark blood trickled around the curved steel, tumbling down the sides of the man's throat, muddying the dust.

The fingers of the Apache continued to tighten on Ryan's hand, making him wince at the clamping pressure. Breath gurgled in the warrior's chest as he tried to lift himself, pushing against the saber that pinned him to the earth.

"Die, you bastard!" Ryan panted. Only a moment ago he'd been eager to spare the life of Dark Cloud. Now every fiber of his soul yearned for the Indian's death.

The hilt of the saber was hurting Ryan's chest, where he was braced against it. The Apache's head rocked from side to side, hastening the ending.

The last scene was suddenly, swiftly over.

Ryan felt the fingers loose their hold, leaving him with swollen weals on his hand. The head stopped its shaking, and stillness came.

The eyes went blank, looking inward. The mouth

sagged open and there was a great sigh of breath, carrying crimson bubbles.

Ryan straightened, leaving the long sword where it was, the brass hilt only three inches from the front of Dark Cloud's throat.

Slow Eagle came toward him, nodding. "It was well done. There was honor."

"Fuck your honor, Chief. It was just another bloody killing."

DUSK WAS CLOSING in across the land. Most of the Mimbrenos had taken away the gigantic corpse of their hero, leaving their chief behind with a couple of the older warriors of the tribe.

Slow Eagle had done everything he could to persuade the Trader to help him and his people against the ruthless tyranny of Alias Carson. Ryan's success seemed to convince him that they were not allies of the baron, but he wrongly assumed that they must therefore be the enemies of Towse ville.

Finally the Trader rose from the boulder where he'd been sitting and shook his head. "No. I sure figure you got a whole lot of righteous grievances against the baron, but the answer's still the same. No. We aren't masked avengers of injustice, coming in to the ville on white horses."

"They are too powerful. Too many men and too many blasters."

Ryan was at the Trader's elbow. "That's how the

world is, Chief. You had it. They come and took it. Now they got it.''

"With help we could take it again. The land is for the people. There have been people there for hundreds of years. Navaho and Hopi and our people. You would not send all baron's sec-men into darkness. Send some. Open doors. We will take the rest.''

The Trader hesitated and glanced at Ryan, who shook his head. The older man spoke to Slow Eagle. "My war captain thinks like me, Chief. No percentage in it. We stand to lose some good men and women, and we might not get the gas we need. What do we win?''

"Honor.''

Ben was standing near them. "Honor," he said. "Who has honor? He that died today. Honor's another word for dying well.''

The Trader sighed. "That's about right, Chief. Wish you luck. Take back your ville and I'll gladly come and trade with you.''

The Apache looked him in the eyes. "There will be no trade. What we have lost will not ever be won again. I see that.''

"Real sorry. But it's getting close to dark and we best get back to the wags. Wasted time visiting the redoubt. Nothing there for us. Nothing at all.''

Over to the west, the orange sun was sinking into a bank of dark thunderheads.

Chapter Twenty-Five

One tanker of gasoline had arrived when the two war wags eventually returned to the pale adobe walls of Towse ville.

Baron Carson wasn't particularly interested to hear that they'd located the redoubt. He asked if it held any weapons or any gas. Once he'd learned that the fortress was completely ruined, he completely lost even minimal enthusiasm.

The deal on the gas meant that the fuel tanks of War Wags One and Two were now partly full, but their consumption was enormous, with a poor miles-per-gallon ratio. Carrying all that steel, the wags were the ultimate gas guzzlers.

Carson shrugged his narrow shoulders when the Trader tried to press him about when the rest of the fuel would turn up.

"You can't eat the chicken until the egg's been laid," he drawled. His slitted eyes peeked out at the Trader and his mouth trembled into the beginning of a grin.

"Could wring the chicken's neck soon as look at it," the Trader replied, "if it don't hurry up and squeeze out the rest of the damned eggs."

"Patience is the greatest of human virtues," the baron uttered with a virtuous nod to the sky.

"A .38 through the eyeball settles most arguments."

Alias Carson finally managed his thin lizard smile. "Guess I like the cut of your coat, Trader. Shame you can't stick around here a while longer. Talk gets precious in Towse."

"I'll give till noon, day after tomorrow. Then I start to get angered some," the Trader warned. "No more extensions."

"Your wish is my command, Trader. Or should that be your command is my wish? I always get sort of terminally confused with that old saying. Know what I mean?"

THE RUN-IN with the Apaches had only raised a flicker of interest from the baron. But his sec-boss had been a whole lot more excited to hear all about it.

"You chilled their fucking giant?"

Ryan and the Trader had talked to J.B. in a council, and they'd agreed that they'd only give the bones of the confrontation with the Indians and avoid any mention of Ferryman or the request to help them against the baron. Ryan's fight was forced upon them as the price for walking free from the ambush. The sec-man accepted the amended version without any question.

"Got lucky," Ryan said.

"Luck like that you made yourself. It's called 'skill' not 'luck,' Ryan."

"Mebbe."

That evening, the Trader beckoned for Ryan to go walk with him around the perimeter of the ville, and the two men strolled through the warm evening. During the afternoon, the temperature had risen sharply and the wind had dropped. Now, close on ten o'clock, the thermometers were showing better than twenty-five degrees centigrade. The crews had all moved their sleeping bags outside, away from the ovens that the vehicles had become. To economize on fuel, the Trader had ordered power units switched off or down to low.

As they crossed the narrow bridge over the river that foamed through the pueblo, the Trader paused and leaned on the handrail, staring down into the water. He reached into the pocket of his combat jacket and fished out a black cigar.

"If things was different, Ryan, this could be a hell of a good place. Guess it was, once. Now...too much edge. Too much closed doors. Too much not knowing what kinda game's being played."

Ryan nodded. Away to their left, in the adobe block that housed the sec-men, a shuttered window was thrown open, splashing a golden rectangle of light across the square. Someone shouted an obscenity, and the lamp was extinguished. But the shutters remained open and Ryan was conscious that someone was standing there watching them.

"Too many eyes, Trader. Not enough mouths."

"How d'you make Baron Alias Carson?"

"Not like most barons. Doesn't swagger around with a pair of matched .45s in a handtooled Mex rig, but he runs a real tight ville."

"What's he want from us, Ryan? You tell me the answer to that."

He didn't reply immediately, sifting and weighing his feelings, allowing them to meld. "Only two possibilities."

"Yeah?"

"He's straight and the gas'll come. Or not."

"Some came, like he said." The Trader picked at his mouth and spit a shred of tobacco into the tumbling stream.

"Guess you trust him...and carry a loaded blaster."

"How about this woman?"

Ryan watched the far-off pattern of silver lightning playing on the peaks of the distant mountains.

"What about her, Trader?"

"Figure she knows his plans?"

"Could be."

"You just seen her the once?"

"Yeah."

"Why not see her again?"

Ryan laughed. "Now, what does 'see' mean?"

The Trader also laughed, a sudden, harsh barking sound. "I don't care what it means. Just spend some time and talk some with her. See what you can find out."

"Spy?"

"Prefer to say it's a recce in a hostile zone, Ryan."

"How about the baron?"

"Steal food from a man's dish, in front of his face, and he'll likely get angered. Take it from the back shelf of his larder and he won't even notice it's gone."

"I'll be careful."

"Know you will."

They stood together in a companionable silence. Ryan noticed that the window had been closed in the sec-men's headquarters. The lightning was becoming ferociously brilliant.

"One of the women who brings us food said there was big storm brewing," the Trader observed. "She was part Navaho and said she could feel it."

"Could be right. The night doesn't feel good. Too quiet. Too sticky."

The Trader took a last draw on his cigar and flicked the glowing butt into the river, where it vanished silently.

THE CHANCE came next morning.

McMurtry wandered over to watch the crews of wags going through their daily ritual of checking and cleaning all blasters under the eyes of J.B. The ville's sec-man was wearing a faded blue sweatshirt with a slogan printed on it that was barely legible—If You Find Me, Can You Tell Me Where I Am?

"How you guys doing?"

Ryan and the Trader were standing together, near

the big front wheels of War Wag One. They turned at the approach of the sec-man.

"Doing fine. How's the Harley?"

McMurtry's narrow face brightened. "Real good. Going out on it at noon. Sharona's off on one of her painting gigs. Baron wants two of us with her in case the skins get a taste to pick her off."

"Painting?" the Trader asked. "You mean like making up pictures?"

"Sure. We don't go far. Baron wouldn't let her. Old ranch near the water at Abbyqu."

Ryan glanced around. "Sure wouldn't mind getting out of this damned place for a few hours myself. Think the baron mind if I came along with you?"

"No. Can you ride a two-wheel?"

"Yeah. The woman ride a two-wheel?"

"Bitch can ride anything." He paused, and the grin broadened. "Or anyone!"

WHEN RYAN went out to join McMurtry, the Trader came with him.

"Don't lose sight of why you're going out with the woman," he said, patting Ryan on the shoulder. "It's a dirty job, my friend, but someone has to do it."

"I'll close my eyes and think about you and the war wags."

The baron came out of his living quarters and joined them as they reached McMurtry by the four motorcycles.

"Understand you'll be joining the art school outing, Cawdor."

"Going along for the ride, baron." The words were no sooner out of his mouth than he wished he'd avoided the word "ride," bearing in mind McMurtry's lewd comment about Sharona Carson.

"There's not been any trouble with Indians up that way for some time, but you all keep your eyes open. Return if there's any suggestion of harm."

Ryan glanced at the machines they'd be riding. McMurtry had his Harley. The other sec-man, called Smitty, was a long-haired, bearded man, carrying forty pounds excess around the guts. His bike was a much-rebuilt Suzuki. Ryan had an antique English Norton, 350 twin, its chrome winking in the patchy sunlight. Sharona Carson had a chopped Harley, which had been converted into a trike with raked sissy bars, and had a small, two wheeled trailer at the rear.

At that moment, the lady herself appeared and posed briefly on the shadowed porch before striding across the patterned sand toward them.

Ryan had once been shown a page from a frail, crackling women's fashion magazine, which had shown a skinny, elegant woman dressed in a bizarre fantasy of how someone imagined pretty Indian girls looked. Sharona Carson seemed to have decked herself out on the basis of something remarkably similar.

Her hair was braided, with tiny beads and semiprecious stones knotted among the strands so that it constantly tinkled. A pair of smoked glasses hid her eyes;

a pale lilac scarf was tied around her throat, chosen, Ryan figured, to match her invisible eyes; her jacket of golden leather was unzipped, showing a low-cut blouse of silver satin; the fringed skirt in light cream suede fell just above the knee; soft boots in matching suede, low-heeled, fitted just above the knee.

"Looks a barrel of jack," the Trader whispered in Ryan's ear.

"Dirty job, Trader," Ryan replied.

They set off in convoy. McMurtry was in the lead, with Sharona immediately behind him. Ryan came third, grateful for the goggles and scarf that J.B. had pressed on him. Smitty, his two-wheeler coughing spasmodically, brought up the rear. The highway was straight and clear leading north, but the mountains had disappeared behind towering chem-clouds of purple.

Chapter Twenty-Six

All four of the bikes were fitted with heavy-duty ribbed tires for off-trail riding. Every now and then the blacktop was in such poor condition that Ryan was thankful that they possessed them. He enjoyed the ride, in spite of the bouncing and jarring.

And despite having to detour around earth slips or fallen trees or washouts, they still made excellent time. They reached the outskirts of the abandoned, scattered village of Abbyqu in less than two hours.

They were surrounded by outcrops of twisted rock, layered in a dazzling variety of colors, ranging from a soft muted gray to vivid pinks and oranges. Millennia of wind and rain had tormented the cliffs, producing sculptured forms that even Ryan could recognize had their own bizarre beauty.

Smitty's Suzuki began to give more trouble, its coughing growing worse. "Mother's blowing too fucking hot!" the bearded man yelled, holding up a hand. He pulled off to the side of the road near a clump of stunted sycamores.

The others all rolled to a halt. Sharona looked back over her shoulder. "We're nearly at the ruins of the old ghost ranch where I want to do some painting.

Mac, you stay with Smitty and get his hog fixed up. Me and the outlander'll go up the trail and stop there."

McMurtry wasn't all that happy about her suggestion. "Best we stick together."

"No. Time's wasting."

"Baron said—"

"I know what he said, Mac. But we're so close now."

Ryan, standing astride the big Norton, was just glad to have the weight off his backside for a few blissful minutes.

"Shouldn't take more than a half hour for her to cool down some," Smitty said, getting off the two-wheel wag and kicking the stand into place.

"Come on, Mac. We all got blasters. Any sign of trouble and I'll shoot off a couple of rounds, and you can come a'running."

The sec-man was clearly unhappy at the suggestion, but he was also clearly frightened of the baron's wife.

"Sure."

"Come on, Ryan," Sharona said. "See you two in a while."

"Take care," McMurtry called.

Just for a moment Ryan wondered whether the parting shout was directed at Sharona or both of them. Or just him.

THE CLIFFS rose gently to their left. The air was stifling, but there was now a breath of roasting breeze coming from the northeast, where the sky was looming black over the Sangre de Cristo range.

Sharona throttled back as the tumbled ruins of an old ranch appeared close ahead of them. A windmill, its tower grotesquely rusted, shuddered and creaked in the rising wind. Dry as ancient bones, the fallen remnants of stock fences lay scattered everywhere. The roof had long gone off the adobe house, but the walls were still secure. At one end there was a solid extension, looking newer, with a workmanlike roof still in place.

It was a beautiful and picturesque place, and Ryan found his imagination stirred by it, wondering for a passing moment what life must have been like in such an idyllic location before the long winters took the land by the throat.

The two engines both cut at once, and silence came flooding in. But it wasn't a total silence. Ryan could hear the squeaking of the weather vane, the rising breeze stirring the top branches of the live oaks where the corral had been and the river, moving determinedly along on its own private business.

Sharona swung off her chopped trike and stretched her arms high above her head. "My sweet Lord," she moaned, "but I'm stiffer than a grizzly's dick."

Ryan also dismounted the Norton, relieved at the peace. "Want me to give you a hand with that painting stuff?" he asked.

"No, Ryan. I want you to give me some good loving with that pork mortar you got tucked into your pants. And I mean *now*!''

There was no time to be wasted.

''We got a half hour, tops. Then them two lame-brain dickheads'll be riding in to protect the baron's possessions,'' she said. ''Inside. No, not the main house. That's long fucked. The storeroom. There's a mattress and some emergency rations there.''

Ryan rode with it. He consoled himself with the thought that he was, after all, merely obeying the orders of the Trader.

Sharona left the door ajar so they could listen for the approach of the bikes, even though the fast-rising wind was already drowning out the sound of the river. As they went inside, Ryan caught a last glimpse of the sky to the northwest, and the sight made him hesitate.

''What's wrong?''

''That storm. Coming this way faster'n a one-legged man in a forest fire.''

Sharona, her dark glasses already in her pocket, stepped back outside to look where he was pointing. ''Yeah,'' she said. ''It'll blow over.''

''I don't know. Those clouds are boiling. Look at them. I never seen...''

The massive nukings of the last and final war had not only had a terrible effect upon the face of the planet, it had permanently upset the balance of the world's climate.

Now there were storms throughout the American

continent that were more devastating than any prior to day-dark. Ryan had experienced many of them during his life, but he'd never seen a sky quite like the one that was menacing them now.

Far above the cloud layers was a line of startlingly vivid silver, and this seemed to be giving birth to a constant cascade of lightning, great spears and sheets of forked lace that dazzled the darkness. It was impossible to make out where sky and mountains were conjoined, because of boiling dust. The clouds themselves were mainly purple to black, but they were streaked with fiery crimson and slashes of a wicked green. Despite the wind, they could both hear the sound of almost continuous rolls of thunder.

"Told you. It'll blow over. Come on, lover. Let's get inside and comfortable."

She turned to him, standing so close that he was enveloped in the musky scent of her perfume, combined with the feral odor of her sweat. Sharona reached out and allowed her fingers to brush gently across the front of his pants.

"Well, I'm glad some part of you wants to get inside."

RYAN DECIDED that afternoon that he really didn't like having the initiative taken away from him during lovemaking. It was good and exciting to find a woman who was as enthusiastic as Sharona Carson, but she only really wanted it on her terms, her way, when and how *she* wanted it.

The first time was standing up, her beaded hair rattling against the adobe wall behind her. There wasn't any tenderness or any foreplay. She simply dropped her panties in the dirt and quickly unzipped Ryan's pants, cool fingers reaching hotly for him.

The second time was nearly as quick.

Sharona was so hot to boogie that Ryan barely managed to reach his own climax before she was hustling him for seconds.

"Sit down, lover. Quick, before those two bastards come 'n catch us."

She pulled his trousers to his ankles, waiting impatiently while he sat down, back against the wall. Sharona stood astride him, the heels of her suede boots easing his legs farther apart. The hem of her short skirt was only inches away from his eyes, and for a moment he considered leaning forward and using his tongue, but she—

"Keep still and let me move," Sharona hissed as she lowered herself onto him, impaling herself with a gasp of pleasure on his swollen maleness. Her gold leather jacket was open, and she shrugged it off so that he could admire the way her nipples thrust hard at the silver satin of the tight blouse.

"Oh, yeah," she moaned, rising and falling, eyes squeezed shut as she lost herself in her own pleasure.

Ryan put his arms around her waist, steadying himself and preventing her from moving so fast that she risked losing him. The Trader's joke about it being a dirty job came back to him at that moment.

Two factors kept Ryan from giving himself up to the delight of their coupling. One was his straining to hear the sound of the two-wheel wags coming along the dirt road toward the ruined ranch, and the other was his awareness that the grandfather of all storms was raging in toward them.

He'd taken the precaution of wheeling his Norton into an angle between the walls of the main building, where it would get some protection, but Sharona's chopped hog was out in the open, not far from the river.

"Oh, yeah! Come on, you son of a bitching bastard, Ryan! Gimme it all, all, all!" Her head was thrown back, the cords in her throat standing out as if she were being throttled. Her mouth gaped open in an expression of near idiocy, and spittle was stringing from her full lips.

Knowing he wasn't going to get there, Ryan concentrated on sustaining his erection to avoid disappointing the gasping woman. Outside, over her heaving shoulders, he could see that sunlight had disappeared, and the day had become dusk. Sand swirled around, and the door began to swing back and forth in the howling wind.

Ryan had expected Sharona to scream her climax, but she simply collapsed on him with a long-drawn sigh of pure delight.

She was kissing him on the lips, the face, his good eye, his neck, his forehead, tiny nibbling kisses that kept him roused.

"Oh, dearest, that was wonderful. Again. We gotta do it again. We got time."

"No, Sharona."

"Yes. Don't worry about the sec-men. They won't get here. Please, lover. Anything you want. I'll be so good for you."

"No. The storm."

"You can be baron of Towse, Ryan. With me to help you."

The noise of the hurricane was so piercing that Ryan wasn't sure he'd heard her properly, even though her lips were against his ear. She had started to move again, little risings and fallings, making him stir with arousal.

"What d'you say?" he shouted.

"You and me, Ryan. You're man enough to take him out."

"Take him? The baron?"

"Chill him, lover."

She was moving more, one hand stroking his face, sliding her index finger into the corner of his mouth. But Ryan shifted away from her touch.

"No. You want me to chill Alias Carson for you? That it?"

Dust was billowing around the small, square building, and the wind was deafening.

"Yes. Chill him. I'll arrange it. No risk. He doesn't even have a blaster. Do it, lover, and you'll have me for always and all the power and all the jack. All of it."

Ryan closed his good eye, blinded by the dust. When he opened it again, moments later, he stared straight into the muzzle of McMurtry's blaster.

Chapter Twenty-Seven

"This is business, Ryan," McMurtry shouted, shaking his head sadly.

"Yeah," Smitty agreed from behind him, also holding an automatic pistol. "We heard what you said, and we seen what you done. What you're still doing by the look of it."

Ryan with Sharona Carson sitting astride him, knew that this was as close to death as he'd come for a long, long while. Either the sec-men chilled them both now, or they got taken back to Towse. The latter might give him some sort of a chance.

"Do it now, Mac? Or take 'em back for the baron? Which?"

McMurtry sniffed. "Fucking dust gets... I don't much like the idea of having to watch this one-eyed son of a bitch all the way back to the ville. Guess it looks like now."

That was the same decision that Ryan would have taken if their respective positions had been reversed. Now was generally best.

And safest.

The hut was about ten feet square. The mattress where he sat, back against the wall, took up about a third of the space. The door was still swinging back and forth, slamming against the latch. A ferocious wind screamed outside, sending spiraling fountains of red dust into the crowded room.

Sharona, her back to the intruders, hadn't said a word, seeming paralyzed with shock. She slumped forward, her left hand at her face. The right was on the blind side, clutching, oddly, at her ankle, just inside the soft top of the suede boot.

Peering through the fog of sand, Ryan tried to make out what kind of blasters the two sec-men were carrying, but his eye was prickling and tears filled it. All he could see was that they were both hefting standard .38s. At a range of six feet, it didn't much matter.

"Ready?" McMurtry asked.

Sharona turned around at last, staring up at the sec-man. "Any use offering you jack?"

"Jack'd buy us good graves with real pretty coffins. Brass handles and all. Won't buy us life if the baron got to hear about what you said and done."

"If Ryan chills him, then you'd be safe."

Her right hand was reaching for Ryan's fingers, as though she sought the comfort of a human touch in the final seconds of life.

"Nobody can chill Baron Alias Carson," Smitty bellowed. "Man lives for ever and ever."

"Amen to that," McMurtry said.

"Please. You can both have me if you let me go. Just chill Ryan."

The sec-men laughed. The eerie shriek of the storm

was all around them, and Ryan couldn't actually hear the noise of the laughter. But he saw Smitty's layers of belly rippling with his amusement.

"You'll fuck with us, Sharona?"

"Yes. Any way you like."

Now her hand was locked into Ryan's hand, and he could feel what she was holding.

McMurtry shook his head. "You don't have nothing other sluts don't have. Not 'nough to buy the farm for. No. This is it."

She passed Ryan a knife, short, with a very heavy blade, shaped like a broad leaf. The slender hilt felt like carved bone to Ryan's fingers.

McMurtry was partly hidden by Sharona, but Smitty was a little to the left, his grinning face and raggy beard hanging over the barrel of the blaster.

Hampered by the woman, and with an unfamiliar blade, Ryan knew that he had to go for the ace-on-the-line throw. That meant the throat.

He powered himself into explosive action.

Bracing his legs and pushing Sharona directly at McMurtry, he simultaneously flicked the small knife toward Smitty's neck, not waiting to see how successful the throw was.

The combat logic was very simple.

If the knife missed, then the fat man would shoot him. If he waited to see whether he'd hit the target, then McMurtry would recover and shoot him.

Sharona sprawled on her back, legs wide apart, arms clawing toward McMurtry, who staggered a couple of paces, banging his shoulder against the swinging door. The blaster went off, almost mute in the inferno of noise from the appalling chem-storm that raged outside. Chips of adobe flew from the wall by Ryan's shoulder, peppering him with the sharp splinters.

A tiny fraction of Ryan's fighting brain was conscious of how vulnerable he was, with his pants down and sand stinging the exposed flesh.

Hobbled, he barely reached the sec-man, his hands snatching at McMurtry's groin. He locked his fingers into the softness and tore at it with all his strength. There was a mewing squeak, and the sec-man tore himself free, stumbling and falling halfway through the door. Ryan chopped with the edge of his right hand at McMurtry's unprotected groin, feeling the jar as he pulped the genitals against the ridge of the pubic bone.

The man's knees came up in an involuntary reaction, and his whole body went into a shocked muscular spasm. Ryan knew that the sec-man wouldn't be taking any interest in things for a while, and he turned his attention to Smitty.

The fat man was kneeling against the far wall, sand smearing his sweating face. The ivory hilt of the throwing knife was stuck in the side of his fleshy neck, blood leaking fast. The pistol had fallen from his fingers, and he was fumbling for it with his left hand, while the right hand touched the hilt of the knife cautiously, as though he feared he would hasten his own passing if he was clumsy.

Sharona lay where McMurtry had kicked her, doubled over, eyes shut tight.

Ryan snatched a moment to hoist his own pants, clicking the buckle closed. Then he stepped across to Smitty. The sec-man squinted up at him through glazing eyes. His lips moved, but Ryan couldn't hear a sound from the dying man. He stooped and picked up the blaster, throwing it into the corner of the hut.

Smitty was rocking slowly back and forth, head moving from side to side. Eventually the knife would take his life, but Ryan wasn't about to stand there waiting.

He bunched his right fist and struck a single, lethal blow to the side of the sec-man's neck, just below and behind the right ear. Smitty slumped on his face, legs twitching, fingers scrabbling in the piled sand.

Sharona had recovered enough to drag the semiconscious figure of McMurtry inside the hut, gesturing to Ryan to close the flapping door and shut out the hurricane.

As he threw all of his weight against the heavy oak door, Ryan glimpsed a scene from hell. The trees of the river were folded double, all of their leaves stripped by the demonic gale. Visibility fluctuated between forty yards and zero. With a great effort, Ryan braced his shoulder against the door and forced it shut, slamming the bolt. A tiny barred window of thick glass, set near the ceiling, provided murky light, enough for him to see Sharona bending over the moaning figure of McMurtry.

The noise outside was still deafening, but inside the adobe walls there was a reasonable level of sound.

"What're you doing?" he shouted.

"Making sure, lover," she replied, straightening up.

She'd drawn the ivory-hilted throwing knife from the neck of the corpse and placed the point inside McMurtry's left ear where he lay in the dirt. The white bone handle was smeared with Smitty's blood. It stood there, like a marine creature probing at the interior of a shell, moving slightly in time with the breathing of the barely conscious sec-man.

"Now what?"

Sharona turned to him, her eyes staring white with shock, her lips folded back off the perfect teeth in a vicious snarl.

"This," she called.

Lifting her right foot and positioning it carefully over McMurtry's head, she stamped down with all of her weight, the sole of the boot driving the sharp steel deep into the sec-man's skull. The impact was so great that Ryan heard the hollow sound of bone bouncing off the stone floor of the hut.

There was hardly any blood from the mortal wound, just a little, very dark, seeping out around the sculpted ivory hilt.

"Now we put 'em out," she yelled.

Ryan immediately saw the cunning of her plan.

Someone, sometime, might want to take a look at the corpses of the two sec-men, and if they found knife wounds then it might prove difficult for Ryan and the woman to explain. But out in the scouring gale...

"Pull that blade," he said.

"I put it in. You take it out," she argued, wiping her hands in the sand to clean off the flecks of blood.

Ryan wasn't in the arguing mood.

He reached inside with finger and thumb and was just able to grip the slippery haft, drawing it smoothly out and wiping it on the dead man's T-shirt. He handed it to Sharona, who tucked it snugly back inside her right boot.

"Lucky you had that," he said.

She pointed to the two dead men with her foot. "They were unlucky. We were better."

IT WAS EASIER to talk about dumping the bodies outside the protection of the hut than it was to actually do it.

The chem-storm was so unrelentingly savage that it whisked away the senses. Once the door was opened again, both Ryan and Sharona were blinded and deafened. The sand lashed at their skin, making it impossible for them to see what they were doing. Communication was out of the question.

Finally Ryan pushed the woman down on the mattress while he stooped and lifted Smitty under the arms. He heaved him a few paces out the front of the ruined ranch, dropped him and went back to fetch McMurtry's corpse.

He battled back into the hut, surrounded by constant thunder and purple lightning. The air reverberated and buffeted him, filling his nostrils with the bitter stench of ozone.

Ryan jammed the door shut, fighting for breath. Sharona sat hunched on the stained mattress.

"Now we wait," he said.

Chapter Twenty-Eight

As far as Ryan could calculate, the eye of the chem-storm passed over them around five o'clock in the afternoon. That was when they were both conscious of a sharp, painful change in atmospheric pressure. Sharona cried out, clapping her hands over her ears. Ryan did the same, swallowing hard to try to minimize the sudden discomfort.

The noise dropped for a quarter of an hour, then resumed again with a banshee wail. It persisted for several more hours, bombarding the sturdy little building. Long after dark, the noise began to ease. The thunder drifted slowly away, and they could no longer see continuous purple lightning through the one tiny window.

"Is it over?" she asked, breaking the long, long silence between them.

Ryan considered his answer. "The storm, you mean? Yeah, that's over?"

"How about what I said?"

"That's over, too. Fact is, it never got itself started."

"And us?"

"Us?"

"You and me, lover?"

"Over."

RYAN OPENED the door and glanced out. The sky was shrouded in unbroken cloud, hiding the moon completely, making it impossible to see what had happened to their hogs or to the corpses of the sec-men.

He closed the door again and went back to the mattress, curling up beside the baron's wife and falling immediately asleep once more.

When Ryan next came smoothly from sleep, he saw the first pallid lightening of the dawn sky through the window above him. He had slept fully dressed and he swung himself upright, stretching the kinks from his muscles.

The movement woke Sharona. "Time to get up?" she asked.

"Storm's done."

"Sweet Lord! I feel like I've been rad-blasted up and down and in and out. My mouth tastes like a rabid cougar pissed in it."

The door was blocked by a drift of blown sand. Ryan levered it open enough for them to get out and look around.

It was a thoroughly beautiful morning, with the air clean and fresh, the peaks of the Sangre de Cristo looking close enough to touch.

The sun smiled serenely from a flawlessly blue sky. At a first glance around them, nothing seemed to have changed.

The contours of the land were the same. Ryan could see that the river was still running, though its waters now looked swollen and muddied. The devastated house and hut were much as they'd been before, though the adobe walls looked as if they'd been scoured clean by a team of sandblasting workers. The trees had gone—not totally, but only splintered trunks remained. Every leaf and twig, and virtually all of the large branches had been stripped away.

"Look at 'em," said Sharona Carson, standing at his elbow.

Ryan looked.

At first glance it was difficult to even recognize the corpses as human bodies. Sand was piled around and over them, almost providing ready-built graves.

Ryan walked toward them, his boot heels crunching through the scattered, glittering sand. He stooped and brushed away at the corpses, checking that the marks of their violent deaths had been removed by the chem-storm.

"Nothing to worry about," he said quietly.

He straightened and brushed his hands free of the orange dust.

The clothing of the sec-men had gone, except for a few ragged threads that had been partly protected by the weight of the bodies. Their skins had been flayed away, often taking the flesh with it. In several places—at shoulder, knee, elbow—the polished whiteness of exposed bone.

McMurtry's face was unrecognizable. His eyes had

been torn out, as had his lips and the soft tissues around his throat and mouth. His jaw gaped, and his teeth bore an unnatural gleam of scoured ivory. Smitty's beard had protected a little of the flesh around the jaw, but the rest of the face was disfigured in the same way as the other sec-man.

"Tell it like it was. Smitty's hog overheated. Mac stayed with him. We went on and got to cover. They didn't make it.'' The woman's voice was calm and totally lacked expression. She stared at the bodies, avoiding any sort of eye contact with Ryan.

"Sure," he agreed. Sharona was quite right. Best lies were the simple ones. You got caught out when you tried to be clever and elaborate. Tell it like it happened.

More or less.

THE TWO-WHEEL wags of Sharona and the sec-men had been destroyed by the insane power of the chemstorm. Not a flake of paint remained on any of the machines. When Ryan tried the starter on the Harley trike, there was just the faintest grating sound. McMurtry's hog and Smitty's Suzuki were totally, terminally mech-dead.

"Where's your…oh, I remember. You put it inside there, didn't you?"

He nodded and walked through the empty doorway. His Norton was relatively unscathed.

Sharona followed him in. "You're one of the most

careful men I ever met, Ryan Cawdor. You wouldn't want to reconsider…''

He didn't even bother to turn round, throwing the words over his shoulder. ''I said it was over, lady. Over.''

Before starting off toward Towse ville, they snatched a hasty meal from the emergency rations in the hut and shared the remaining drinking water from the metal canteen. Ryan opened a couple of the cans, none of which bore any labels.

''Corned meat in this one,'' he said, ''and I guess this is some kinda squash. You got a preference, or can we eat half each?''

''I don't care.''

''How about if I eat it all, if you really don't care?''

''Fuck you…lover,'' she spit, snatching the tin of meat from him.

IN THE END Ryan decided that it would be wise to drag the stripped corpses into the hut and push the door shut on them. The wind and sand had almost tanned what flesh remained, and they were light and easy to move.

''Keep them away from the wolves and the coyotes,'' he said.

''Wouldn't hurt them. Not now.''

He stared at the woman. ''You get your mouth working before you get your brain engaged, lady. Suppose your husband wants to see the bodies. Suppose he doesn't believe our story. Those scoured bodies are like…like silent witnesses. Leave them out and they disappear, and our story gets to grow a few more holes in it. That what you want?''

When she didn't reply, Ryan strode outside.

After he'd given the Norton a thorough cleaning, he kicked it into reluctant life, beckoning for Sharona to join him. Despite the ordeal, she still looked like a fashion plate. The dark glasses were in place and the scarf was knotted casually about her slender neck. She picked her way daintily through the loose sand. Ryan let the engine idle quietly.

''Ready to go?''

''Why not? Nothing to keep us here, is there?''

''Nope. And we got the story straight. Wouldn't want the baron to think that we couldn't be trusted.''

She was about to swing her leg over the pillion seat of the bike, but she paused, looking at Ryan with her head on one side. ''I really like you, outlander. Truly. Enjoyed the good time, and you handled the bad time better than anyone I ever met.''

''Thanks. Come on. Baron'll be sending out a search party anytime now.''

Sharona put her hand on his shoulder and leaned to kiss him softly on the cheek.

''Don't worry about whether the baron trusts you and Trader. I should worry more about whether you and Trader can trust Baron Alias Carson.'' She went on quickly. ''And before you ask, lover, I'm not saying any more. My husband has a long arm and a mean disposition. Let's go back to Towse.''

The Norton left a long pillar of red dust rising behind it into the bright morning air.

Chapter Twenty-Nine

Ferryman was leading the search party himself, driving one of a trio of small, fast armored wags. They braked to a halt across the highway, halfway between the ghost ranch and the ville.

Ryan slowed down and pushed up his goggles. Sharona eased her grip around his waist, peering around his shoulders. Her face was masked with dust, and she coughed and spit as Ryan finally braked the 350 twin bike.

"Where's my men?" the sec-boss shouted.

"Chilled."

A light machine gun was mounted on the front of each of the wags. Without a word being said, the nearest one dipped and swung right until it covered Ryan.

"Chilled?"

"Both."

The sec-boss swung his legs out of the driver's cockpit of the wag and jumped down. He pushed up his goggles as he walked toward Ryan.

"You chill 'em?"

"No."

"You and the woman? You and Sharona Carson? Chill them 'tween you, did you?"

"No." Ryan fought hard to keep his self-control.

"Coldcock them. Mebbe the woman offered herself. Smitty didn't have the brains of a fence post. Show him a hole in the ground, and he'd likely start trying to fuck it."

"You got a big mean mouth, Ferryman," Sharona snarled. "Baron'll hear about what you're suggesting so damned loud."

The sec-boss ignored her, keeping his eyes drilling into Ryan's face. "You got a real hard look to you, outlander. I seen hard and I know hard. McMurtry wasn't nobody's fool. Day he fell easy's the day shit stops smelling. So, how'd you do it, Cawdor? I'm real curious about that."

Ryan hadn't moved. "Like the lady says, you got a mean mouth on you, sec-boss. Wind from your lips helps keep me cool. But I had enough of that, for now. Smitty's hog broke down, a coupla miles from the ghost ranch. McMurtry stayed with him."

"I wanted to try and get some of my picture done before the storm came swooping down onto us," Sharona added.

"Two of you went on ahead, cozylike," Ferryman said. "And then?"

"Storm came," Ryan replied flatly.

"Just like that?"

"Yeah, Ferryman, just like that. Looks like the

storm only skirted south toward Towse ville. That right?"

"We seen clouds. Thunder and some lightning. Not likely enough to get a couple good sec-men down and chilled."

Ryan's anger began to move from smoldering toward glazing. He pointed an accusing finger at Ferryman. "You go take a look, you son of a bitch! You'll find big trees stripped to the core. Two-wheel wags with every grain of paint scoured clear. And two corpses, Ferryman. Two corpses looking like they been blasted out of their skins. You go and look, and you fucking look good!"

He kicked the motor of the Norton into throbbing, vibrant life, and Sharona clutched him around the waist again.

A haze of dust burst from the rear wheel as Ryan gunned it, leaving the sec-boss standing in the dirt, watching them go.

RYAN AND SHARONA had only one brief opportunity to talk.

They rolled through the fine sunny day, finally halting in the center of the ville's plaza. A couple of sec-men started to run toward them, as did the Trader and half the crew of the war wags. And Ryan glimpsed the shadowy figure of the baron, emerging from the porch of his living quarters.

The engine died and the noises of the ville swept in all around them.

"Won't ask you again, Ryan. Not ever. But just watch your back," Sharona told him.

"Thanks," he said.

"Take care...lover."

Then they were swallowed in the crowd, surrounded by questions.

The Trader gripped Ryan by the arm, his fingers like brass bolts. "You all right?"

"Sec-men got chilled in the chem-storm. Ferryman's gone to look."

"What'll he see, Ryan?"

"What there is. Two dead men, bodies stripped by sand and wind. That's all."

The melancholic voice of Alias Carson came droning in, silencing the rest of the voices.

"I counted four people leaving the ville, day before today. Now I count just about half of that number returning. I set my mind to wondering just how that can be."

His wife told him the story, sticking to the simple scenario that she and Ryan had agreed upon, finishing up by explaining that they'd met Ferryman on the way to Towse, and that he was going to the ghost ranch by Abbyqu to check out the bodies.

Alias Carson watched her through his thick-lensed spectacles, his pale blue eyes never moving from her face.

"Interesting tale, my dear," he said. "Like most things in life, I guess we got us a mess of truth beans with just a sprinkling of chili lies. Best a man can hope for."

There was something about the tall, immaculately dressed baron that made Ryan's fingers itch for the butt of his Ruger Blackhawk.

"I just got me some news about the gas convoy," Carson said.

The Trader gazed at him as though he'd just jerked a white rabbit out of a hat.

"Said I got news on the gas," he repeated.

"What news, Baron?" the Trader asked.

Ryan and the woman's adventures in the chemstorm were immediately forgotten. Two sec-men chilled didn't weigh in the balance against the possibility of filling up War Wag One and War Wag Two with precious gasoline.

And Ryan didn't mind at all that the light was turned away from Sharona and himself. No questions was always a whole lot better than any questions— Better and safer.

"Be here tomorrow. Big problems in the processing plant out Westexas way. Got 'em sorted."

"Tomorrow?" Ryan asked.

"Sure, son. Sure as the golden sun rises up there in the east and goes falling down into the west. There'll be gas tomorrow."

"I'll count on that, Baron," the Trader said. He turned to face Ryan. "Looks like some sort of a cleanup'd be good."

"Right."

THE TRADER debriefed Ryan, with J.B. listening nearby, as the one-eyed man took a shower. The needle jets of water drove the grime from his pores, forcing tiredness out of his aching muscles.

"You chilled the sec-men?"

"Caught me with the woman."

"That mean you had to kill them, Ryan? I keep telling you about your temper and about finding ways out of a situation. Over, under or around. I tell you that, don't I?"

Ryan shook water from his long black hair, reaching for the control handle in the tiny shower unit.

"Sure, you do, Trader. Wasn't just they caught us ramming away."

"What else?"

"Sharona had asked me to kill her husband and take over the ville. Didn't whisper it, either."

"Fireblast," the Trader swore.

"And Smitty and McMurtry heard that?" J.B. probed.

"Yeah, and before you ask, there was the rad-blasted father of all chem-storms going on outside the hut where we were."

"Stupid," the Trader said. "You're too bastard old to get your dick caught 'tween a rock and a hard place, Ryan. Now there's men dead."

"No way they'll track how they were done."

"How'd you get them?" J.B. asked.

Ryan considered his answer. The Armorer and the Trader were already seriously angry with him. If he told them that Sharona's hidden knife had saved them both, and that she'd terminated McMurtry herself, it wouldn't sound good.

"Hand chopped the fat guy. Knocked him into McMurtry. Took 'em both."

Trader nodded grudgingly. "Least you got that right. But what else d'you find? She wanted Alias chilled?"

Ryan started getting dressed again, grateful for the feeling of the fresh clean clothes on his skin. "She's triple-crazed, Trader. Wouldn't trust her as far as I could throw her."

J.B. passed him his shirt. "She say anything else, Ryan?"

"Yeah."

"What? Dark night! It's like trying to get honey from a granite boulder with you."

"Said not to trust the baron. He's got some sort of game up his sleeve, Trader. He wants the wags to tighten up his power base. They'd let him drive free and easy all over the land, end the threat from the Indians."

The older man nodded slowly. He winced slightly and eased himself down, as though his clothes felt uncomfortable. "Keep getting these kind of pinches in my gut. Like I swallowed something real small with claws." He shook his head. "I guessed all along there was something up. But now you know for certain, we can plan extra careful. Double guards tonight.

If it comes it'll be tonight. Or maybe during the fueling."

"Or after that." Ryan suggested. "Just when we figured it was safe to leave."

The Trader grinned and patted him on the shoulder. "That's better, Ryan. Shows your brain cells ain't all died."

"I'll set double watch," J.B. said. "Spread the word to take extra care. Ferryman said earlier on something about a kids' party. Asked us to go sit in on it."

The three men looked at one another in a momentary silence. The Trader broke the stillness.

"Why not? Be such an obvious time to try and raid us, the son of a bitch might even try it. We'll go along, but we step light."

"What time?" Ryan asked. "This evening? Fine. You guys don't mind, I'm going to hit the bunk. Could use some sleep."

Chapter Thirty

Nearly six hours had crept by since Mildred Wyeth had given Ryan Cawdor the injection. She'd hoped for some sign of success within a couple of hours, maybe four hours at the outside. But the botulism held the unconscious man gripped in its scaled claws with a remorseless and unrelenting cruelty.

The best she could see was that he didn't seem to have become any worse, but there wasn't any evidence that he was getting better.

Everybody was restless.

Jak had asked the doctor to give him some sleepers. "Can't sleep, Mildred. Want to. Can't. Not with Ryan like…"

She'd taken pity on the teenage boy, touched by the desperation in the dark-rimmed ruby eyes. Now he lay on his back, white hair tumbled around his narrow skull, snoring gently.

J.B. had fieldstripped his blasters a dozen times, going through the mechanical motions, sometimes with his eyes shut, sometimes with them open. Every half hour or so he'd walk over and stand by Ryan's bed, looking down silently at the unconscious man, taking his glasses off and rubbing his eyes.

Doc Tanner couldn't sit still, and he couldn't stop talking. He'd start a halfhearted, half-remembered conversation with Krysty or with Mildred, then his tired mind would lose its way among all of yesterday's clutter and he'd wander away again.

"Did I tell you about the time that me and Harry Dean Stanton went off to San Francisco and…and I fear that I don't recall what we did there. My memory is more addled than a bucket of sun-dried eggs. Whatever it was we did there was… No."

Krysty sat in a plastic chair, leaning against the wall of the redoubt room where Ryan was deeply asleep. She'd tried praying to Gaia, but she knew in her heart that it was futile. The power of the Earth Mother could do wonders, could almost move mountains. But it couldn't combat the lethal toxins that were crushing the life from Ryan Cawdor.

For some of the time, Krysty slept, starting wakefully whenever Mildred came quietly into the room.

"Any change?" she asked.

"No. Not worse."

"Not better?"

She shook her head slowly. "I don't know, Krysty. The injection… He was closing in on death. I'm certain of that. I didn't figure he'd hang in there more than two or three hours. It's now—" she checked her chron "—six hours. He's still alive, and that's a victory. We got to cling to the small victories, if we can."

"And hold off the big defeat?"

"Right."

Krysty saw that Mildred was out on her feet. "Get some sleep," she said.

"Have to keep checking the patient—professional responsibility, you know. Lose my post as house surgeon if I don't."

"I'll watch him. I know what to do. It's easy enough. Wash him if he needs it. If he dies, I'll know, Mildred. And if he starts getting better...well, I guess I'll spot that as well."

Reluctantly the other woman went off to her own bed, extracting the promise from Krysty to call her if there was even the tiniest indication of change in any of the vital signs.

Krysty sat back and watched the still figure under the blanket. The coma was so deep that it was no longer possible to detect any sign of life. The woman leaned forward and rested her hands on her face, feeling the calming rustle of her own hair gathering around her cheeks.

"Come on, lover," she whispered. "Never known you to turn away from a fight. Do it for me, lover."

The movement was almost imperceptible.

If she hadn't been staring with all her concentration at his face, Krysty would have missed it. Even with her incredible, mutie-enhanced sight, she still wasn't sure.

"Lover!" she said.

The lid of his good right eye had trembled, as

though a speck of dust had touched the cool skin. Krysty stood and moved closer, leaning over the bed.

"I saw that, Ryan, you bastard. Now do it again. Move your eye!"

This time the twitch was much more pronounced. She could see the glimmer of chillingly pale blue beneath the lid. He had opened his eye a fraction of an inch, and was looking at her. She was certain.

"Mildred!" she shouted. "Mildred! Everyone! Come here, quick!"

In her heart Krysty knew that this was the beginning of the big victory.

Chapter Thirty-One

Someone banged hard on the door of Ryan's sleeping capsule, jerking him instantly awake. A voice that he didn't recognize shouted out the news. "Gas! The gas's come!"

It took him moments to heave on his boots and tie the laces tightly. He plucked the heavy, long-barreled pistol from beneath the pillow and slid the door open.

The passage was bustling with people, pushing past one another. He made his way quickly along to the command deck of the battle-wag, where J.B. and the Trader were already waiting.

"Ah, the sleeper wakes," the Armorer said. "Glad you could make it."

"Thought baron said tomorrow. I didn't sleep the chron around, did I?"

"No. He sent a messenger a half hour back. Said that the gas-wags had put on extra speed to get through that chem-storm. One that chilled them sec-men. They're here now."

"Ready to fuel us up?"

The Trader looked around him. Most of the ob-slits and blaster ports were open, letting in the light breeze that relieved the stifling heat. He rubbed his chin thoughtfully, glancing down at his chron.

"Said it'd be an hour or so. By then it's going to be closing up on the dark."

Ryan eased his shorts where they were pinching him. "Cutting it fine if we wanted to get on the black-top tonight."

"That's what I think. J.B.?"

"Not worth the sweating, Trader. Better to fuel up tonight. Go to this kids' party. Triple up the watch to red and get away safe and clear at first light. Way I see it."

"Way I see it, too. We all agreed? Fine. Let's get to it."

THE WHOLE OF Towse stank of gasoline. In the failing light the refueling of the war wags hadn't gone as smoothly as they'd all hoped. A valve at the end of one of the long canvas hoses had broken a thread and snapped, tearing open the connection. A hundred gallons of precious gas had soaked into the sand of the plaza before anyone had the presence of mind to spin the lock-off wheel.

Ferryman had been in overall control of the operation, and his yell of rage and warning could have shattered crystal at three hundred paces.

"Nobody fuck up! I want every cigarette and cooking stove in the whole ville out and now! Watch steel on steel for a spark. No electric switches. No rad-contact anyplace!"

A team of men and women came swarming out of the adobe buildings to help. The walls of the ville were dappled rust red by the setting sun, and the water that streamed through the center of the plaza was slashed with blood.

They shoveled heaps of clean sand on top of the dark stain of gasoline, mixing it in until the immediate threat of a catastrophic explosion had been diminished and the refueling could be concluded.

It was only a few minutes away from full dark before the gauges on the two war wags finally leveled at Full. Tanks were locked tight and adjustments made to the pressures of tires, with the heavy extra load affecting drive and balance.

Baron Carson came striding out from his quarters, his wife, a lyric ballad in elegance, on his right arm.

She was wearing a dress, reaching nearly to the ground, of crushed violet silk that was embroidered with tumbling streaks of black and white satin. A shawl covered her shoulders, made from lace so fine it looked as if a careless breath could ravage it. A comb of lacquered tortoiseshell held up her blond hair, and rings of precious stones circled her long fingers.

Her eyes, matching her dress, raked the assembled crews of the wags, not settling on any one man or woman for more than a heartbeat.

Ryan had never seen anything quite as beautiful as the delicate masterpiece that was Sharona, wife to the Baron Alias Carson. It was hard to reconcile this image with the rutting alley cat that he knew she could become in the wink of an eye.

"I hope that it all went fine, Ferryman?" the baron said.

His sec-boss came close to bowing. "One hose got tore, but we fixed it."

"Place sure has the flavor of gasoline. No danger, is there?"

"Nope. Not now."

Baron Carson turned toward the Trader. "If any of my men had caused you an upset, friend, I'd have had their eyes removed with white-hot hooks and their skin peeled off with blunt flensing knives."

The Trader kept his face straight. "Mighty kind, Baron, but none of that's necessary. We got loaded up with gas and ammo, and food and water. You got our jack. We can be on our way."

Ryan happened to be glancing in the direction of the sec-boss as his boss said that, and he saw the start, the dropped jaw and the narrowed eyes that darted toward the baron.

"On your way?" Carson asked in the same, unaltering, monotonous drawl.

"Dawn tomorrow. If that fits with you, Baron?" the Trader replied.

Ferryman relaxed, looking away with a vague disinterest toward the distant tips of the Sangre de Cristo, still holding the last rays of the tumbling sun. It had been an intriguing bit of body language, and it kept Ryan's suspicions ticking over.

"Sure. And watch out for them Indians. They keep haunting us, waiting their chance to strike back, I guess."

"Not all bad, Baron," Ryan said.

He drew the lizard's eyes to himself. "You figure, Mr. Cawdor, do you? If I chanced upon one of them Apaches on fire, I would not even piss upon him."

With that he turned and walked slowly away, his wife at his side, teetering on high heels.

Ferryman watched them go, then looked at the Trader. "Party for the young'uns starts in an hour. Won't last long. You can all get to rest early if you aim for a dawn start."

EVERYONE was relaxed. The evening was pleasantly mild, the wind dropping right away to a gentle zephyr. A round moon rose through a rack of thin clouds, throwing sharp-edged shadows around Towse ville.

Ryan hadn't been to a children's party for more years than he could recall. He'd organized the rotation of sentries with J.B. and the Trader, and felt fairly happy that the wags were secure for the night. So there was a space to unwind and enjoy the festivities.

Hun, July, Otis and Matt went around the ville with him. In the morning they'd be back on the road, living on the honed edge of danger. For now they could all take it easy.

It was surprising how many of the youngsters around Towse showed definite ethnic signs of Indian blood. Ferryman himself was dark-skinned, with hooded, dark eyes. Three of his own children were at the festivities, scampering around and sliding quickly from being excited to becoming overexcited.

One thing that Ryan picked up on was an unmistakable atmosphere of tension among the sec-men. The short hairs at the back of his neck prickled expectantly, and he could almost taste the adrenaline in the cool evening air.

"Feel it?" J.B. asked from beside him, watching as a handful of harassed women fought to control the children and get them to play a version of pass the parcel.

Ryan didn't need to ask his friend what he meant. They both knew.

"Yeah. Figure it means trouble?"

The Armorer pursed his lips and took a slow, raking glance around the plaza of the ville. "Got to be tonight, or first light."

"If it comes at all."

"Woman said—"

Ryan interrupted him. "Sharona said a mess of things, J.B., and not all of them worth a fistful of sand."

"But you can feel it?"

"Sure. But you got to look at the other side of the jack."

"How's that?"

"Two heavily armed war wags, fuelled up, with trained crews. Run by the Trader. And everyone in

Deathlands has heard of the Trader. Here we are. Could have a fine ace on the line at taking over the whole of the baron's ville.''

J.B. nodded. ''Guess that's so. They could just be plain scared.''

Ryan laughed as one of the children ran weeping to its mother at getting knocked out of the game. But the woman wasn't looking, and the charge knocked her over in the soft sand.

''Then again,'' he said, ''could be that the trigger edge is 'cause they aim to blast the living guts out of us in the next ten hours.''

Chapter Thirty-Two

A mediocre magician dropped bunches of bright paper flowers from under his damp-stained black-and-scarlet cloak; a puppet show fascinated half the children and bored the other half. Ryan kept moving, muttering a warning word to any member of the crews that he passed. In the background was the distorted, nasal squeaks of the puppet master, and the whoops and shrieks from his audience, interspersed with the occasional flat sound of a slap as one of the children was disciplined by its mother.

Ferryman, flanked by female sec-guards, loomed from out of a narrow alley between two of the square adobe houses, nearly bumping into Ryan.

"Enjoying the party, outlander?" he asked.

"Makes a change to be able to relax for a few hours. You be up and ready to see us away at first light?"

The sec-boss smiled, his teeth white in the dimness. "Wouldn't miss it. Smitty and McMurtry would've liked this party. Smitty had two young'uns."

"You buried them?"

"Sure."

"You checked them first? Find any blaster holes? Any knife cuts?"

Ferryman shook his head. "Sure didn't, Cawdor. Think you'd be here like this if I'd found anything? Just some sandblasted bones and muscle. Hardly knew either of them. That chem-storm did a good job for you."

"For me?" he asked innocently.

The sec-boss took a half step toward him, his hand striking for the butt of his pistol. He checked himself with a visible effort, shaking off the warning from one of the women.

"You're a cold-eyed killer, Ryan Cawdor. You chilled those two friends. I know that. Fucking well know that!" His voice was a venomous hiss. "And one day, mebbe soon, mebbe not, I'll take you down for it."

"Threat or promise, Ferryman?" Ryan said mockingly, trying to push the man nearer the edge in the hope of provoking him into some kind of word or action that might blow the scene open.

"Promise, outlander. Fucking promise."

The first of the fireworks exploded into the clear New Mexico sky, with firecracker ripples of cracking noise, filling the night with magnesium silver and flowering patterns of crimson and green.

Ryan tensed, wondering if the display might be the signal for the beginnings of a bloodbath. But Ferryman simply stared upward with a childlike innocence, the two sec-women also gazing at the beautiful lights and colors.

"Fucking lovely, Cawdor," said the sec-boss. "Baron does a good show."

"Can't argue with that," Ryan agreed. "See you around, Ferryman."

He turned on his heel, feeling the momentary tightness of waiting for a round between the shoulders. But none came.

THE TRADER was standing by the bridge over the river, leaning on his elbows and smoking one of his small cigars. Ryan noticed two dim shapes lurking in the shadows by the sec-headquarters. Even at a distance he was sure he recognised Remmy Stedman and Long Dog Hodgson.

"Good fireworks, Ryan," the Trader called. "Some of them cherry bombs could be blaster fire."

Ryan joined him on the narrow wooden bridge. "Yeah. I thought of that, too."

"See any signs of a raid?"

"Not up front. But bodies sometimes say more'n words."

The Trader nodded, taking a last draw on the butt and flicking it into the water. "Know what you mean, son."

A salvo of rockets hissed into the sky, bursting into crackling star bombs.

There was a long pause, and they could hear the chattering of the children. Out of the corner of his eye

Ryan noticed that the brace of sec-men had vanished into the darkness.

"Think it's over?" the Trader asked, sounding a little disappointed.

"Looks like... No, there's another of them big mortar rockets."

It was a single, immensely powerful firework, blasting hundreds of feet into the air. Ryan had seen the long tubes that the rockets and mortar shells were being fired from, set in the earth. The bore was at least nine inches in diameter, and the whole plaza shook when they were triggered.

It was a dazzling silver flare, spreading its light across the whole sky, throwing the entire ville into clear, crisp relief.

There was a loud "Oooooooh!" of delight from the children.

"And that concludes the entertainment for the night, I guess," the Trader said, straightening and grinning at Ryan.

The star shell still hung over Towse, burning brightly, suspended from a tiny white parachute that kept it floating. It was a beautiful climax to the display and to the children's party.

Ryan glanced at his wrist-chron. "Just before ten."

"Time for bed. Party's done."

But they both stiffened at the sound of more fireworks going off, crackling all around the ville, backed by the eager cries of the children.

But they weren't fireworks, and it wasn't just children who were crying out in the shadowed ville.

Ryan felt the rail of the bridge vibrate under his hand, and a long white splinter of wood, several inches long, miraculously peeled away and fell into the river.

"Fireblast!" he cursed, drawing the Ruger before he even realized his hand was moving to the holster.

The firefight was on.

Chapter Thirty-Three

Sharona Carson's warning to Ryan hadn't honestly made a lot of difference to the reactions to the treacherous attack. Nobody in the Deathlands ever trusted a baron, and Alias Carson was simply proving himself true to his breed.

The war wags that Marsh Folsom and the Trader had discovered so many years ago were devastatingly powerful pieces of mobile weaponry, with a unique overchill capacity. If the Trader had been so minded, there was scarcely a ville in all Deathlands that could have withstood a serious attack from War Wags One and Two.

Sharona had simply amplified the Trader and Ryan's awareness of the high-risk situation they were in at Towse ville.

At a moment of frozen violence, all the Trader's drills and iron discipline came into its own. There wasn't a man or woman from either vehicle who wasn't honed and ready for a firefight. The wags themselves were locked down sec-tight, and a skeleton crew was ready to repel any hijackers.

Used to scabbies, stickies and the local poorly armed Indians, Baron Alias Carson had made a grave and costly error of judgment. His forces were spread around the ville with orders to launch a general attack at the signal of the single, final skyrocket.

Ryan had been thinking about how he might play that sort of assault, and he decided he'd have placed marksmen to pick off the Trader, J.B. and himself, and try to establish a wedge between the two wags and the bulk of the scattered crews.

Carson had gambled on the shock of the firing producing panic in the outlanders. His gamble failed him. The Trader and Ryan were standing on the bridge. An Uzi chattered, and a trail of lead furrowed across the wood. Both men dived for cover, landing with their legs in the freezing water, sheltered by the slope of the bank. The Trader's beloved Armalite was back in War Wag One, but he'd drawn his Browning FN-DA, a big fourteen-round double-action blaster that he carried for its reliability and stopping power.

Ryan had the Ruger Blackhawk cocked and ready in his right fist.

"Make for the wags!" the Trader yelled.

"Together?"

"Hell, why not?"

Just as they readied themselves to make a move, the parachute flare finally burned out and the whole area was plunged into relative darkness. There was still a good hunter's moon, but after the mag-bright rocket, it was like being shrouded in black velvet.

"Now!" the Trader shouted.

Ryan was at his chief's heels, powering out of the

clinging mud, running in a half crouch. The air seemed filled with whining lead, and the ground around their feet exploded in shards of stone. Most of the firing seemed to be coming from their right, where the sec-men had their main barracks and both of them snapped off a couple of shots in that direction. Their reward was a scream of pain from one of their attackers.

A grenade bounced off a low adobe wall in front of them. The Trader dropped flat, and Ryan followed him, hunching his shoulders and opening his mouth slightly to minimize the damage from the blast.

In the second of waiting, Ryan recalled something that J.B. had once told him about the killing capacity of grenades—"Explode a gren in a group of men all six feet away from it, and only about half get injured. Less than a ten percent chill rate. Course, the M-26 got notched wire wrapping and that fragments. More effective."

The grenade went off with a stunning blast but failed to injure either man. The Trader was immediately on his feet again, darting and dodging toward the bulk of the two wags.

Trails of bullets erupted from the machine guns on both port and starboard sides of the war wags, interspersed with the golden light of tracer rounds.

Ryan saw a lot of dead.

What might have seemed a pretty clean operation when it first filtered through Alias Carson's calculating mind was becoming messy on the ground. Nobody had thought about clearing the children out of the way once the bullets began to sing, and many of the corpses scattered around Towse were very small and frail.

J.B.'s slight figure could be seen at the center of a defensive ring of men and women, covering the retreat of the other crew members from all over the ville. He spotted the Trader and Ryan sprinting toward the wags and gave a yell of warning to the rest of the perimeter.

A bullet plucked insistently at Ryan's sleeve, stinging his skin. Although he was very fond of the Ruger, he was painfully aware that six rounds wasn't what you needed in this kind of all-out, knock-'em-down-and-gouge-'em firefight.

With only two rounds left he spotted the stocky figure of Remmy Stedman coming at him, firing his Renato Gamba Trident Fast Action .38 from the hip.

One of the last pairs of .357 rounds hit the sec-man through the left side of the body, under the ribs, knocking him down sideways. But Stedman was tough, and rolled on one knee, steadying his own blaster in both hands. Ryan paused a moment and drilled him through the upper part of the chest, kicking him backward, turning him instantly into two hundred pounds of dying meat.

It wasn't a good place or time to think about reloading the Ruger, and Ryan concentrated on getting to the wags.

Hurdling a corpse with its left arm completely

missing, he realized with a shock of recognition that
the white frozen face was Rodge, the cook's assistant
on War Wag One.

There was Dexter, ace guitarist, one of the nicest
guys on War Wag Two, lying on his side, the top of
his skull shot away, a mixture of blood and brains
frothing out of the gaping cavity. His outstretched
hand was on the bottom step of the main entrance to
the war wag, and Ryan actually trod on the fingers as
he leaped aboard. Bones cracked under his heel, but
he had vastly more important things to center his
mind on.

"Hun!" he yelled. "Hun, you there?"

"Ready, Ryan. Want me to start her up?"

"Sure. Cohn?"

"Yo!"

"Get onto Two."

"Right. What message?"

"Fire engines. Get ready to roll. Wait for the
Trader's word. Or mine."

The engines of War Wag One coughed a couple of
times, then the ignition fired. The Trader had made
sure both wags turned their engines over every day
that they were in Towse.

"Ready!" Hunaker shouted, stooped over the main
driving controls, peering through the narrow ob-slit.

With bullets pounding on the armored flanks of the
vehicle, it was like being inside a bucket being
punched by a crazed stickie.

The night was filled with screams and explosions

and the moans of the wounded being helped up the stairs into the relative safety of War Wag One. Suddenly the Trader appeared at Ryan's elbow, assuming command of the war center. There was blood all down one of his sleeves, and a bruise on his temple.

He saw Ryan look down at the sticky crimson mess on his arm. "Not my blood. Lex. Gut-shot. Engines running? Great."

The vehicle rocked at a near miss from something larger than an ordinary grenade. Ryan glanced at the Trader. "Time we was going?"

"Yeah. They can pick us off here. Ram the gates on my word. Huh. Cohn?"

"I told 'em, Trader."

"What about the dead?" Beulah asked, sliding into her seat at the nav-console. Her eyes were wide with shock at the butchery all around her.

The Trader was looking to make sure J.B. was pulling in the last defenders. He turned to Beulah. "Dead and wounded stay here." His face was hewn from the coldest stone, silhouetted against the green light of the command deck. "But I'll come back, lady. Carson pays for this. I swear he pays."

The noise of the engines was rising to a full-bellied roar, but the sound of gunfire was also intensifying. Another mortar went off close by, and someone tumbled from her gun position, hands squeezing at her eyes. Blood gushed out from between the fingers. Ryan didn't see who it was.

"Wait!" the Trader shouted.

Ryan moved to the side of the door, seeing that J.B.'s defense had cost dear. There were at least five motionless bodies there, and the last of several wounded were just coming aboard. Beyond the Armorer, Ryan could see half a dozen sec-men making a desperate charge to try to prevent the war wags from making their getaway.

"Bite on this, bastards!" J.B. shouted, throwing a small implode gren into their midst.

Covered by the sucking burst of the gren, he darted up the stairs and signaled Ben to close the arma-door.

The Trader was leaning over Cohn's shoulder, listening into a spare earpiece, checking that as many of the surviving crew of War Wag Two were aboard and their doors sealed shut. The moment he got the all-clear from them, he gave the order for the two wags to roll.

"Chill anything that moves. Chill anything, anyone! Full power, Hun, through the main gates. Let's get the sweet Hades out of here!"

THEY TOOK a running count as they headed north out of Towse ville. War Wag One had eight chilled, three missing and a half dozen with serious wounds. At least half of the rest of the crew had some kind of injury, but nothing bad enough to stop the wag from functioning.

The voice crackling over the intercom told everyone the toll on War Wag Two.

"Nine chilled. Four missing, but there's dispute

about two of them. Some say two were caught in tracer cross fire near the church. Three critical on board. We got trouble with an axle running ragged, but the temp's okay. We're doing good, Trader.''

''Acknowledged.'' He switched off his handmike.

''Not far to the gorge bridge,'' Beulah called.

Ryan hadn't been able to snatch a moment to talk to the Trader about what had happened, and about their course of action. The miles had been eaten up with status reports from both wags, detailing every aspect of logistic multifunctions.

Now, with no sign of any pursuit behind them, there was a moment of comparative peace on the command deck.

''Trader?''

The craggy face turned to him, still smeared with blood and smoke. ''What is it, Ryan? No, don't tell me. You want to know where we're going and what we're going to do when we get there. That it?''

''That's it,'' Ryan replied.

''Two miles to gorge,'' Beulah said.

''I don't know. Got to get my mind clear. Revenge can be a bastard costly thing to dine on, Ryan. Soon's I decide, you'll know about it.''

''There's a block on the highway,'' Hun reported. ''Looks like a couple small wags. Half a dozen blasters behind it. Could go around it, cross-country.''

''No. They'll have talkies with them. Slow down. J.B.?''

''Yeah?''

"You see them?"

"Sure. Nightscope on the gren-launcher works real well. It's like Hun says."

"Slow it down to a walk. See any other sec-men, away from the block?"

"No."

"Fine. Stop around one-fifty yards, Hun. Wipe them away, J.B. Hardest with the mostest."

Ryan knew that the Trader was deadly serious. The forward gren-launcher also fired a small rocket. They only had three of them left, and to consider using one on a piss-ant roadblock showed that the Trader wasn't going to mess around.

The war wag jerked to a stop. The sec-men ahead of them had fired half a dozen ranging rounds that pinged off the armor. J.B. was working the cross-calibrated comp-sight, whistling softly under his breath.

Nobody spoke.

"Ready. Sure you want to use this big baby on six sec-men, Trader?"

"Do it."

The blaster absorbed the detonation, and there was only the faintest noise inside War Wag One. At such short range, the impact was almost simultaneous.

"Got 'em!" Hun yelled. "Triple ace on the line, J.B.!"

They rolled forward, slowing past the blazing trucks. The ragged remains of five corpses lay crumpled on the ground. A sixth man, terribly burned, was still making feeble movements. Everyone on the port side of the war wag could see him clearly.

"July."

"Yeah, Trader?"

"Chill him."

Despite their strict discipline, the crop-headed blonde still queried the order.

"Chill him?"

"You getting deaf, or stupid? You chill him or move the fuck out and let someone else pull down on the trigger."

"He's near dead, that's all."

"Near dead…he might still use a talkie back to the ville. Do it."

The light machine gun spoke in a brief burst of a dozen bullets.

"Chilled, Trader," July reported, her voice carefully unemotional.

"Now we know the bridge is safe. Hun."

"Yeah?"

"Turn her around."

"South?"

"You got it."

Ryan hesitated, then asked the unnecessary question. "We're going back to the ville?"

The Trader smiled like a starving wolf. "Yeah, Ryan. We're going back."

Chapter Thirty-Four

A half mile from Towse, the Trader ordered Hun to pull off the snaking blacktop. All driving lights on both war wags had long been extinguished, and they'd been making cautious progress by the light of the moon.

The ville was just out of sight in a shallow decline in the land.

Ryan was stunned by the Trader's instinctive flair for combat strategy. To actually return now, barely an hour since they fled the treacherous attack, would be the last thing that Baron Alias Carson would be expecting.

The orders snapped out—who would be in command of War Wag One and who would be responsible for Two; who looked after the wounded and how many men and women would stay; what sentry pattern they would run; who'd check out both wags for any unsuspected damage; ammo count and blaster service, and what their strategy would be when they reached Towse.

One thing that Ryan had spotted as they rumbled southward was a number of shadowy figures moving down onto the plain from the foothills of the Sangre de Cristo. Scattered groups on horseback headed in a looping curve toward Towse.

"Apaches," he told the Trader. "Must scent the ville's in trouble, and they're coming out of the mountains to see what they can scavenge."

The Trader nodded. "They wait a short while, and they might get themselves the best pickings they ever imagined."

THE ATTACK PLAN was simple. The Trader drew a big circle on a rough pad—three arrows, one at the back—J. B. Dix and a small group. Second arrow on the right flank, the Trader with the main attack. The third arrow was going directly in the front, to the heart of the defensive complex.

"Through the gates?" Ryan said, peering at the scribbled diagram.

"No gates there. They won't be looking for us coming back. Leastways not tonight. They'll be treating wounded and laying out the dead. We blasted the gates to hell and back. Come in at an angle, from the side here. Keep behind the walls. Then straight in. Moment you open fire I'll bring in my force. J.B.'ll wait ninety seconds and then go for the rear wall. Easy as that. Questions?"

J.B. cleared his throat. "Yeah, Trader. I got a question."

"What?"

"Tell us about what we do inside."

The Trader's deep-set eyes were like chips of

obsidian. "Children and women...not this time, friends. Once was enough for that. But the men."

"All?"

He looked at Ryan. "You use your blaster for a baron, then you rise or fall with that baron. He dies, they all die."

J.B. had another question. "If any escape...do we follow them?"

"Why? There's a hundred miles or more of Apaches out there. They'll pick up any scraps that fall off our plate."

"Slow Eagle," Ryan said. "Yeah. Be the kind of meal he'd enjoy."

RYAN HAD SIX handpicked gunners with him—Ben, Otis, July, Francis, Lou and Hunaker.

Despite J.B. urging him to take one of the machine pistols from the war wag's armory, Ryan stubbornly insisted on sticking to his Ruger. But he eventually, and reluctantly, took along one of J.B.'s personal favorites, something they'd picked up from the basement of a blaster freak's ruined house on the outskirts of old Des Moines. It was a Heckler & Kock CAWS model, an automatic 12-gauge, ten-shot scattergun.

Searchlights illuminated the interior of the ville, and they could see shadowy figures rushing around. The wrecked gates hadn't been replaced, and there was no sign of any sentries. As they drew closer, Ryan and his small group could hear shouting and cries of pain beyond the adobe walls.

"Not got the wag back on the wheels," Hunaker whispered.

"There were a load of kids dead, as well as some of the mothers," Ben said. "Be digging graves for a week."

"Make it a month if we get in there first," Ryan contradicted.

IT WAS absurdly simple.

Preoccupied with the results of Baron Carson's disastrous ambush on the two war wags, nobody was on guard anywhere around the ville's defensive perimeter. Ryan took his group along a draw, which led in turn to a row of old outbuildings. From there it was easy to cross a hundred yards of mesquite to reach the shelter of the walls.

The moon had almost disappeared, but there was no trace of the first hint of light in the eastern sky that would herald the false dawn. It would be full dark for some time.

"Everyone ready?" It wasn't really necessary to whisper the question. All six had ridden with the Trader long enough to know what was going down, and how they were supposed to act.

"Can we wait just a minute?"

It was Lou, one of the starboard gunners from War Wag One. He was a chubby young man with the latest in a long line of failed mustaches decorating his upper lip.

"What?"

"I gotta fart."

Otis giggled, partly from the tension. Ryan sighed. "Can't you hold it in, Lou?"

"Guess not, Ryan. Pork and beans with them green peppers sort of worked on through me."

"Fireblast! I don't want the life history of your bastard guts, Lou. Just do it and keep quiet about it."

"Silent but violent." Otis sniggered.

The joke wasn't that funny when Lou finally lived up to his threat. "I think something's died up your ass, Lou," Hun joked, holding her nose for effect.

"Come on, guys," Ryan pleaded. "We're going in to do some serious chilling here. Kind of simmer it down."

Someone screamed inside the ville, a high, terrified sound.

Ben was the only one to speak. "Hope that isn't one of our people," he said.

The gateway was only forty yards away from them, to their left. Ryan cocked the Ruger and made sure the shotgun was secure in its sling on his shoulders.

"Lets go."

IT WAS AN extraordinary feeling. Earlier that night the occupants of the ville had launched a cowardly and treacherous attack on the crews of the war wags. Now Ryan was able to lead the group straight in through the gateway without being challenged. The one damaged sec-door hung from its bent hinge, swinging slightly from side to side. The torn metal squeaked softly.

At the council of war, before they split into their groups, Garcia had suggested they might go in behind smoke grenades.

J.B. had vetoed that. "Not going to be that much light. We're going to need to see who we're blasting at. Smoke'll hide too much."

Now Ryan wondered whether that had been the right decision. He felt like a buffalo in the middle of a frozen lake, totally exposed to any member of the Towse sec-forces who might glance in his direction.

From where the group stood, pressed together in the mouth of a narrow alley just inside the main entrance, they could see the plaza beyond the looming bulk of the burned church. They hid in deep shadow, but the generating plant of the ville was flooding the central area with bright light.

"Kids' bodies." Hun pointed with her 10-gauge scattergun at the flatbed wag with at least a dozen small corpses piled carefully on it.

"Yeah, and there's the baron." Ryan could see Alias Carson, stalking like a gray raven through the scene of carnage. His head was stooped, and he didn't seem to be speaking to any of his people.

His lizard head swung around, and his glasses glittered in the direction of Ryan and his companions. Though he knew they were safely hidden in the blackness, the one-eyed man withdrew with a shudder. There was a strange and sinister mutie quality to the baron of Towse. Ryan could almost believe that Alias Carson could actually see them lurking in the alley.

But the baron's head turned away again, and the moment passed.

"Triple-creep bastard," July hissed.

The baron was beckoning to Ferryman, who appeared magically and stood listening to orders. The long arm of Carson swept out and pointed momentarily to Ryan Cawdor, darting on past him and stopping at the gate.

"Worried about his front door," Otis said, gripping his M-16 expectantly.

"Time we started the action," Ryan stated. "Follow me, and chill anything that moves."

The alley was between the adobe walls of linked houses, winding to left and right, and finally opened into a small square. Ryan figured they were only a block away from the main plaza.

Hunaker was the most experienced of the six, and she was bringing up the rear. He waited until she'd joined them. Ryan's idea was to get into the plaza and start blasting, take out as many of the sec-force as possible and distract the rest so that the Trader and J.B. could get into the ville.

"We're going to—" he began.

"Behind you!" Ben yelled, squeezing the trigger of his Uzi and spraying lead at the doorway of one of the small houses.

Ryan spun, dropping into an instinctive crouch, and saw five or six sec-men erupting into the dark square.

Ben put most of them down in that single burst, but the others were already opening fire at the attackers.

"Bastards!" Ryan shouted, not even aware that he had spoken. He fired off two rounds from the Heckler & Koch 12-gauge, feeling the kick against his hip. The boom of the powerful blaster was deafening in the confined space, and the impact was devastating.

The surviving sec-men went down in a jumble of flailing arms and legs, twitching among the other dying bodies.

The next few minutes were a chaos of tangled images—darkness and dazzling light; dealing and dodging death; hot blood and the cold shudder of controlled fear; threats and begging; moments of startling silence and piercing screams.

A lot of pain and dying.

Ryan had seen old vids and read old books that described firefights, and none of them got within a thousand miles of the reality. Fiction made them seem clear-cut and simple. During the five minutes or so that the assault on the ville lasted, he had no real idea of what was going on, or whether they were winning or losing.

He could tell that the Trader and J.B. had launched their attacks, because he heard shouts and more firing from other parts of Towse. Toward the end, he also began to see other crew members around the alleys and moving across the bright plaza.

It was absurd to try to keep his group of six together amongst the maze of lanes and twisting passages. As soon as the brief skirmish was done, he gave them their orders.

"Split up. Watch your backs. Good luck."

ALONE, he doubled back, reaching the alley that overlooked the main entrance. If it became necessary for a talkie message to go to the wags for assistance, it was important that the defenders weren't given the chance to barricade the open gateway.

He recognized the sec-man leading the group that was hesitating by the entrance, listening to the noise of the assault and not certain whether to stand or to move.

It was Long Dog Hodgson, waving his customized blaster in the air. The searchlights caught the ten-inch barrel of the Charter Explorer 3, making it appear like a silver magician's wand.

The group of two men and three women were less than twenty feet away from Ryan. He slowly brought the shotgun off his shoulder and slipped the Ruger back into its holster.

He'd reloaded the Close Assault Weapon and it was ready to go.

The other thing he'd seen in vids of battles was that men were always shouting warnings before they opened fire. That always got a good laugh on War Wag One when the crew was watching an action vid.

The first blast hit Long Dog in the small of the back, almost slicing him in two. He died not even knowing who'd administered the savage death blow.

Fitted with an effective muzzle flash suppressor, the scattergun delivered its deadly gifts from cover. The baron's people had no way of knowing the sniper's position. One by one Ryan picked them off, steadily working the action of the weapon, moving calmly from target to target.

As the last man went spinning down, blood spurting from torn flesh, a young girl, barely ten years old, ran screaming from one of the houses. She stopped and picked up a heavy pistol that had been dropped by one of the sec-women.

"Fuckin' bastard!" she yelped, turning to where Ryan stood at the corner of the alley. The blaster was an old Smith & Wesson 9 mm revolver, much too heavy for her small hands. But hatred drove her on, and Ryan heard the sharp click of the hammer locking back.

Ryan hesitated, staring at the dark muzzle of the pistol, his own finger slack on the trigger of the shotgun.

"You dead, dead, dead," the girl chanted.

A 10-gauge scattergun round hit her in the side, opening up the fragile bones of her chest, bursting her heart. The blaster dropped to the dirt with a heavy, thunking sound.

"Wrong, kid," Hun said, breaking her smoking weapon. "You dead." She ejected the spent round and expertly thumbed in another. She looked at Ryan, standing beyond the pile of corpses. "No good chilling all but one, lover."

"I know it. Thanks, Hun."

"No survivors!" Francis yelled, eyes wide with the savor of the slaughter, grinning at Ryan as he ran by.

Out of the corner of his eye, Ryan spotted a familiar figure, dodging across the flat roof of one of the houses by the old church.

"Ferryman," he whispered.

Chapter Thirty-Five

Nobody ever found out who started the fires. The first serious explosion came as Ryan began to chase the fleeing sec-boss. There wasn't any special personal hatred against Ferryman. It was purely business. One thing that the Trader had drummed into Ryan was that a man never ever left an enemy alive. If he did, then one day he'd have terminal cause to regret his generosity.

As Ryan made his way through a wide lane that ran parallel to the direction Ferryman was taking, a building to his right erupted in a mushroom of orange fire. Huge chunks of shattered adobe flew around him, and he caught the smoky odor of burning gasoline.

Almost immediately there was a second massive concussion, from further toward the center of the ville. Ryan had to duck and protect his head from tumbling pieces of broken clay and brick.

Dust and smoke billowed around him, and Ryan paused, trying to clear grit from his good eye.

The shouts and screams continued, but the noise of the guns seemed to be gradually diminishing. A woman came stumbling from a doorway just ahead of him, holding a little boy by the hand. Both were badly burned around the arms and faces. She saw Ryan standing there, like an inflexible apostle of death, and she tried to cry out. But all she could manage was a faint moan as she fell to her knees.

"Mom's real bad, mister," the little boy said in a shocked, piping voice.

"Yeah. Go get her some help, son. That way." He pointed behind him, toward the main plaza.

"Thanks, mister. You know you only got one eye, mister?"

"I noticed, kid. Move it!"

The boy darted off, followed more slowly by his mother, who kept her face averted from Ryan.

From the direction Ferryman was heading in, he was probably making for the transport section of Towse, expecting to grab an armored wag or a two-wheel to make his escape.

A corpse of a naked man, grotesquely fat, almost filled the alley. Ryan leaped over it, noticing as he passed that the hilt of a carving knife protruded from the rolls of fat that rippled across the body. He wondered, as he moved on, whether someone had taken advantage of the general mayhem to indulge in a little domestic murder.

A bullet struck the wall a yard from Ryan's face, showering him with splinters. He pressed himself into a doorway, trying to see where the attacker was hiding, but the moon was almost down and it was extremely dark.

"Lucky, outlander!"

"Ferryman?"

"What a surprise." The voice mocked him. "You mean you didn't know who you were chasing, Ryan? Hard to believe!"

"We've taken Towse."

"I warned the baron." The mockery was replaced by a deep bitterness. "Figured you might try and come back tonight. Once the ambush didn't work I *knew* you'd come back. Everyone knows the Trader's reputation where revenge is concerned."

From the voice, Ryan put the fleeing sec-boss at the corner of the church, near a side entrance to the ville.

"Wanna give up, Ferryman?"

The quiet laugh revealed genuine amusement. "Sure. The Trader shakes my hand, gives me a boot-ful of jack and wishes me luck."

Ryan wasn't ready to lie to the sec-boss. He didn't doubt that the Trader would shoot Ferryman dead at his feet if he caught him, a clean death by a bullet through the back of the head—if the Trader was feeling in a merciful mood.

At last Ryan had spotted him. Another pillar of reddish flames from behind him provided just enough light to pick out the pale blur of the sec-boss's face. He cocked the Ruger and leveled it carefully. But Ferryman realized the fire had revealed his position, and he pulled back out of sight, snapping off a shot at Ryan as he did.

"What sort of blaster you got?" Ryan shouted. "Sounds like a big .38, or mebbe a .45."

"Star Model PD, .45. Most compact man-stopper I ever had."

Ryan had heard of Star blasters, but he didn't know enough about them to know how many rounds the mag held. Ferryman wasn't likely to tell him.

"Why not just turn around and walk away, Ryan? Let it lie. Let me get a two-wheel and make a run for it. Nobody'll know."

"I'll know, Ferryman. Your baron tried to back shoot every man and woman in the war wags, including me. And you're his sec-boss."

Again the laugh, but this time it had an undertone of strain. "Yeah. Too much on the table 'tween us, ain't there? So what do we do?"

Behind him, Ryan heard the fourth of the catastrophic explosions as the ville self-destructed. The old church was at his shoulder, across the alley. If he could get inside, then he had a real chance of outflanking the sec-boss.

To think was to act. He powered himself off the wall, hearing the bullet whiz by within inches. Then he was safe inside the roofless building.

Now he could move the length of the nave, and he'd be in a position to hit the sec-boss from the shelter of the damaged wall by the alter.

But Ferryman was on his own turf, and he moved even faster.

Ryan never saw him. There was a triple explosion

of shots and a pain that felt like fire across his lower ribs. He went down, unable to supress a gasp of shock.

Ferryman whooped in delight. "How'd you like them apples, outlander?"

Ryan's fighting instinct had enabled him to keep hold of his blaster. If it had dropped to the debris-strewn floor in the stygian gloom, he might never have found it again. With his left hand he cautiously explored the wound, feeling stickiness around where his shirt was torn. He gritted his teeth and probed deeper.

It was a long, lancing tear, but he couldn't feel an actual hole. The bleeding wasn't serious, and he crouched against the wall, ready to fight on.

There'd be time to treat it later—if there was going to be a later.

"You there, Cawdor?"

Another tremor and a fountain of flames threw the interior of the church into momentary stark relief.

Ferryman was caught, halfway down the aisle, cat-footing toward Ryan, his stubby automatic in his right fist. A tight smile was frozen on his lips.

At a range of a dozen paces, Ryan felt a surge of triumph, knowing he couldn't miss him. He fired three rounds without the sec-boss managing a single round in reply.

The flames from the burning building to the north of the ville gave enough light for Ryan to see that all three of his rounds had hit the man.

The first one, aimed as the stopper, caught him in the chest, high on the right side. The second one clipped Ferryman's right shoulder, his instinctive dive for cover nearly throwing Ryan's aim. But he instantly adjusted, and the final .357 round smashed into the falling man's face.

Ryan heard the beginnings of a scream, saw the Star .45 spin for a moment in the air, then hit the left-hand wall, yards away from where the sec-boss had gone down. Ryan didn't rush in, knowing that someone like Ferryman could easily have a hideaway somewhere on him—a small, concealed pistol, maybe a .22.

But his experience also told him that nobody could fake the sort of noises that were coming from the thrashing figure on the heap of rubbish. Three magnum rounds slowed a man down.

Ferryman was yelling, crying and choking. Ryan could hear cans tumbling and rattling, as well as bottles splintering. The sec-boss held both hands to his face, as if he were trying to hold it together. Ryan couldn't see clearly what damage that third bullet had done. He rose cautiously and took a couple of steps toward the stricken man, the Ruger preceding him, covering Ferryman.

The fire outside was dying down, and he noticed that the shooting had become even more sporadic. There was still enough light coming through the shattered windows, though, for him to see his victim.

The sec-boss was locked tight into his own nightmare world of pain and horror. He rocked from side to side like a child with a toothache, kicking out his legs in front of him, stiff, as though he were having a fit.

Through the clasped fingers, Ryan was able to see enough to appreciate the rending damage the last round had caused. From the blood on the man's chest, it was probable that the first bullet would be the one that eventually killed him.

But it was the last round that had destroyed him.

From what Ryan could make out, by the hellish glow of the burning ville, the bullet had hit the sec-boss as he was diving for cover. It had struck him on the left side, where the jaw articulates, below the cheek. Its progress then became random, but it had almost certainly smashed the joint, dislocated the jaw, angling sideways, and took out most of the upper teeth on that side. The splinters of bone would have shredded the tongue. The bullet, tumbling and distorted, must have gone spinning upward, ripping through the soft palate. Ferryman's left eye was missing from its bloodied socket, which meant the round had exited there, smashing the cheekbone again on its way out.

The frantic scrabbling and kicking was slowing down as the sec-boss became sucked into the mystery of his own ending.

Short of putting him out of the final misery, there was nothing Ryan could do—nothing that he wanted to do. The coup de grace bullet remained unfired beneath the hammer of the Blackhawk.

THE ENTIRE VILLE was now covered in a smothering shroud of gas smoke, several fires blazing uncontrollably. The shooting had stopped, and some of the crew of War Wags One and Two were going around checking for anyone hiding from the Trader's righteous vengeance. Bodies were being dragged into piles, and the wounded were being treated.

The Trader was standing in the center of the plaza, with J.B. and a few of the senior crew members. Standing in front of him, arms folded, was Baron Alias Carson.

Ryan walked toward the group, knowing that the drama was nearly played out.

Chapter Thirty-Six

"Ferryman?"

Ryan flicked his right thumb downward in the universal gesture for someone chilled.

"He say anything about the fires?"

"No." He looked at Carson. "How about the baron? He start them?"

The Trader shook his head. "He's saying plenty of nothing."

The baron spoke in his slow, sardonic drawl. "Only thing I'm interested in right now is whether any of you terminal fools have a supply of an immortality drug. If not, then I guess I don't have too much to say."

J.B., his shirt torn from shoulder to wrist, looked at Ryan. "Seen anything of the baron's woman? She's not among the dead."

"No. I was sort of tangled with Ferryman. Got a crease across the ribs. We lose many?"

The Trader answered. "Too many." There was a wave of heat and shock as a building on the far side of the ville went up in flames. From the size of the explosion and the color of the flames, it was obviously a gas store. Fiery rubble cascaded across

Towse, starting a dozen fresh fires. The Trader sucked on his lower lip. "Place is done. We're getting wounded together. I got a burial party standing by. Wags have been called in. It's over."

"How about him?" Ryan asked looking at Alias Carson, amazed that the man could be maintaining his cool.

"No time for a real job," the Trader replied. "Most of the sec-men are finished. Some others caught bullets. Blood price is paid."

Carson spoke. "The buildings go. Captains and kings depart. But the land remains, Trader. You and me can't do shit about that. Nothing else matters. The land's what matters."

Without comment, the Trader lifted the muzzle of his Armalite a few inches and shot the baron three times through the stomach and lower chest.

Alias Carson staggered back a dozen paces, glasses tumbling from his narrow nose. Blood marred the perfection of his light suit. His slender hands waved helplessly at the watching circle of men and women, and a low moan escaped from between his lips. He dropped to the ground, rolling onto his face in the trampled dust of his own ville. His body shuddered once then lay still.

"Talks like a baron. Walks like a baron. Acts like a baron. Dies just like you and me," the Trader said, shouldering the warm gun.

DAWN WASN'T far off, though the skies around the burning ville were still dark. Only an occasional diamond star glittered coldly through the cirrus clouds. The two wags had come lumbering cautiously along the blacktop, manned by the skeleton crews and the lightly wounded. The shooting had virtually stopped. Hun put a last merciful bullet through the head of a woman she found hideously burned, crawling along a narrow alley, blinded, hairless, her scorched skin peeling off and trailing behind her like grotesque rags of vanished finery.

The bodies of the war wags' dead were already being buried in a shallow draw a hundred yards outside the adobe perimeter wall. The Trader's scouts reported a number of Indians standing patiently in the darkness of the desert, waiting for them to depart and allow them to reclaim their own.

Nobody had found the corpse of Sharona Carson, and it was assumed that she'd either managed to make an escape during the confusion of the raid or, more likely, was a burned and unidentified body in one of the ruined buildings.

Alone, Ryan wandered along the one flank of the ville, past the church where Ferryman's corpse still rested, looking back at the huddled mass of women and children who stood with their few possessions, watched by a couple of guards. The Trader had grudgingly agreed that the wags would escort them a few miles north, over the high bridge, to keep them from the vengeance of the Apaches. But then they'd be on their own, and there was a lot of wilderness to cover before the next ville. The war wags didn't carry passengers.

Smoke swirled around Ryan, making his eye water. He stopped near the entrance to the baron's two-wheel wag store—and heard someone cough, the noise nearly muffled. If he hadn't been standing right by the open door he'd never have heard it.

Ruger in hand, Ryan eased himself around the open door, trying to see who'd made the noise. The building had obviously once been an old stable for horses, years before sky-dark, and some of the partitions remained. The 350 twin Norton stood in the nearest stall, on its rest.

"Come out. You won't get hurt," Ryan shouted, raising his voice to compete with the crackling of the advancing flames.

"Knew you had a sense of humor, lover."

He couldn't see her, but he guessed she was hiding in the second or third compartment down.

"Come out, Sharona."

"Turn around and walk away from me."

"Why should I?"

"Got an eight-inch barrel on a .38 Colt Python that says it's a good idea."

"Six good ideas," Ryan agreed, straining his eye to try to see her position.

"Alias is dead." It wasn't a question, and Ryan didn't reply. "Stupe bastard. Could've been him who started the fires. If he couldn't take it with him, then I guess Alias didn't want anyone else to have it."

"Come out and join the other women. Trader'll see you all safe across the bridge."

The laughter sounded genuine. "Sure. Full of tricks like that, lover. Rather suck on the barrel of this friendly old Colt. No, thanks. I'll tell you how it is, Ryan."

"How is it, Sharona?"

"I get on that Norton hog and take my chances outside."

"I'll stop you."

"Then I'll shoot you down, lover. Sure, I'll grieve about it, but I'm not going to give in. Not my way."

"Be sorry to chill you."

She laughed again, but this time it was laced with tension. Behind her, the flames were hungrily devouring the roof, racing toward her hiding place.

"I could put six clean through your guts right now, Ryan."

The one-eyed man was uncomfortably aware that the woman was probably telling the truth. Silhouetted against the open doorway, at less than a dozen paces, he'd be hard to miss.

"Better do it. Pull down on the trigger. I'm not moving."

Suddenly Sharona stood before him, dressed only in jeans and a parka. Her hair was tied back in a ponytail, and she wore no makeup, looking more beautiful than Ryan would have believed possible. He caught his breath.

"I mean it, Ryan," she said quietly. "I'm going to live. Not just for me. For..."

"For what?" he asked, puzzled.

"For...reasons. Real special reasons."

"That doesn't affect me."

She smiled. "That's where you're real wrong, Ryan. Real wrong."

"Still got to stop you."

"Why?"

"Man gives his word to his partner."

"Macho shit."

"Maybe."

"I'm going. Easy or hard, I'm getting out of here."

Ryan half lifted the Ruger, then lowered it again and slid the pistol back into its holster. Sharona Carson smiled, holstered her own gun and stepped in close. She kissed him once, very lightly, on the cheek.

"Thanks, lover. Won't forget it. Won't forget you. Take care now. See you again one day."

There was a burst of sparks as the end wall fell, bringing down a sizable part of the roof. The woman swung her leg over the saddle of the Norton and kicked the motorcycle into life. Other than the blaster, it looked as if she wasn't taking anything with her.

Ryan stood back and watched the woman leave. The roar of the engine was engulfed by the noise of fires all around them, and nobody else saw the two-wheel wag leave the ville.

Ryan knew that he would never see her again. He also knew that he'd never forget her.

TWO HOURS LATER, in the flushed light of full dawn, Sharona Carson braked the Norton and eased it to a stop. She was nearly sixty miles southwest of what remained of the once-proud ville of Towse. The road had been rough, and she'd twice been lucky to dodge attacks by bands of marauding Indians. Now she hefted the bike up on its rest and stretched.

Behind her, just visible as a gray smudge of smoke, fast disappearing into the clear morning sky, was Towse. By now she guessed that the Trader would have pulled out in convoy, moving north. The unburied corpses of Baron Alias Carson and his sec-forces would already be attracting the vultures and the ravening packs of coyotes. Ryan Cawdor was gone from her life, forever.

Before trucking on toward the far west, the woman sat down with her back against a boulder. The rock, chilled by the night, was just beginning to warm under the sun's heat. She felt a wave of sudden nausea and clasped both hands to her stomach.

Sharona had known almost from that first thrusting moment.

The sickness passed and she stood again, giving her past one final look before climbing once more onto the chromed Norton.

She gave a secret smile and patted her stomach, utterly content in the certainty of the new life and who its father was.

Sharona rode away from her past into her uncertain future.

Chapter Thirty-Seven

"Welcome back, lover."

A blur blocked out the ceiling light. Someone stood over him, and a hand stroked his forehead. Red hair. A voice calling him "lover," that he thought he recognized.

"Sharona?" he tried to say, but his mouth and throat were still numb and wouldn't respond to his vocal bidding.

"Don't try and talk, lover. You've been triple-sick. Relax."

He blinked. The voice was a woman's, and she had red hair. Ryan felt obscurely proud of himself for working that out.

"Hun? That you?"

"Did he call you 'honey?'" Mildred asked, leaning anxiously over her patient.

"I don't think Ryan ever called me that," Krysty replied. "You don't think something's happened to his brain, do you?"

The black woman looked away. "I don't know, Krysty. All I know is that Ryan ate some poisoned food that gave him what I think was botulism. As far as I could tell, he was off to shake hands with the widow maker. His breathing and pulse were about as low as they can go without nailing the box down.''

Ryan could hear the second voice, but he couldn't see who was speaking. He tried to move his head, but the effort was too great. The words came filtering through the gravel beds of his mind, but only a tiny fraction of them made any sense.

''But he's going to get better now, Mildred, isn't he?''

''Hope so. I didn't know what I could do to try to save his life. I mixed up every combination of the drugs in the medicine chest, and one of them seems to have worked. Can't honestly say more than 'seems,' Krysty. His pulse has lifted out of the basement, and the stiffness of his muscles isn't quite as severe.''

''But he is...''

The other voice became sharper. ''I don't know! He's certainly not out of the woods yet. Let's leave it at that and keep a careful watch.''

Ryan was aware only of a silence. It was so restful after the confusion of the women's voices that he was happy to relax into it. He closed his eye and fell asleep.

Over the next thirty hours, his breathing became a little stronger and steadier. His heartbeat was faster, without the faltering that had made Mildred think that his race was nearly run.

Krysty and Mildred took turns massaging the stiffness from the muscles of his face and throat. Relaxation was slowly and painfully won. At his lowest ebb, it had been as if his sinews and flesh had been cast in bronze.

Mildred had discovered a way of administering an IV drip to feed him, because he was still not capable of swallowing even the thinnest of liquids. During the days of his illness, in the stale air of the sealed redoubt, he had clearly lost muscle tone.

Doc Tanner tended to hang around, offering help with cleaning the unconscious man and generally trying to find some way of making himself useful—and rarely succeeding.

J.B. and Jak roamed the sections of the rambling fortress that they were able to enter, looking for a way to get into the locked gateway or a way to escape from the ruined redoubt.

The day after Ryan had first showed a glimmering of recovery, the five friends held a council.

"Jak reckons there could be a way out," J.B. announced.

"Where would that be?" Doc asked. "From the wretched lack of fresh air, I doubt that there is any contact with the outer world. Indeed, we have lived here so long that I swear I am turning into a cave dweller."

The albino teenager grinned at the old man. "Love funny words, Doc. You mean think no way out here?"

"That sums it up admirably, my parchment-haired bird of youth."

"Found place, far as can go. Roof fall like all passages. But sure way out through fall."

J.B. nodded. "Jak took me there. I'll swear the air's cleaner. Can't see light or anything, but it just feels right."

"How about the gateway?" Krysty asked. "Can't you get that sec-door open somehow? Use grens on it?"

"Boobied. Whole place is. Jak and me've been all around and covered every single yard while we waited for Ryan to come back to us. I'll try it if we decide that's best."

"I don't understand the danger," Mildred said, frowning. "If we all take cover from the blast, the worst that can happen is that the door won't open."

"No," J.B. replied. "We've come across a few places during the years me and Ryan have been together. Some still got active booby traps. One redoubt was wired a bit like this one. Linked up to some central control. Break into it and a timer starts. Unless you got the comp-code to stop it, the whole place'll go up. I just worry that this might be the same sort of thing."

"We'll wait and see what Ryan thinks," Krysty said. "When he comes all the way around."

Nobody argued with that.

HIS EYE opened.

It wasn't War Wag One and it wasn't Towse ville.

In fact, it wasn't anywhere that he could remember seeing ever in his life before.

His throat felt like it had been given a twice-over by a maddened stickie. When he tried to swallow, it hurt. Cautiously Ryan attempted to move his hands and feet, and was relieved to feel some sensation of life in the extremities. But a similar try at sitting up got him nowhere. The effort made him tremble, and the breath rasped painfully in his chest.

By rolling his head sideways, Ryan could make out a little of his surroundings. He was on an iron bunk and covered with gray blankets. It looked like some kind of institution or a dormitory in the deeps of a...

"Redoubt," he croaked.

Then, very slowly, it all began to trickle back into his mind.

KRYSTY FINISHED her tasteless soup and pushed her chair away from the table. "Guess I'll go check on the patient," she said.

The heels of her boots clicked on the stone floor of the short corridor. As she entered the sickroom, she saw Ryan lying as he had done for the endless days of the coma, flat on his back, hands at his side, his black hair curling over the pillow. His face was lined and thin and had a deathly pallor.

As she stared at him, his eye snapped open and his right hand lifted a few inches from the blankets.

"Hi, Krysty," said a frail, dry voice.

Chapter Thirty-Eight

"Botulism?"

Mildred nodded. "That's what I guess it was. Or something very like it."

"Never heard of it. You figure it was like a real bad gut rot?"

"Worse than gut rot. It wasn't ordinary food poisoning, Ryan. That shouldn't have presented any serious threat to someone in your condition. No, botulism can be a stone killer."

"Neck still feels sore, and my face is still stiff. Like...like I've been smiling for five days solid."

Krysty grinned at the idea of Ryan smiling even for five minutes solid.

Jak was leaning against the wall, picking at his nails with the tip of one of his throwing knives. "When we go?" he asked.

"I suspect that our nearly departed comrade will require a few days of rest and recuperation before embarking on any journey away from this keep perilous," Doc suggested.

"Means I'm not strong enough yet, Jak," Ryan translated.

Mildred was sitting on the end of the bunk. "If you

were a patient in my ward, Ryan, it'd be a week before you got out of bed, and a month before you ever thought about setting foot outside the hospital. You have to realize what a damned close thing this has been."

"Felt the wings of the death angel," Ryan agreed. They'd managed to prop him up against a mound of pillows, and he was already looking better. "But Jak's right. We been here too long. Have to try and get into the gateway real soon."

J.B. had briefed him on the scouting that he and Jak had done, explaining slowly to Ryan that there were only two possible options, and both of them were fraught with potential danger.

"Try the sec-door first. Mebbe any booby'll be long dead."

"Maybe not," J.B. said, "but I agree we try that first. We clear out our route to the place Jak found. If there's some sort of autodestruct defense, then it could mean a fast exit."

"Sure. Now if you'd all like to go find something to do some other place, I want to get on with getting well again."

"Not too much too soon," Mildred warned. "Your heart and lungs have taken a beating, Ryan. Remember, nobody loves a smart-ass."

THE IMPROVEMENT in Ryan's health was amazing. If he'd been outside with some decent food and the sun on his face, then it could even have shifted up a gear into miraculous.

Mildred searched the shelves of dried and canned food, trying to find anything that was even vaguely high in protein, and made sure that Ryan took plenty of liquids with extra glucose and fructose to help the muscles rehabilitate.

Apart from that, it simply took a little hard work: forty minutes' exercise—sit-ups, push-ups and some general loosening, then a ten-minute break. A brisk walk for a mile was next, trying to draw health from the dusty, ailing air of the redoubt. He jogged for a hundred yards, then sprinted a hundred, followed by walking a hundred. Over and over.

In the first couple of days, Ryan did a whole lot of puking.

First time he got out of bed, the room went spinning. His head felt like he'd been on a three-day drunk in a pest-hole gaudy, and he would have fallen if Krysty hadn't been standing by his side.

Exercise brought instant nausea. After just six push-ups he lay flat on the cold floor with clenched fists, as close to tears as he'd been in years. He was angry and frustrated at his own appalling weakness, frightened that he might never get close to his previous level of fitness.

At the end of the third day Ryan could manage a hundred sit-ups, with Jak holding his ankles. Muscle tone was coming back, with the softness of the sickness being replaced by the beginning of the iron sinews. He could manage to jog a full mile before running out of stamina.

On the debit side, his throat was still painful, and he found it difficult to keep solid food down. The muscles of his face had relaxed again, and Mildred reported that pulse and respiration were both very nearly normal.

ON THE EVENING of the fifth day the companions sat around the table, the unwashed dishes in front of them. Doc Tanner, to keep himself occupied, had calculated that day how long the supplies of food could last them.

"Assuming that we each live to something approaching a normal life expectancy," he announced in his best rhetorical, ringing tones, "I estimate that young Jak, as the putative final survivor, would happily still be here in sixty years, thus leaving enough food for another dozen people for at least eighty-seven years. You see, I imagine the possibility of the patter of tiny feet in these dank corridors."

"Don't bring me into the 'tiny feet' crap, Doc," Krysty snapped. "Not now, and maybe not ever. You got that?"

She rose to her feet and walked quickly out of the room. They sat in silence for a few moments, hearing her stalking down the passage.

"Guess the strain's getting to her," Mildred suggested.

Ryan stood. "I'll go see her. I'm not that much in the way of pattering feet, either, Doc."

As he went into the corridor, he could hear Krysty's heels, clicking away from him around a corner. He jogged after the sound, seeing her near the next bend of the corridor.

"Krysty!"

She paused, half looked around, then walked on out of sight.

Ryan ran faster, almost bumping into her, where she'd stopped and was waiting for him.

"Don't say anything, lover," she said.

"Fireblast, Krysty! Think I don't know why you blew up at Doc back there?"

"Why?" She was tense, her whole body language radiating hostility.

"One day you want us to settle down. Start a family someplace it's safe and clean."

Krysty nodded. "That's right, Ryan. And when's that going to be? Tomorrow? Next day? Next week? Next year? Sometime, never!"

"Sometime," he said quietly.

"You want children, lover? Do you really and truly want to stop running, fighting and chilling? Do you?"

"Sure. Heard a song once about how you get one time around, then they nail the lid down on the box in the ground. One chance, Krysty. Want that to be with you. I want kids. Want to leave some mark on the land. Not just piles of unmarked graves. I'd love to have a child."

Krysty suddenly shuddered, hugging herself around the middle.

Ryan reached out and touched her arm, relieved when she didn't pull away from him. "What's the matter, lover?"

"When you said about wanting a child it... Gaia! Like a feather across the back of my neck. Don't know why."

"Come back to the others."

Ryan folded her into his arms, feeling the brittle tension as she resisted him. He kissed her on the cheek and rubbed his hand across her nape. The tightness of the crimson sentient curls brushed against his fingers. Slowly he could feel Krysty relaxing.

Her mouth was close to his face and he was aware of her breath on his skin. "Thought you were gone, lover," she whispered.

"Yeah. I didn't know too much about it. I was locked away into another time and another place. Way, way off."

"Where?"

He shook his head. "Can't tell you for sure. It was like I was living another life inside my head. But it was real. Real times when that really happened to me."

"Memories?"

"Dreams. Nightmares."

"Good and bad, lover?"

Ryan took a half step away, holding Krysty at arm's length. He nodded. "Yeah. Some good and some bad, I think. Can't remember all that much. There was a lot of darkness. Thing I know best is that it's great to be here again, with you.''

A half smile touched her lips. ''Come on. Let's go back to the others.''

''Right.''

Krysty's smile broadened. ''You're looking a touch more like the son of a bitch that I used to know, Ryan.''

''Know and love?''

''I was coming to that.''

''Guessed you might.''

''Now you got some of your muscles into something like working shape, I was sort of wondering how you felt about some night exercise.''

Ryan matched her smile. ''I could manage something if you was to come calling.''

''*Were* to come calling,'' she corrected. ''Your grammar's been worse since you recovered consciousness.''

''Sorry, love. But I still say I could manage something later on tonight.''

''I'll be there. Hope you can live up to your promise, lover. Talk's cheap....''

''But action costs. Trader used to say that a lot, you know. Funny but... No, guess it's nothing.''

''I just hope you can deliver tonight, Ryan. Been a long time since you could raise more than a smile.''

KRYSTY WOKE FIRST and padded along the corridor to make some coffee-sub, bringing it back to where

Ryan was still dozing. There was no sign of life from any of the other four members of the group.

"Here. Wrap yourself around this, lover, while I go shower."

"I'll follow you. It's time to try the gateway."

"Think we'll get out?"

Ryan pulled the blankets up to his chest. "One way or another, we will. J.B.'s checked out the sec-door and the place where Jak thinks we can do us some digging."

"You sleep well?"

"Like a baby. No dreams. No nightmares. Just a long rest. How about you?"

Krysty threw him a mock curtsy. "Exceeding well, thanks, lover. Eventually."

"No complaints?"

Krysty hesitated in the doorway, head on one side, as if the question were peculiarly hard to answer. "With another few weeks' exercise, you might be back to something like normal, lover."

The mug of coffee-sub missed her head by less than a yard, and Ryan could hear her laughter all the way down the corridor.

Chapter Thirty-Nine

An hour or so later, Ryan began to feel sick again. He was sweating and his stomach churned. Pains in his lower gut sent him running to the toilets three times in an hour. Krysty immediately called for Mildred, who took Ryan's temperature and checked his pulse against her chron.

"What is it? Not the botulism back again?" he asked.

"No. I've been keeping up the daily injections of the antibiotics, just as a sort of precaution. Now that all the toxins have left and you're getting back to health, I think your body's rebelling against the drugs. I'll stop them and see how that goes."

"Death is nature's way of telling you to slow down," Doc remarked. "I'm sure I once read that in some digest or other."

"We still going to try and get out?" J.B. asked.

Ryan sighed. "It's all I can do to keep a tight ass and make it to the toilet without losing all control. Figure we should wait another day. Sorry, friends, to keep you all hanging around."

J.B. HAD DONE a dummy run. Moving as fast as he could, and making allowance for the speed of the rest of the group, he'd gone the shortest way from the damaged sec-door up to the point that offered a chance of escape. They'd discussed whether they should make a trial dig at the rubble, but Ryan had felt that the route was only a last resort. There was a clear risk of a roof collapse, and he didn't think it was worth taking the risk.

"Best time I made was eighteen minutes. For all of us I reckon we should allow something close to twenty-five."

"What sort of time would they put on a booby timer?" Ryan asked. "Two hours?"

The Armorer took off his glasses to polish them while he considered his answer. "Got to allow everyone time to evacuate the complex. Plus destroying any of the files and codes and comp-tapes. Can't be less than two hours. Could be three."

"Not long," Krysty said. "Not if we're digging our way out."

"No. Any way we can find out if we have triggered a main destruct alarm, J.B.?"

"Doubt it, Ryan. We set the charge. If it blows the doors then we're in, straight to the gateway and make the jump. If not..." A thought struck him. "I guess there must be some sort of audible warning. Klaxons, or mebbe lights. Mebbe even a recorded message. Yeah. I'd bet there'd be that."

Ryan nodded. "Makes sense. Well, if everyone's ready? Let's go."

THE HUGE DOOR was just as it had been when Ryan had last seen it. In fact, he'd never even asked Krysty just how many days had crawled by while he was in the coma. It seemed as if he'd only left the gateway a couple of days ago, yet he guessed it was closer to two weeks.

Deep down in the bowels of the redoubt the air was cooler and damper. And more stale.

"I got the grens primed and ready. Put them on a five-minute fuse. No point in risking anything shorter. The blast in a confined space like this is going to be powerful. Farther away we are, the better."

Jak tugged at J.B.'s sleeve. "Why not longer? Why take fucking chance? Why not half hour?"

Ryan answered the question. "Farther away we go, then the farther to come back. We need to know if the doors are boobied. Time's going to be real vital, Jak. Five minutes is about right."

"You all go. I'll set them," J.B. offered.

"No. Four hands are better than two handling plasex and grens and detonators. I'll stay. Rest of you go. Know what to do?"

Krysty replied for the others. "Course. Flat down. Heads away. Mouth open. Hands over ears."

Doc tried a joke. "I recollect that one should place one's head between one's legs and then kiss one's ass goodbye."

"Doc, say 'Good night,' will you?" Mildred grinned.

THE ASSUMPTION was that the hinges and the main lifting and lowering mechanism had been damaged when the door slammed down. The main problem was in the very nature of armor-plated doors. They were specifically designed so that they wouldn't easily blow. Given enough explosive, there was nothing in the world that couldn't be destroyed.

But any demolition was a shifting equation with any number of variables.

In this case they didn't have unlimited power at their disposal. And if they used too much, then it could likely have wrecked the delicate machinery of the gateway—as well as bringing down the rest of the roof on top of them. It was like trying to use a sledgehammer with all of the delicacy of a watchmaker.

J.B. worked fast and carefully, setting the charge halfway up one side of the door where it should do most damage. He glanced at Ryan once the work was done. "Ready?"

"Yeah."

The small red button was depressed, and a tiny light began to flash once every second. Three hundred flashes to detonation, give or take a few clicks. The little chron-detonators were notoriously unreliable, and it was always better to give yourself a margin of safety.

"Move," J.B. said.

The others had got farther away, out of sight in the maze of passages. J.B. was counting out loud as he and Ryan sprinted away from the explosives. They passed under a section of roof that had already partly fallen, and Ryan had a moment to wonder if the shock would bring it all down.

"Two hundred and sixty and one and two and three… This'll do."

Both men dropped, keeping to the center of the corridor where the impact was likely to be less. Walls set up pockets of violent turbulence. Ryan closed his eye and tried to relax. Hands pressed tightly over his ears, mouth slightly open, he continued counting under his breath.

He felt himself lifted momentarily by the blast. Dust swirled all around him and brought back a fragment of memory of the chem-storm at the ghost ranch by Abbyqu. He strained to hear if there had been any major falls, but the cascading echoes bouncing off the ceiling and walls distorted sounds.

The moment the shock wave had passed, he stood and brushed dust off his clothes. The force had been greater than he'd expected, probably because of the confined space. J.B. also stood, wiping away a thin worm of blood from below his nose.

"Quite a bang," he said.

"Yeah. Let's go see if it did the trick. The others'll follow us."

Some rocks and concrete had fallen from the weak part of the roof. Ryan looked up at it before moving underneath. He could see twisted bars of rusted iron and some raw, reddish-orange rock. Dust was still dropping and the two men didn't linger.

"Rad-blast it!" J.B. rarely showed his emotions, but he couldn't conceal his anger and frustration as they confronted the sec-door into the gateway.

The air carried the bitter flavor of plas-ex, and a haze of smoke drifted aimlessly in the corridor—not enough to hide the fact that the attempt to blow the entrance had failed.

Part of the wall had caved in, and the door now hung crookedly. Where it had slipped at the top, was a narrow gap, perhaps four inches at its widest, showing the light from the interior control room. But the arma-door was now more firmly jammed then it had been before, one corner dropping into a metal trough beneath it. Even if they could have blown the lock, opening it was now an impossibility.

"Around?" Ryan asked, hearing the sound of feet behind them as the other four arrived through the swirling smoke.

"The wall, you mean? Take a lot more explosives, and it would do some serious damage in the room behind the door. No." J.B. shook his head.

Krysty, hand over her mouth against the fumes, was the first to join them, taking in the situation in a quick, raking glance. "Didn't work," she said. "Nearly, but not nearly enough."

Jak was second. He slapped his hand against the inflexible steel. "Fucking door!"

Mildred arrived third. She stood for some moments, trying to weigh up what had happened, and saw the glimmer of light at the top angle. "Can't we..." she began. But she read the look on Ryan's face. "No. No, I guess it looks like we can't."

Doc joined the others, his lion-headed cane rapping smartly on the stone floor. "Upon my soul, but the stench is extraordinarily noxious. Far worse than dynamite and black powder used to be. Do I assume from the gloomy expressions on your faces that our little experiment has not been a success? Yes. I believe that I do. Ah, well, back to the drawing board."

The noise from the explosion and the various sections of falling masonry was finally dying down. The flat stillness of the abandoned redoubt came creeping slowly back around them.

"Least it doesn't look like we set off any megadeath alarms," Ryan said.

"Put out a lot of the lights, though." J.B. pointed along the passage. Three-quarters of the ceiling lamps had gone out, and others were flickering.

"That light inside the control room's started to flicker as well," Krysty observed, "pulsing in a rhythm."

Everyone looked up at the ribbon of gold. With a tremor of unease Ryan saw that Krysty was right. And the light was also tinged with red. He turned to Jak.

"Here." Ryan cupped his hands and stood against the door. "Climb up and see what you can see."

The boy stepped up, balancing himself with the ease of a born acrobat. He hung on to the top of the door and heaved himself up, feet scrabbling on the smooth metal for a grip.

"Some kind red flashing light," he reported.

Ryan was hesitant to abandon the gateway. Not every redoubt had a mat-trans facility. If they managed to claw their way out of this fortress, it could be months before they managed to get themselves back into the network of gateways—maybe never.

"Got to be some way in," he said. "I hate the idea of just walking away from it."

Jak vaulted lightly down. "Don't like red light. Angry."

J.B. looked worriedly at Ryan. "Jak's right. I don't like it."

"Should be an audible warning though," Ryan commented.

"We broke big red wire in ceiling."

"What? What's that, Jak?"

"Broke wire. Looks like speakers wire."

"More lights going out," Krysty cautioned.

J.B. and Ryan looked at each other. If the teenager was correct, then the broken wire could lead to a system of loudspeakers for their section of the redoubt.

"Jak, can you join the ends?"

"Sure. Help up. Easy."

Ryan held him, and they all waited in silence. Suddenly there was a piercing screech of crackling feedback. Jak jumped and nearly fell.

A booming woman's voice erupted all around them.

"One hundred and fourteen minutes to destruct. Proceed immediately to evacuate. Without override, the complex will destruct in one hundred and fourteen minutes."

Chapter Forty

There wasn't a moment's hesitation from any of them.

"I am the bringer of death," Doc panted, hobbling along with surprising speed, his knee joints cracking like a fusillade of flintlock muskets.

"Save your breath," Ryan snarled. "J.B.! You and Jak go fast as you can and start digging. We'll get there as quick as we can."

With less than two hours before the fortress disintegrated, there was no point in the fastest waiting for the slowest.

Parts of the fortress's speaker system had decayed over the past hundred years, but other parts still functioned. So the run through the redoubt was a dash at the edge of panic, sprinting through corridors of silence, then encountering the recorded voice once more.

"One hundred and four minutes remain to termination. Move quickly without panic to the nearest exit point. One hundred and three minutes."

Under pressure, Ryan was only too aware of the danger of someone taking a wrong turn and vanishing into the maze of corridors, so he kept his speed down to that of Doc Tanner's, trying to hustle the old man along without actually driving him beyond his limits.

"I am doing my best, my dear friend. Why do you and the ladies not press on at your own speed and leave me to make my best time?"

"Disengage your mouth, Doc, and keep the feet moving. We get out together."

"Or we vanish into the ether, together," Doc replied, but he moved along a little faster.

"Ninety-one minutes. Self-destruct procedure is progressing without override. Use approved comp-code to check termination sequence. Ninety minutes. Ninety minutes remain ... main ... main ... main ..."

"Shit," Mildred gasped. "Just what we need. A malfunctioning computer."

JAK WAS OUT of sight, but J.B. was lying on top of the earth fall, reaching into the gap near the ceiling, dragging back the stone and dirt that the boy was excavating. He hardly glanced around as the rest of the companions arrived, throwing the news over his shoulder.

"Doesn't look so good. Block of concrete fallen directly ahead. Jak says he can feel air, and thinks he can make out light."

The albino boy found seeing difficult in bright daylight, but in the gloom his eyes were at least as good as Krysty's.

"Can he shift it?" Ryan asked, leaning over and

battling to steady his breathing, trying to ignore the reproachful voice warning them that only eighty-three minutes remained.

"No way. But he's trying to tunnel under it to the right. Says there's a gap."

"A gap for him and a gap for me aren't necessarily the same thing," Doc panted, his face drawn and tired.

"Gaia! I wish we could find some way of turning off that woman's endless voice," Krysty complained.

"It'll turn itself off in around eighty minutes from now," Ryan said.

"SIXTY MINUTES. The time is now one hour and still counting. This is not a drill. This is not a practice evacuation. The self-destruct clock is running, and now shows fifty-nine minutes."

The gentle feminine voice could easily have been giving out a recipe for making a blueberry sponge cake, not conveying the slightest hint that a cataclysmic explosion that would totally destroy the redoubt was now less than an hour away.

Exhausted, fingers bleeding, Jak Lauren had reluctantly agreed to be relieved at the rock face and allowed Ryan to take his place. The others took turns clawing back the piles of loose stones and red dirt that were being pushed from the gap above the fall.

It was desperate work.

Ryan tried to lock his mind onto the compressed earth ahead of him, forcing away the knowledge that there could be anything up to a mile of solid rock poised above his head. He half expected a slide, a tiny, tiny movement that would smear him into instant eternity. Doc had waved him into the cramped tunnel with the encouraging words that if anything happened he probably wouldn't feel any pain.

The long panga was useful to jab out gobbets of dirt, but there was little space to use it effectively. Every handful had to be pushed behind so that someone else could drag it, in turn, into the open tunnel.

The working area was about eighteen inches high, and about four feet across at its widest. The long block of crumbling concrete that J.B. had mentioned was almost a finite obstacle to their escape route. But Jak had been right. It could just be circumvented. Twice Ryan was certain that he felt it move against his legs and winced, anticipating its forty-ton weight coming across his knees.

But it held.

"Fifty-one minutes until termination. Make sure that you have switched off all electrical equipment and removed all classified material. If you are not sure where to go, check with your manual, page two hundred sixty-eight, paragraph two. Please make your way to the appropriate departure point. You have precisely fifty minutes."

"Fuck off!" Jak yelled, shaking his fist at the nearest speaker. He stooped to pick up a chunk of concrete as big as a baseball, winding up ready to throw it.

"No," Krysty said, pausing from shoveling dirt with her hands.

"Want shut fuck up!" he shouted.

"Better to let it run. Keep track of the time without having to keep stopping to check a chron. Leave it be, Jak."

Reluctantly the boy dropped the hunk of jagged stone.

Ryan crawled out and made way for J.B. It was oppressively cramped, and everyone was touching the far edge of exhaustion.

"Thirty-six minutes. Evacuation is proceeding smoothly, and most of the personnel have been removed to places of safety. Will anyone still remaining in any part of the complex go immediately, and I repeat that word, immediately, to the nearest exit. Thirty-six minutes remain to autodestruct."

Ryan was back in the hole, digging away with the blunted point of his panga. The air seemed fresher. He rested a moment, then jabbed once more at the packed earth. Some slid loose and he blinked. The tunnel was dark and he could now see...

"Light. I can see light!"

TIME WAS becoming desperately short.

At thirty minutes a siren began its banshee howl. It started as a whining, low note, then rose up the scale to a crescendo of noise, sometimes drowning out the monotone of the woman's recorded voice.

The pinprick of light had become the size of a

hand, then the size of a child's skull. But there was bedrock on either side, and it was becoming impossibly tight to work.

Ryan was close to giving up. The gap wasn't big enough for any of them, even Jak, to wriggle through. The redoubt would be vapourized in less than half an hour and they would die, trapped in its entrails. The consolation that death would be swift was very small. Even if they got out, the sand was running through the hourglass with such speed that they wouldn't have time to get a safe distance away.

"Let me take over, Ryan," J.B. called close behind him.

"No. If I can just break this angle of..." His voice vanished into a grunt of strained effort. He pushed his feet against the sides of the escape passage, bracing himself and putting his hands flat against the corner of the chipped rock. Slowly, using every fiber of his fading strength, Ryan straightened his arms. Nothing happened and then...a tremor of movement. Another tremor.

The rock broke away, leaving a wider gap. It was no more than a foot high, and barely two feet wide, but it was enough.

It had to be.

"Through!" he panted. "Come on."

Behind him he could hear the muffled voice of the self-destruct announcement.

"Twenty-one minutes remain. Without comp-code

override the complex will be subject to controlled termination in twenty minutes.'' The screech of the siren
drowned it out.

Ryan wriggled forward.

Chapter Forty-One

The fresh air was almost like a triple shot of top-grade jolt. It surged into the lungs and raced through the body, rushing into the brain.

When Ryan tried to stand up he became dizzy, overwhelmed by the air and by the brightness of the golden sun.

He was vaguely aware of a crimson land, stretching below, but his entire preoccupation was with helping the others to escape from the towering sarcophagus of the doomed redoubt.

Doc was out first, panting and wheezing, dragging his cane behind him, the bulky Le Mat pistol snagging on the raw rock on the left. As soon as he was clear the glasses of J.B. glinted in the opening. He pushed through Ryan's Heckler & Koch G-12, followed by his own MP-7-SD-8 automatic rifle. He took Ryan's forearm and slipped easily out into the fresh air.

Then Mildred was through, her face beaded in sweat and covered in gray and orange dust. She collapsed on hands and knees, fighting for breath.

There was a brief delay, then Krysty's flaming hair appeared in the darkness. She wriggled her way out, snakelike, cursing as her ankle got trapped against some loose rock.

"Jak's right behind me."

"How long?" Ryan asked.

"Eighteen," she replied.

Like some mythical cave dweller, Jak came through last, his face whiter than ever, his ruby eyes glowing like coals in the sockets of scoured bone.

Ryan's mind was racing.

In eighteen minutes, on level ground, a fit man could probably run something like two and a half miles. Maybe manage three. In eighteen minutes.

There had been a moment to look around at where they'd emerged from the naked rock. Just to one side was the obvious remains of an emergency exit from the redoubt, but the door had been twisted out of shape by some massive earth movement, probably at the time of the mega-nuking. And the corridor leading to it had been distorted, leaving only the slender gap that they'd managed to find and exploit.

Now they stood on a narrow ledge, less than six feet in width. Ryan had already checked the drop, which was nearly seven hundred feet, onto spires of crumbled sandstone. The cliff above them rose two hundred feet, nearly vertical. In any case, since the redoubt was going to explode in a big way, it seemed a bit pointless to think about climbing up. It would be like sitting on the nose of a missile and striking it with a large hammer.

Despite their tiredness there wasn't a second to waste.

"Come on," Ryan said, leading the way along the ledge, moving to the right, where he'd seen a goat path that zigzagged across the face of the mountain.

J.B. was keeping an eye on his chron. "Sixteen minutes, Ryan," he said quietly.

"Keep the count."

In his heart, Ryan knew that their chances weren't that good. There was no way they were going to be able to get far enough away from the redoubt in the short time left to them.

The Trader had used to say that it didn't matter if the odds against survival were a million to one. You still tried for that one chance.

Frequently glancing over his shoulder to check that the others were keeping up with him, Ryan led the companions on a breath-stopping descent. Slipping, sliding and tumbling, they ignored the cuts and bruises and the dust that stung their eyes. They kept moving.

"Seven minutes," J.B. announced.

Very soon Ryan knew they'd have to stop and try to find some cover, however minimal. If the redoubt self-destructed while they were out on the exposed hillside, then they'd all be pulped.

Several hundred yards below them were the ruins of some buildings. But it was obvious that they'd been destroyed long years ago. They were useless for shelter and safety.

"What's that?" Krysty called, pausing a moment and pointing to something just beyond the farthest building. It looked like a huge saucer of white metal, streaked with orange rust.

"Radar dish," J.B. said.

"Satellite receiver, I believe," Doc panted. He was nearly done. A little blood trickled from his mouth where he'd bitten his lip.

"Five minutes," J.B. counted.

Ryan made the decision.

"There," he said.

THERE WAS just room for all of them to squeeze under the fallen metal dish, pressed against one another.

"What if it's not strong enough?" Mildred asked, and immediately answered her own question. "Kind of stupid, Mildred. We get killed if it's not strong enough."

"Inside two minutes," J.B. said. "Can't be too sure about accuracy within a minute or so. Could be any moment."

Krysty had her arm around Ryan's shoulders. "If we don't make it, then it's been good. Wish we could've found a place to settle, lover."

Ryan held her tight, his cheek against hers, not saying anything.

Waiting.

"I make it around thirty seconds," J.B. announced. "Hang on, people."

"Farewell, comrades," Doc muttered. "I would just like to remark that—"

The explosion of the world interrupted him.

The concussion was unimaginable.

Ryan blacked out and guessed that the same happened to all of them. There was a shock wave that moved the earth beneath, behind and all around them. They were lifted up and slammed down, and the metal disk above them rang like a bell. Despite the amazing power of the huge underground explosion, there was very little noise. There was a pressure that hurt the ears and a vague, booming sound that seemed to swirl around between sky and earth.

When Ryan came around he was deafened by rocks and stones pounding on the satellite dish above them. He instinctively curled partway into a ball, grabbing for Krysty to try to protect her.

It was impossible to see beyond the circular edge for the whirling dust. The ground beneath Ryan was still trembling from the shock and what he guessed were some minor detonations in the remains of the redoubt.

It crossed his mind that this was what it must have been like when the United States of America died and the Deathlands was born.

THE TREMORS continued for half an hour. Ryan had ordered everyone to remain within the relative safety of the metal shield. It had been visibly dented and battered by the hail of stones that had struck it, some of them having obviously been hurled hundreds of feet in the air. Without its protection there wasn't much doubt that all six of them would have died.

Ryan tried to swallow and hawked up a mouthful of thick red spittle. His head ached, and his good eye was sanded sore. Jak had begun to bleed copiously from both ears, but it had finally stopped and the boy seemed little the worse for the experience.

"Nearly thirty minutes since the blow," J.B. said.

Ryan nodded. "Okay. Let's move. Come out real slow and easy. Don't know what the mountain's like up there above us."

"Sweet Jesus on the Cross," Mildred breathed, rubbing at her eyes.

The rest of them stared in silence.

A whole section of the hillside above them had completely vanished, as though a giant excavator had bitten a monstrous slice from the rock.

Millions of cubic feet of stone and concrete had disappeared in the cataclysmic explosion. The prevailing wind was blowing the pillar of dark smoke away toward the east, away from the six companions, obscuring the horizon. There wasn't the least sign that there'd ever been a redoubt.

All around them the land was scattered with smashed stone, some pieces the size of a small wag. The metal dish that had saved their lives was pitted and scarred, with dozens of chunks of rock all over its battered top.

Ryan turned away and, for the first time, was able

to take a more leisurely look at where they were. It was a bleak desert landscape, blood-hued and inhospitable. There were more mountains toward the south, across a featureless plain, dotted with stately saguaro cactus and yucca. As far as the eye could see there was no evidence of any human activity.

"Don't look much," he observed.

Krysty laid a hand on his arm. "Looks good to me, lover. Looks like life."

Doc was hypnotized by the ravaged mountain beneath which they'd lived for so many wearisome days. "I am death, the destroyer of worlds," he said. "By the three Kennedys! That is power too great!"

"No rad-count," J.B. commented, as cautious as ever.

"Where now?" Jak asked, picking at a small cut on his cheek.

"Check where we are first," Ryan replied. "You do it, J.B. Once we know that we can decide what to do. Where to go."

While the Armorer began to take the necessary observations with his microsextant, the others sat down on the sun-heated rocks. Krysty and Ryan smiled at each other.

"Lover?" she asked.

"Yeah."

"Could be worse."

"Sure. Could all have died there. Like ants under a wheel."

"You nearly went with that poison."

"Too close." He held her hand, warm in his fingers.

"When you were out, in that long sleep… Where were you?"

Ryan kissed her hand, tasting the roughened skin and the dust. "I was in the past."

"Your own past?"

"Yeah. Good place to visit for a while, but I sure wouldn't want to go and live there."

Epilogue

Somewhere in Deathlands, if it had survived, the child of Sharona Carson, fathered by Ryan Cawdor, would be about ten years old.

An enemy within...

STONY MAN™ 41

SILENT INVADER

Stolen U.S. chemical weapons are believed responsible for attacks on Azerbaijan and on a merchant ship in the Caspian Sea. While all indications point to Iraq, Bolan and the Stony Man team are sent to track a much more insidious enemy....

Available in July 1999 at your favorite retail outlet.

Take
2 explosive books
plus a
mystery bonus
FREE

Follow Remo and Chiun on more of their extraordinary adventures....